WHITE STAR

WHITE STAR

Beth Vaughan

Copyright © Elizabeth Vaughan 2009

The right of Elizabeth Vaughan to be identified as the author
of this work has been asserted by her in accordance with
the Copyright, Designs and Patents Act 1988.

First published in Great Britain in 2009 by Gollancz
An imprint of the Orion Publishing Group
Orion House, 5 Upper St Martin's Lane, London WC2H 9EA
An Hachette UK Company

A CIP catalogue record for this book is available
from the British Library

ISBN 978 0 575 08422 3 (Cased)
ISBN 978 0 575 08424 7 (Trade Paperback)

1 3 5 7 9 10 8 6 4 2

Typeset at The Spartan Press Ltd,
Lymington, Hants

Printed and bound in Great Britain by CPI Mackays,
Chatham, Kent, ME5 8TD

www.orionbooks.co.uk

The Orion Publishing Group's policy is to use papers that
are natural, renewable and recyclable products and
made from wood grown in sustainable forests. The logging
and manufacturing processes are expected to conform to
the environmental regulations of the country of origin.

ONE

He was weary.

Orrin Blackhart strode through the great kitchen, past the cold hearths and scullery boys, past the cooks with their stained aprons, cold kettles and wide eyes. Silence followed him as he emerged to march across the small courtyard, scattering the geese and chickens before him. His stride was long, his steps strong and steady, an old habit not to show exhaustion or pain. He was soul-weary, truth to tell, although his lips curled in derision at the thought.

As if he had a soul.

Men watched as he crossed the yard and angled towards the door to the dungeons beneath. He could have avoided their gaze, for there were other ways into the depths of the keep of the Black Hills, but those were dark, filthy and guarded by the Odium. They were the undead guardians of this place and though he appreciated them as a weapon, he could do without the stench. He'd wanted a bit of air before plunging into the depths of the prison, where light and breath were precious and rare.

A puddle of something foul lay in his way, but he stepped square into it with his black boots, determined to take the straightest route. After all, the Scourge of Palins never wavered in his duty: to protect his Baroness and his people. He took whatever means was necessary, used whatever weapon was at hand, to accomplish that goal.

Hadn't he?

Pah. He was weary of the filth. Weary of stupidity, weary of trying to preserve the lives of his men. Bone-deep weary, that was the worst of it. No amount of sleep brought him rest or ease.

Orrin set his jaw and kept walking.

They knew where he went, his men. They knew full well what lay in the depths beneath the courtyard. Word would have flashed through the keep, from the lowest scullery to the highest tower. He could almost feel their questions on his skin. Why had High Baroness Elanore left with a small force when the men were needed on their borders? What use would this prisoner be for their cause?

They looked to him, Orrin Blackhart, Lord Marshal of the Black Hills.

Pity he had no answers.

He strode to the door, bearing the burden of their regard. He'd served Lady Elanore, Baroness of the Black Hills, for years now, but the weight was heavier with each passing day. Each passing hour. It didn't help that since her injury, Elanore had grown obsessed with her power and the undead Odium that she could create with it.

Orrin scowled. Of late she'd grown even more focused and secretive. The Baroness had come up with this scheme to take one of the leaders of the rebellion prisoner. Once that had been set into motion, she'd used her magic to make even more of the Odium than he'd thought possible. Then she'd left, with men and Odium he needed for defence. Left, damn her, against his advice, and no reasoning would convince her otherwise.

His fist was hard clenched before he even raised it to pound on the door. Three blows, then a swift turn to sweep the yard with a stern glance.

Men turned quickly back to their tasks and the normal business of the keep resumed. Weary he might be, but he was Lord Marshal. None would challenge or question.

For now.

Reader looked up from his book. 'That's him coming.'

As Archer lifted his head from his work, he saw Sidian raise one of his bushy white eyebrows, a move Archer always watched with quiet amusement. Sidian was black-skinned, his face, chest and arms covered with ritual scars, and so dark that his bald head and thick white eyebrows were startling. When one brow moved like that, it was as if a fuzzy bug had crawled over his eye.

'How so?' Sidian asked in his clipped accent. 'You've no way of—'

The pounding at the door cut him off.

'Why do you doubt, friend?' Archer asked quietly. 'He's always right.'

Sidian snorted as Reader jumped up, thrusting his book into his pack. The small man wiped his palms on his pants as he darted to the door and jerked it open.

Blackhart stood framed in the doorway, silhouetted against the day. As he stepped in, his hazel eyes pierced the room.

Archer was unmoved by Blackhart's glare. True enough, the darkness of this place was no match for Orrin Blackhart, Lord Farentell to Lady High Baroness Elanore and death incarnate to her enemies. But Archer had known the man and been part of his hearth-band for years, and the impact of that glare had worn a bit around the edges. It had been aimed in his direction a fair number of times over the years. Not that he was used to it. Not that at all.

'Well?' Blackhart growled.

'Very well,' Archer replied calmly. 'She walked right into our trap. Your information was good.'

Blackhart grunted. 'Should be, considering the source. Anyone hurt?' He looked at the other men.

'No.' Archer gave the man the reassurance he needed. 'Timothy and Thomas are taking care of the horses. There wasn't even a fight, it was that easy. There was another priest with her, but she pushed him back through the portal before we could grab him, too. It closed before we could blink.'

Blackhart's shoulders relaxed a bit. 'We've got her. That's all that matters.'

'Sidian probably scared her,' Reader piped up, 'what with them scars and all.'

Sidian raised that eyebrow again, but didn't rise to the bait.

'Where is she?' Blackhart moved farther into the room.

'Below. Mage is keeping an eye on her.' Archer nodded towards the door that led below.

Blackhart frowned again. 'The spell chains are—'

'Working fine,' Archer assured him. 'But she's prayin', and that's got Mage nervous.'

Blackhart grunted and grabbed a torch. 'For all the good praying will do . . .' He opened the door that led to the cells and headed down the stairs. Archer settled back and returned to work on the arrow in his hands. The dungeon was a mite close for his taste. Besides, Blackhart could handle one small priestess by himself, now couldn't he?

Torchlight danced on the walls as Orrin stomped down the narrow staircase. The heels of his boots clicked on the stones, echoing in the spiral that descended into the depths. The stench filled his nose, leaving an acrid taste in the back of his throat. The men posted to duty in these tunnels claimed that the damp cut clear to the bone.

They were right.

The guard at the bottom nodded him towards the right passage. The dungeon was a warren filled with tunnels and cells. One could wander lost if one wasn't careful. Done by design at some point, Orrin was sure. Hard to rescue someone when you can't find yourself, much less their cell.

One of the warders led him to the very end of one of the corridors and there, in a niche in the wall, sat Mage, wrapped in his cloak against the cold and damp. Mage jumped to his feet with a youthful vigor Orrin envied.

'Sir,' Mage said softly.

'Which cell?'

Mage gestured and Orrin moved to look through the tiny barred window. The cell held a small candle, and in the centre of the pool of light knelt a woman dressed all in white, her head bowed, her white hair glowing in the light.

Orrin stepped back and kept his voice down. 'The spell chains working?'

Mage nodded. 'I used fresh ones, just to be sure. She can't use any magic. Been praying since we put her in there. Thought maybe I'd keep watch, her being a high priestess and all. I mean, so far she's not trying to cast magic. But the praying . . .' The youngster shrugged. 'Not sure what I'd do if her gods appeared, but I thought—'

Orrin rested a hand on his shoulder. 'A good thought.'

Mage lifted his head and straightened his shoulders. Orrin suppressed a chuckle, then turned to the warder. 'Open it.'

The warder moved quickly, fumbling with his keys. Orrin eased back to give the man room and waited patiently. Once the door was opened, he handed the torch to Mage and bent down to enter the cell.

The woman looked up as he entered, regarding him calmly. Her hands were folded before her. The manacles were tight on her wrists and the chains that linked them dangled before her robes. Orrin noted the chain that ran along the floor and secured her ankle to the wall.

He'd heard the tales, of course, but it was a surprise to find her hair thick and white, and her eyes the barest blue. She was younger than he'd expected, maybe a few years younger than himself.

She seemed to magnify the glow of the candle, but he was sure that was a contrast to the darkness about her and not her innate goodness. Not that it mattered, either way. Innocence would be no protection here.

She endured his scrutiny, studying him at the same time. He knew full well there was a contrast, with him dressed all in black and towering over her.

'Lady High Priestess Evelyn.' Orrin's voice grated as he broke the silence. 'The Baroness will dance when she learns of your capture.'

'No doubt.' Her voice was soft, yet stronger than he expected.

He was caught off guard by the blue of her eyes and the life that sparked there. No despair or fear, just calm, light blue eyes like a clear sky. Uneasy, he continued, 'She will return to the keep, and then your fate will be determined. Do you know what to expect?'

The Lady High Priestess lowered her eyes and Orrin noted that the clasped hands were trembling ever so slightly.

'Rape, torture.' She paused for the barest moment. 'Death.'

'Yet you do not fear,' Orrin said.

'I fear.' Her voice was quiet. 'I fear the pain and rape. As all do.' Orrin caught a glimpse of her blue eyes and a flash of humour in them. 'I do not fear death. I suspect I will welcome it.'

Orrin frowned. 'There will be no rescue, Priestess.'

Her head came up, her eyes widened and she laughed, a clear sound that rang against the stones. 'Well do I know that, sir.'

Orrin stared at her, still hearing the echoes of the laughter from the surrounding walls, the first honest laugh he'd heard in many years.

The prisoner made as if to rise, but had some difficulty. Without thinking, Orrin extended his hand in its black leather glove. She looked up in surprise, but accepted his hand and assistance. She wasn't tall; the top of her head came to the level of his eyes.

As she stood, Orrin saw that her white robes were stained where she had knelt on the damp floor. The robes were heavy ones, thick and white with gold trim. There was a flicker of silver on the woman's hand, a ring of some kind.

She stepped back from him and clasped her hands together again, her face composed. The brief glimpse of humour was gone. 'I take it, then, that you are Blackhart, Scourge of Palins?'

'I am.' Orrin gave her a nod. 'As you are the leader of the rebellion and the creator of the false prophecy.'

Ah, that made her eyes narrow. 'Hardly as false as the Usurper and his promises.'

'His title is Regent.' Orrin gave her a grim look. 'I'll not argue the point, Lady High Priestess. I have you, and I'll use you to whatever advantage I can.'

The lady gave him a thoughtful look. 'What advantage can there be to my torture and death?'

He frowned, angry that he'd given away too much. 'We'll see, when the Baroness returns.'

The priestess sighed, looking around at the rough cell. 'I half hope it's sooner, rather than later.'

She looked at him then and met his gaze, and somehow he knew that for all her calm appearance, she was doing all she could to hold the terror at bay. He frowned again, suddenly uncomfortable. 'Warder!'

The door opened and Orrin once again bent down to emerge from the cell. He waited for the door to close before he spoke. 'This prisoner is to be moved.'

'Moved?' Mage asked. His uncertainty was to be expected, since Orrin himself was surprised at his snap decision. He wasn't sure where the impulse had come from.

'Am I bewitched?' Orrin asked the lad sharply.

Mage opened his eyes wide, then muttered a few words, casting his spell. His eyes glowed for an instant. 'No, Lord Blackhart.'

Orrin grunted. 'It makes no sense to keep you down here, watching her. Have her taken to one of the tower bedrooms and secure her there.' Orrin turned and leaned in, nose to nose with the warder. 'The prisoner is not to be touched, and nothing is to

6

be removed from her person. That privilege belongs to the Baroness. Am I understood?'

The warder jerked his head, clearly aware of Orrin's reputation as a killer. Orrin spun on his heel, satisfied that he would be obeyed, and left the cell, climbing the stairs out of the darkness. Elanore would be pleased, and upon her return the Priestess would die. But in the meantime, she could be housed in a better location, easier for his men to guard. Made no sense to go to great length to capture her then lose her to illness. No telling when the Baroness would return from her little jaunt.

As he climbed the stairs, back towards the air and the light, he admitted to himself that he felt odd. Suddenly, he longed for something he had not wanted or thought about in a long time.

He wanted to hear that laugh again.

TWO

She was terrified.

Evelyn's hands clenched tight as she watched Blackhart leave. It was all she could do not to fling herself at the door and pound on it, begging for her freedom.

She closed her eyes and forced herself to hold still as muffled voices came through the door. With any luck her captor hadn't seen her terror. Her heart was pounding in her chest and her mouth was so dry it was a miracle she'd been able to form words at all.

She was exhausted, which made it harder to keep the fear at bay. At the very least, she could die with dignity. After all, she was a priestess, wasn't she? A high priestess, for all that.

Little good that did her now.

She licked her lips and made herself take in a slow, shuddering breath. Lord of Light, this place stank. Of fear, of the undead these people had raised, of foul fluids and rot. She let the air out slowly and took another breath, trying to relax her tight shoulders. With a grimace, she knelt on the damp floor. Prayer would help.

Not that she truly expected aid, divine or otherwise. She'd brought this on herself. The Chosen had warned her of the danger, but she'd blithely continued on, sure of her path. Evelyn could see her own arrogance now, to her shame. She could only pray that it would not harm their cause, would not prevent the Chosen from claiming her rightful throne.

Blackhart had surprised her with his talk of a rescue. The look on his face when she'd laughed right out loud – nonplussed was the best way to describe it. There was some degree of satisfaction to that, if a prisoner could be said to have any.

Evelyn rolled her shoulders, trying to relax them, and took another conscious breath. She swallowed too, to wet her mouth. 'Prayer focuses our thought on the Gods, and opens our minds to their will and their wishes,' she whispered, reciting an old lesson her mother had taught her, trying to regain her calm. 'Give your heart and mind to the Lord of Light and the Lady of Laughter and they will answer, in ways seen and unseen.'

Focus on the Gods. Easy to say, but hard to do when the clawing fear in her gut threatened to take her by the throat.

Nonetheless she closed her eyes and tried to pray.

'Hail, gracious Lord of the Sun and Sky, Giver of Light . . .'

Evelyn opened her eyes just enough to see the flame of the candle they'd left with her. The tiny thing barely held back the darkness of these depths. Of course, it was more for their convenience than her comfort, so they could keep an eye on their prisoner.

Not that she could do anything. Her gaze fell to the manacles around her wrists, grey and tight. Whatever they were, they somehow drained her magic away, leaving her helpless to cast any spell. She had never heard of such a thing, but any power she could summon was gone in an instant, as if pulled into the metal. Its effect could also explain the sick feeling in her stomach, and the headache. Maybe it wasn't just her fear.

If they removed the chains, it was possible that she might be able . . .

She was fooling herself and she needed to admit it. Even if she could win free of the chains, there were guards, both human and Odium, between her and freedom. It would take precious seconds to cast a spell and open a portal, and they'd probably be upon her before she could escape.

Odium. Her stomach clenched at the thought. She'd never fought them, but she'd seen what they could do to a man: seen men rendered, their flesh torn, seen the horrible gaping wounds that the Odium inflicted with tooth and nail.

Soulless ones, the Odium were, made worse because they were created from the living, their souls stripped from their bodies. They fought with no need for food or rest. Worse, their filthy hands and rotting flesh left corruption behind in the wounds that they made. A man could survive a battle with but a scratch and be dead in days when the wound soured and spoiled.

Odium could be stopped only by severing the neck or chopping the limbs. Or killing the one who created it. She shivered.

These people created and used them. What would they do to her?

The gnawing fear rose once more, and she looked at the candle again. Her father had taught her the first of her spells with a candle. The old lessons helped her to concentrate and she closed her eyes once more. *'Hail, gracious Lord of the Sun and Sky, Giver of Light and Grantor of Health. Your priestess beseeches you for forgiveness . . .'*

For her pride, her arrogance, her stupidity. For putting five years of work and toil at risk by allowing herself to be captured. The fear in her stomach turned to sick worry. Did her fellow rebels know she had been taken? Would any of the High Barons withdraw their support of the Chosen? Their forces were in the field and there was no turning back now . . .

'Hail, gracious Lord of the Sun and Sky, Giver of Light and Grantor of Health. Your priestess beseeches you for mercy . . .'

For High Baroness Elanore would have none. She had plotted with the Usurper to ambush the other High Barons and, in the confusion, attack the Barony of Farentell, laying waste to the land and taking its people as slaves, or worse. For the Baroness had turned to necromancy, had raised the Odium, using slaves and prisoners that Blackhart and her armies had brought her.

With Farentell destroyed, they had turned their attentions to Summerford and Athelbryght. Lord Fael of Summerford had fought them off, with the assistance of the armies of Lady Helene of Wyethe.

Athelbryght had been destroyed, its baron left dying in the ruin of his farmstead. The memory of finding her cousin, Lord Josiah, there in the mud, swept over Evelyn. She'd decided there and then that she'd find a way to restore the throne.

So many years of work, so much effort. They were so close.

Evelyn should have known that the talk of plague in the hills had been a lure to trap her, but she'd felt compelled to aid those she'd thought in need. The Archbishop had sent her . . .

Who had betrayed her?

There was a scrabbling sound in one of the corners. Evelyn flinched, darting a glance to the side. Rats, probably.

She shuddered and licked her dry lips.

'Hail, gracious Lord of the Sun and Sky, Giver of Light and Grantor of Health. Your priestess beseeches you for aid . . .'

For the cause, for the warriors, but especially for the children she'd rescued from the Usurper's schemes. They were safe, hidden in Soccia. She'd protected them, loved them these last five years, and she could see their grief as she tasted her own in the back of her throat. They'd be devastated, and had she thought of that? Had she given a moment's thought to . . .

'Hail, gracious Lord of the Sun and Sky, Giver of Light and Grantor of Health. Your priestess beseeches you for courage . . .'

Courage for all. For every man taking up arms against the Usurper. For the children, for the Chosen, for herself. She swallowed hard as pictures of what they'd do to her flashed through her mind. And truth be told, what she feared most was the waiting. It was one thing to face death. It was another thing entirely to kneel in a cell with nothing to do but anticipate what was to come.

She brought herself back, focused on her breathing, tried to ease tense muscles, tried to let the fear go. Tried to pray . . .

'Hail, gracious Lord of the Sun and Sky, Giver of Light and Grantor of Health. Your priestess beseeches you for grace . . .'

For the grace to wait, and endure. As long as she had to. For the grace to hide her fears from that man. Lord Blackhart, Scourge of Palins, who'd aided the High Baroness and the Usurper.

Odd. She'd expected him to be tall and brooding when he'd filled the door of her cell. But for the inhuman monster he was reported to be, his eyes held a weariness that she hadn't expected. Those eyes had been dark, grim . . . she'd seen no hint of colour in the dim light, other than the black he wore. Still, it was . . . unsettling. She'd expected cruelty and hate. How odd to think such a monster might have feelings beyond a lust for power.

Was she guilty of that as well? Of assuming that all of her enemies were monsters?

Evelyn's face grew warm. She'd worked so long to unseat the Usurper, to bring the prophecy to fruition, had she fallen into the trap of blind hatred of an enemy? Was that what took Blackhart down his path of darkness?

As she was lost in thought, the grating of the door took her by surprise. Her head snapped up. Two men with torches stood in the doorway.

'On your feet.'

THREE

'Have your way with her, then and be done.' Archer huffed out an exasperated breath.

'No,' Blackhart snapped, 'no rape.'

'Who said anything about rape?' Archer growled. 'I'm thinking she's as interested as you are.'

Blackhart turned on him, his face filled with anger. 'She's no common whore, to be used for a moment's pleasure,' he lashed out before turning to stomp off.

Archer rolled his eyes as Blackhart walked away from him along the battlements. Since he'd ordered the prisoner moved the day before, Blackhart had been snapping heads off and growling like a bear at everyone and everything. Archer gave the man's back a thoughtful look as he followed. 'You sure you ain't bewitched?'

'Mage says not,' Blackhart said. 'I'm not stupid.'

'Depends on which head you're thinking with.' Archer chuckled, then fell silent as they passed a sentry. Blackhart paused long enough to look the man in the eye and receive a nod in return.

They moved on and after a few steps Archer pressed his point in a soft voice. 'There's none to say you nay, with the Baroness gone,' he pointed out. 'More than like she'll wonder that you didn't when she gets back.'

'*If* she gets back,' Blackhart growled. He stopped for a moment and looked out over the battlements. 'Where the hell is she?'

Archer moved to stand beside him. 'No word, I take it.'

'None,' Blackhart said. His face was as grim as his tone.

'Any movement on the border?' Archer asked.

'The rebels are harassing the troops, but nothing else so far. If the Baroness wants us to move in support of Edenrich she'd better get back here fast.'

'Not that we can offer much support,' Archer pointed out. 'We don't have much left in the way of men.'

Blackhart grunted, but made no response as they moved off. Archer didn't blame him. It was a mess, and they both knew it.

Archer stayed silent as they walked. Didn't matter how bad things got; he'd made his decision a long time ago.

They made their way around, checking the walls and the sentries. Blackhart allowed only humans up here, living men smart enough to use their eyes and their brains to spot trouble at a distance – unlike the undead that guarded the rest of the keep. Blackhart tended to take these little strolls at random, keeping everyone on their toes.

Blackhart hesitated only once, when Archer caught him staring at the central tower, up towards the window of the room where the priestess was kept. Archer chuckled.

Blackhart's back stiffened for an instant, then with a swirl of his black cloak he moved on, yanking open the door that let them back into the keep. Archer followed as Blackhart strode down the hall towards his private chambers.

Archer shook his head in mock despair. 'You might as well have her, seein' as you can't stop thinking about her. Not that she's much to look at, to my way of thinking, with that white hair and all. Not to my taste.'

'What with your taste running to men and all,' Blackhart pointed out.

'There is that.' Archer gave him a grin. 'Use her and get her out of your blood, Blackhart. This is getting old. There's a nice bed up there – hell, ya chained her to it. She's probably expecting ya, and wondering why ya haven't shown up. Hell, we all are.'

'Your sense of humour is going to get you killed.'

'You been saying that for years,' Archer said, 'and so far—'

Blackhart yanked open the door, stomped into his sitting area and strode over to the fireplace. There was a fire keeping back the chill of the black stone walls and floors.

Archer followed silently. The chairs were old wooden ones, the padding worn around the edges, the wood scratched and nicked. Comfortable and strong. He set his bow to one side, the quiver next to it, and sat, stretching out his long legs.

Blackhart went to the mantel and took down two cups and a large ceramic jug before settling in his own chair. He splashed a generous amount of wine into one cup and held it out. Archer took the cup with a nod of thanks and relaxed as the familiar dryness filled his throat.

Blackhart settled in the chair next to him and took a sip from his own cup. 'We're going to die. All of us.'

Archer jerked around, caught off guard by that brutal statement. He gave Blackhart a startled glance, only to see those hazel eyes narrow in satisfaction.

'You've been lying to me,' Blackhart growled.

'No more than you've been lying to yourself,' Archer hedged.

'So we've been lying to each other.' Blackhart stared into his cup. 'I want your honest assessment.'

Archer sighed and watched as Blackhart took another sip. The look on his face made it clear he wasn't going to be the first to speak.

Archer put his head back against the chair. 'If we're being honest, I'm not sure I realised how bad things were until the last few weeks. Then wasn't sure I was right, and then wasn't sure how to tell ya.'

'All these years and you were afraid to tell me.' Blackhart scowled. 'What kind of bastard does that make me?'

'You're trying to protect us, and what's left of the living people of the Black Hills,' Archer rasped.

'The truth. Now.'

Archer nodded and held out the cup.

Blackhart splashed more wine into it.

'Baroness ain't been right for about five years, since she sent our mages and some of our forces into Athelbryght. We lost all those spell-casters in that attack, and the only reason Mage wasn't in on it was 'cause you held him back.'

Blackhart grunted his agreement.

'At the start, Baroness used the prisoners to make Odium, to strengthen our forces. We all thought that was a good idea at the time. We needed the help. And it worked, for a while. But it takes power and energy to control them, and she's been doing it all for a while now.' Archer pulled his legs in and leaned forward. 'I ain't sure she can do it much longer. Her power over them seems to be getting weaker, like she's trying to do too much. Besides' – Archer looked over at Blackhart – 'she keeps needing the living to feed the dead, and she's started using our own people. Prisoners first. Lawbreakers. But now . . .' He sighed, rubbing his hand over his face, and took another drink before he spoke again. 'That Chosen they got, she's cagey smart. She's not coming at us direct. She's using Lord Fael's men to hold us off while she goes for the Regent's throat. Might work, too – if we don't get moving to reinforce them.

'You ain't got enough control to order the Odium out on your own. And the Baroness ain't here. And if the Chosen takes Edenrich, the first thing she and the other High Barons will do is come for us.' Archer took another sip. 'Ain't good.'

'Put extra men on the walls,' Blackhart said. 'If there's no word by this time tomorrow, we'll risk sending out messengers.'

Which meant the talk, and the honesty, were over. Archer stood and picked up his gear without another word. But even as he closed the door, he caught the movement of Blackhart's gaze towards the ceiling.

Blackhart laid his head back on the chair and stared at the ceiling as Archer closed the door behind him.

He could see no way out of this trap. His men, their families, the people he'd worked so hard to protect . . .

And he couldn't get the sound of her laughter out of his head.

Blackhart took another drink and let the bitter wine lie on his tongue for a moment before he swallowed. It was dry, bitter – all the land could offer in these times.

The Baroness would return, that bright light of a priestess would be extinguished, and he'd go on towards the end. There was no other way that he could see at this point. All the possible doors were closed, locked and barred from one such as he.

And one such as she should curse his name. The attraction he felt . . . that was dangerous. He should just forget it – and her. He had other things to worry about.

His stomach rumbled, reminding him that he hadn't eaten. Orrin stood, deciding to go down to the kitchens rather than send for something. He could check on supplies that way – yet another concern. Then maybe some of Reader's brew, to help him sleep.

As he left his chambers, he found himself wondering if the Priestess had eaten.

*

15

The tower bedroom was just as much a prison, but far more comfortable. There was light and air, for one thing. Evelyn sighed as she knelt on the rug by the fire. It was hard not to feel grateful, but she resisted the feeling. It was still a cell, for there was no way out other than down. The fetter on her ankle was attached to the wall with just enough chain to prevent a dramatic leap from a window.

The flames of the fire licked at the wood and basked her face with its warmth. Warmth, light, air . . . and no rats.

She was still afraid, but it was easier to concentrate now, easier to think. She tested the chain that ran between the manacles; it was strong, but not so short that it impeded her.

Didn't impede movement, that is. The manacles were still draining her of her magic. She could cast no spell; her hands might just as well have been tied. But the sick feeling had faded a bit. She still didn't feel right, but she could at least move without wanting to throw up.

If a chance came for freedom, she vowed to take it, whatever the risk. The Chosen would expect it of her, and she'd rather die fighting than not.

Evelyn closed her eyes, bowed her head, clasped her hands and tried to pray.

The door opened, but Evelyn didn't bother to open her eyes. Her jailers made a habit of checking on her regularly, so the only precaution that Evelyn had taken was to cover the silver ring on her right hand with her other hand. So far, she'd been able to keep it, apparently at Blackhart's command, but that would last only so long. She'd keep it no longer than she'd keep her life.

She'd thought of destroying it; the idea that it might grace Elanore's hand made her ill. But when she'd gone to pull it off, the star had appeared in the gemstone, and she'd stopped. Where there was life, there was hope . . .

'Eat now. You can pray later.'

Evelyn's eyes snapped open. Blackheart was seated on a corner of the bed, a tray of food beside him. Evelyn rose slowly, looking at the plain fare. Bread and cheese, butter and dried apples, with a flagon of wine.

'They tell me you aren't eating.' Blackhart pulled off a hunk of bread and spread it with butter.

Evelyn said nothing, but her stomach grumbled.

'You have my word that nothing is poisoned,' Blackhart added.

Evelyn looked at him.

Blackhart gave her a sardonic look. 'Not sure I'd take my word either.'

'It has nothing to do with your word,' Evelyn said softly. 'If you wanted me dead, you'd have no need to use poison.'

Blackhart nodded. 'True enough. Still . . .' There was a glint in his eye as he tore off a hunk of bread and took a bite. 'Eat,' he commanded, offering her the remainder.

Evelyn sat on the other side of the bed, the chain dragging across the rug behind her. She reached out and took the bread. She held it for a moment, hesitating. 'There seems little point—'

'You are hungry. There is food.' Blackhart offered the cup of wine. 'Stop thinking and eat.'

Evelyn looked into the cup. 'Is this wine looted from Athelbryght? I won't—'

'Those bottles are gone, or kept for the Baroness's private use.' Blackhart grimaced. 'This is what passes for wine in the Black Hills.'

There was bitterness in his voice, and Evelyn thought that odd. She took a sip, only to be taken aback by the taste. It was very dry and acidic.

'And this may not be the fine white bread of Edenrich, but it fills the belly,' Blackhart said.

The bitterness was still in his voice. She made no comment, just started eating the bread. It was coarse and dark and chewy, but it tasted wonderful.

They ate silently for a moment. Blackhart took a bite of everything, even going so far as to sample each piece of dried fruit.

'Tell me of the ring.' He gestured at Evelyn's hand.

'The ring?' Evelyn blushed slightly. 'It was a gift from a merchant. I healed his son's high fever and he gifted it to me. I'm told that by keeping it, I am too vain, too materialistic, but it gives me joy.' Evelyn extended her hand slightly. 'It's a white star sapphire. In certain kinds of light, there's a star that shines within the stone.'

Blackhart snorted. 'Seems a small token for saving a man's heir.'

Evelyn smiled wryly. 'A man who stole it told me that it's

worth only a few silvers at best. The stone is flawed. But I love to see that star shine.'

'When did he tell you the value of the ring?' Blackhart's eyebrows went up. 'As he removed it from your hand?'

'When he returned it.'

Blackhart gave her a long look, then stood and left the room without a word.

Evelyn studied the door, but when Blackhart did not return, she finished the food in silence.

Orrin cursed under his breath as he descended the tower stairs. Archer was right, he should just take the woman and get her out of his system. Elanore would not mind, since the Priestess would surely be raped before she was killed anyway, but for some reason Orrin could not bring himself to do it. Because though he could perform the physical act – hell, he *ached* to perform the physical act – he'd destroy the laughter in those eyes.

He'd made his choices long ago, and the darkness of his soul was a result of those choices. He'd commanded the human warriors for Elanore, and aided her to create undead abominations to use against her enemies. He'd watched a woman he had been intimate with turn into a monster, and had followed her down into the mire without hesitation. He cursed again, thinking of the woman in white.

Archer waited at the bottom of the stairs, an eyebrow arched. 'Did you—'

'No,' Orrin snapped, trying to step around him.

Archer blocked his path. 'You and the Baroness, both smitten fools. She's being stupid, haring off to secure her Josiah in the midst of a war. And now you, with this priestess. You can't afford to be distracted, especially—'

'Was there something you wanted?'

Archer stepped back. 'Riders in the distance – coming hard. They're ours, from the look of things.'

Orrin hesitated for a heartbeat, a pang of regret filling his heart. But he clamped down hard on that and turned towards the main hall. He strode carefully at a set pace, making sure his steps were calm, strong and even. Finally, word had come. If Elanore was but a day or two behind, they could still make this work, protect his people. If she was close . . .

The main doors were already open and men were gathering in the courtyard beyond. The Odium were there as well, lining the walls, their grey flesh falling from their bones. They would stand there and rot until commanded to move or attack. Orrin walked out to stand at the top of the stairs, grateful to feel a breeze. It would keep the stench down. He could see the riders passing the outer wall and spurring their horses forward.

More noise and Orrin knew that Sidian, Mage and Reader had arrived, along with the brothers Timothy and Thomas. His hearth-band, ready to support him.

Archer was a step behind, and a soft sound told Orrin that the lanky blond had nocked an arrow, ready for anything. A wise precaution, but not necessary; he recognised the lads.

'Lord Blackhart!' one of them called as he reined his horse to a stop.

'How far behind you is she, lad?' Orrin called, even as Archer eased his stance. The boy almost fell from his horse in his haste, scrambling to kneel on the black marble steps.

'Lord Blackhart.' The lad took a gasping breath, swallowing hard. His voice was the merest rasp. 'The High Baroness is dead.'

FOUR

Time froze. Orrin's heart seemed to stop in his chest. His worst nightmare had come to pass, and for the barest instant he wanted to turn and run. But then the lad before him held out his fist and unclenched a filthy, blood-encrusted hand to show him Elanore's golden signet ring.

Behind him, Mage sucked in a breath. 'How . . .'

'Are you pursued?' Orrin said, looking at the exhausted group milling in the courtyard.

'No,' the lad responded, 'but Lord, we are all that are left.'

Rage washed over Orrin. Elanore had taken thirty good men, and Odium on top of that. There were fewer than ten in the courtyard. Damn the bitch.

He swallowed the rage. He looked at the ring, then scanned the courtyard with a rising dread.

Archer stepped forward, hand extended to take the ring still displayed in the lad's hand. 'You look exhausted, warrior. Let's see to your needs, and to the others'.'

The lad flushed with pleasure as he stood with Archer's help. Archer turned swiftly to put the ring in Orrin's hand, then called out to the men in the yard, 'Someone see to the horses. I'll take these men to the kitchens for a meal and some of Reader's brew.'

Men nodded. Some turned to their tasks, others ran forward to lead the horses away. Archer had a hand on the lad's shoulder as he guided him and the others towards the kitchens. He gave Orrin a look and Orrin knew Archer would get the full story out of the boy and then report. In the meantime . . .

'Timothy, Thomas, get down to the main gates. Any other stragglers come in, you bring them to me. Don't let them spread word of this.'

The stocky brothers nodded and headed off at a trot.

Sidian stood watching over the courtyard. Reader was there as well, looking very nervous. 'This ain't right,' the little man said, 'they're still—'

Orrin turned. 'Let's stay calm.' He looked at the young apprentice. 'Mage,' he said softly, 'how can the Odium still be—?' He stumbled over the words.

'Odium are destroyed when the spell-caster who created them dies.' Mage's eyes were wide, but he met Orrin's gaze without a flinch. 'If she's really dead—'

'That's the only way this came off her finger,' Orrin said. He opened his hand again, checking the heavy gold ring with its blood-red stone. For a fleeting moment, a contrasting image of a slim silver ring with a flawed white stone flashed in his mind's eye.

'I know,' Mage said, swallowing hard.

'If she's not controlling them, and I'm not controlling them, then who is?' Orrin growled, clenching his fist over the ring.

Mage trembled, but he didn't move. 'I don't know.'

'What if they turn on us?' Sidian rumbled.

The moment froze again as Orrin's gaze went towards the tower where the Priestess was imprisoned. Elanore was dead, he felt that in his bones. The very tool she had made to gain her power would destroy her people. There were more Odium than living men in the keep. And if they started to go into the countryside . . .

There was one chance . . . for his men . . . for his people. The cage doors had opened and he caught a glimpse of a way out. A chance for his men and their families to survive.

'Sidian, Reader, summon my sergeants.' Orrin stalked back into the keep. 'Mage, you're coming with me. We need to send a message.'

Sidian and Reader were already moving, calling for the army leaders. Mage scrambled to stay beside Orrin as he strode off. 'Where do you want the message to go, sir?'

'To the Chosen,' Orrin said.

She'd been left alone for most of the day, alone with her thoughts. One would think a priestess of the Light would prepare for death with meditation and prayer. Evelyn sighed as she knelt by the fire, at the length of her chains. She was trying to pray, but her mind kept drifting to Orrin Blackhart.

For a man who'd plotted her capture and death, he'd treated her decently enough. And though the Baroness would take great pleasure in Evelyn's death, it seemed that Blackhart would not share in that joy. Odd. She'd spent only a few moments with him, but he . . . interested her.

Orrin Blackhart, Scourge of Palins. A warrior, certainly. She tried to think of what little she knew of him. Mostly rumours. He bore the title of Lord Marshal, and people said he'd worked his way through the ranks to earn the position with a ruthlessness that all feared; that under his command, the people of Farentell had been slaughtered. Ezren Storyteller had said that the Baroness was using Odium, and that she'd used prisoners to create her army of undead with the support of the Usurper. Evelyn had denied it, but now she'd seen it with her own eyes.

She shuddered. That anyone would engage in those black and evil practices was unthinkable. How could she be . . . *interested* . . . in a man who would—

The crashing of the door brought Evelyn to her feet, heart pounding.

Blackhart stood in the doorway, a ring of keys in hand. 'Time to go, Priestess.'

Startled, Evelyn watched as he moved around the bed to where her ankle chain was attached to the wall and reached to unlock it. She hadn't heard any fanfare to announce the arrival of the Baroness, yet it seemed the time of her death had come. But if those keys opened the manacles on her wrists . . .

She didn't give herself time to think. She just moved as quietly as she could. Blackhart spoke as she stepped behind him. 'I'm going to—'

She threw the chain over his head, planted her knee in the middle of his back and yanked back hard. At best she might kill him, at worst . . .

The chain caught in his mouth, cutting off his words. But he didn't budge, even when she threw her full weight back, putting everything she had into it.

It wasn't enough.

He moved then. Evelyn heard the keys fall to the floor as Blackhart's hand gripped her wrist and pulled. He turned in her arms and she found herself facing a very angry man whose glare pierced her heart. She tried to step back, but the chain around his neck pulled her short.

Blackhart's free arm wrapped around her, pressing into the small of her back, forcing her against the length of his body. He took a step and the edge of the mattress hit the back of Evelyn's knees. She cried out as he pushed her down, covering her with his body and pinning her wrists to the bed.

Furious, she struggled, opening her mouth to curse him.

'Stupid—' Blackhart cut off his own words and covered her mouth with his own.

She tasted like spring, like new green leaves and the scent of warm rain on the air.

He kissed her, wanting more, demanding more. And she responded, exploring his mouth as he plundered hers. Her body softened under his, legs opening to cradle him. His hand drifted down to cup her breast. Even through the fabric of her robes, she filled his hand, and his fingers brushed over—

'Oh, fine. *Now* you take her.'

Archer's voice cut Orrin's spine like a knife. He jerked his head up, staring down at the Priestess he'd just defiled.

Her blue eyes were wide with shock and confusion, her mouth still open, still wet from his—

Orrin stood abruptly, pulling her off the bed. 'Count yourself lucky, Priestess,' he snarled as he pulled her towards the door.

Archer stepped back from the doorway. 'The Chosen's envoy is on her way. Already passed the first gate.'

Orrin nodded and pulled the Priestess along behind him. He marched her through the halls and down the stairs to the main throne room. She never said a word, but he could feel the trembling of her hand.

He was too afraid to stop and answer her questions. Everything depended on the next few moments, and if she tried asking him about the kiss, he wasn't sure he wouldn't press her against the wall and take her right there and damn the consequences.

They entered the throne room and he rushed her up the dais, placing her on the throne. She stared at him, then frowned. 'What—'

Archer knelt and chained her ankles, using a short chain. He rose and stepped back quickly.

Orrin nodded to Mage. He then moved back from the throne, making a swift gesture that stopped the woman from moving.

Mage had his book in one hand, loose pages poking out the sides. He raised the other hand and gestured, muttering the words of the spell. There was an odd sparkle around the throne and then Evelyn stiffened, a startled look on her face.

'Did it work?' Orrin asked. He had his answer as Evelyn's lips moved but no sound emerged.

Mage closed his book, a slight frown on his face. 'She can't hear us and we can't hear her.'

'Good work.' Orrin moved to stand at the base of the dais, looking around at his men. 'Everyone, pull up your hoods. I don't want her to see any face but my own.'

His men obeyed as they moved into position. Archer entered the shadows behind Blackhart, bow at the ready. 'I don't like this.'

'You don't have to.' Blackhart turned to look at him, pleased that the hood concealed his features completely. 'You've passed the word? The men are ready?'

Archer nodded, his eyes gleaming from the darkness. 'They're ready. You give the word, and the keep will empty before you're out the gate.'

'Make sure that they gather the living in the fortified villages,' Orrin said. 'Take this.' He tossed the gold ring with the red stone to Archer. 'Melt the damn thing down and sell the stone.'

Archer faded back into the shadows. 'You sure the Chosen's gonna agree to this deal?'

Orrin glanced back to make sure that the Priestess hadn't moved. Her eyes were wide and she was staring at him, clearly trying to figure out what was happening. He turned back to face the doors, a grim look on his face. 'Let's find out, shall we?'

FIVE

The doors of the chamber opened of their own accord.

The figure that appeared out of the darkness of the main corridor was a tall blonde woman wearing plate and bearing only a simple white flag. No weapons, as he'd requested. Orrin relaxed a bit, seeing that she'd obeyed that part of his message.

She was tall and impressive. Her armour had a sheen to it that made it glow in the torchlight. A warrior, and one with experience. Good.

The woman's gaze flicked from the Priestess to the men in the shadows before she focused on Orrin.

He arched an eyebrow, well aware of her scrutiny. 'Lady Bethral, I assume.'

'Blackhart,' the woman replied coolly. 'You asked for a parley.'

'I did.' Orrin gestured to the throne. 'You see the Lady High Priestess, as promised.'

Bethral looked at Evelyn. 'Lady High Priestess, are you well?'

Evelyn almost couldn't breathe when Bethral walked into the throne room. What was she doing here?

The Chosen had made it clear that there'd be no rescue. But there stood Bethral, fully armoured, with no weapons and a small white flag.

Evelyn strained to hear, but the spell cast by the young apprentice had effectively stuffed up her ears and silenced her voice. All she could do was watch as they talked.

Bethral faced her and asked a question. Evelyn sighed and shrugged. She pointed to her ear, shaking her head.

Blackhart gestured as if explaining. Bethral turned back to face him. Evelyn watched as Blackhart stepped off the dais and moved closer to Bethral, as if confiding in her. Their expressions told her nothing, to her growing frustration.

Finally, Bethral nodded and Blackhart handed her a set of keys. She took them and walked towards the throne. As she drew close, there was a pop in Evelyn's ears as the spell around her was released.

'Are you well?' Bethral unlocked the wrist chains first.

As the first manacle loosened, a wave of repressed pain passed through Evelyn's bones. She swallowed hard at the sensation, barely able to manage an answer. 'Well enough.' Evelyn looked into Bethral's concerned eyes. 'What—?'

'Can you work magic?' Bethral asked urgently as she unlocked the second manacle.

'No.' Evelyn shuddered, rubbing her wrists. 'Whatever those chains are, they've drained me completely. I'll need rest before I can do anything.'

Bethral handed the keys to Evelyn and gestured for her to free her legs. She turned slightly, keeping an eye on the people around them.

Evelyn bent down to unlock the chain on her ankle. She glanced about and saw Blackhart talking to a group of the hooded warriors who were darting off in all directions.

Blackhart looked their way, but he didn't meet Evelyn's gaze. 'Leave with her,' he said to Bethral. 'You can do nothing with this place.'

'I'm free?' Evelyn whispered as she sat up, confused. What had happened?

Blackhart gave her a long look, then jerked his head in a nod. Evelyn grabbed Bethral's arm and stood as he continued, 'I will give the orders to my warriors, and then I will emerge from the gates and surrender myself. Your men will let my people pass?'

'I will give the orders myself,' Bethral replied as Evelyn took a few shaky steps. 'I have your word?'

Blackhart gave her a grim smile. 'For what it is worth, Lady.'

Evelyn jerked her head up and focused on Blackhart. Now he met her gaze, and those hazel eyes were filled with determination and . . . regret. She stared at him for a long breath, and he returned the look.

Evelyn released Bethral's arm and walked forward, never letting her gaze waver. 'I thank you, Lord—'

'No, there's no time. Go, and quickly.'

Evelyn made no move to obey.

Bethral reached for her arm. 'Lady High Priestess, we must go.' She took her by the elbow and urged her forward. Bethral bent down, grabbed the spell chains from the floor and wrapped them around her wrist.

'I will be at the gate within an hour.' Blackhart was looking at Evelyn as he made the promise.

Bethral took Evelyn's elbow and headed for the corridor.

His men were evacuating the keep as fast as they could.

Blackhart forced himself to move calmly and smoothly. The Odium still lined the halls; silent, dark, and more threatening than ever. He ignored them.

His men, his hearth-band, waited at the main doors, horses ready, their gear packed. His horse bore no gear. He didn't need any, did he? Blackhart smiled grimly as he walked out into the courtyard.

Archer was holding the reins of two horses. Everyone else was already mounted, their eyes on their surroundings, keeping watch.

'Everyone out?' Blackhart asked quietly.

'If they ain't, they's too stupid to live.' Archer handed him the reins of his horse.

Mage was up on his horse, shivering slightly. The lad's cloak had always been thin. Blackhart removed his own and handed it to the lad.

Mage looked down in surprise. 'Lord—?'

Blackhart turned away and mounted his horse.

'Put it on, lad,' Sidian said gruffly. 'He won't need it.'

Blackhart turned his horse and started it walking slowly down the road to the main gate. 'We'll take it slow. Give the stragglers time to get out.'

Archer fell in beside him and the rest followed. They rode in silence for a moment as Blackhart scanned the grounds.

'You can still escape,' Archer said softly. 'We get out of the gate and make a run for it.'

'No.' Blackhart pulled his horse to a stop just shy of the gate. He could see the Chosen's forces on the road ahead. 'We'll stick with the terms.'

'The Chosen's gonna kill ya,' Archer pointed out. 'For stuff you ain't necessarily done.'

'My terms. My choice.' Blackhart leaned over and offered his hand. 'Keep them safe.'

Archer clasped it hard. 'Do my best.'

With that, he urged his horse forward and the others followed fast, galloping out of the gate and turning north, disappearing into the night. The Chosen's forces made no move to follow.

Blackhart took a deep breath as he waited for a moment to let them get clear. The air was crisp and cold, and it felt oddly clean. Or maybe it was that his heart felt lighter. They were almost clear of this trap. One more thing he had to try to do.

When he reached the lower gate, he stopped and gestured to the side. A figure emerged, an Odium, shuffling forward.

'Guard,' he demanded in a loud voice.

The figure stood there.

'Guard,' Blackhart said again. He expected a nod, the usual response to a command.

This time, the figure nodded its head. 'Gaard,' said a dry, empty voice.

A chill went down Blackhart's spine. None of the Odium had ever spoken before. But he returned the nod and rode forward.

The gates closed behind him, but the chill didn't leave his spine.

He kept his horse at a walk and drew up next to the warrior-lady. Evelyn was mounted behind her, staring at him, her blue eyes alight with confusion.

With a flourish, he handed Bethral his sheathed sword. 'We'd best be on our way.'

Bethral nodded and issued orders. He was surrounded in an instant, his hands grabbed and bound.

Blackhart wasn't looking at the men taking him prisoner. His eyes were fixed on the lovely High Priestess. He allowed himself a smile then. His men were free to protect their families as best they could. Better still, the Priestess was safe with her own people.

And who knew? With any luck, he'd hear her laugh again before he was executed.

SIX

The tower bedroom was just as much a prison, but far more comfortable. There was light and air and warmth. But this castle belonged to the Chosen and now he was the prisoner.

Orrin Blackhart paced barefoot before the fireplace. The room was a cell, for there was no way out, other than down. Furthermore, the fetter on his ankle was chained to the wall, just long enough to prevent a dramatic leap from a window. There were two guards at the door, and two farther down the hall. He had to give credit to the Lady Bethral, now Warder of this castle. She knew her job well, and hadn't permitted anyone to abuse him.

Wouldn't do for the prisoner to be all bruised and bloody for his execution.

He'd known, of course, what his fate would be. It was just the thrice-damned waiting—

The door opened and Orrin's eyes shot to the doorway. The Lady High Priestess Evelyn, dressed in white, stood there with a tray in hand.

Orrin's eyes narrowed.

The Priestess moved forward and placed the food on the table off to the side. Slices of bread, cheese and pears were arranged on the plates, and there was a flagon of wine. She seated herself, her heavy white robes swishing the floor as she settled in one of the chairs. 'Eat. You can pace later.'

Orrin's mouth quirked before he could control it and he moved over to settle in the other chair, the chain dragging on the floor behind him. 'Well, at least I need not fear rape and torture at the hands of your Chosen. Nor poison. A very quick, very public execution will be my fate.'

Evelyn poured wine for them both. 'Yet you knew this when you surrendered the castle and returned me safe to my people.'

Orrin picked up a slice of pear. 'I knew.'

Evelyn reached for a slice of yellow cheese. 'I had to cut this in the kitchens. They would not let me bring a knife to cut it.'

He tilted his head. 'You had to fix the plate?'

Evelyn shrugged. 'I thought it best, Lord Blackhart.'

'Orrin,' he said on impulse. He wanted to hear her say his name. 'My name is Orrin.'

'Orrin,' she said as she reached for the bread. 'I thought it better if I prepared the food.'

'Smart of them not to allow the knife,' Orrin said as he looked at the pear slice in his hand, 'but I would not take my own life. I accept responsibility for my actions, Priestess. My soul is stained with blood and pain, and I welcome death.'

'If you wish to plead for mercy, I would support—'

Orrin shook his head. 'No.' He gave her a wry look. 'They would not even fix the plate for you to bring to me. Do you really think the Chosen could pardon me?'

Evelyn looked down at the food. 'I have heard talk. Men do foolish things for love.'

Orrin laughed at that. 'Foolish? More like dreadful, Lady High Priestess.' His face grew grim. 'Not that love had much to do with it.' He looked at her calm face, suddenly curious. 'Besides, what would you know of love?'

'We are sworn to obedience and chastity, not celibacy.' Evelyn's face was still serene as she spoke. 'We are permitted to marry with the approval of the Archbishop.' She looked at him, and her blue eyes met his.

For a moment, Orrin had the oddest sensation of hope. A wave of desire washed over him as he thought of the possibility that she might—

But then reality crashed back over him. 'Do you know . . .' – he had to clear his throat – 'when will—?'

She looked away. 'They will bring you before the Chosen after her coronation tomorrow.'

'My thanks.' Some of the tension flowed out of Orrin's body. 'It makes the waiting easier.'

'I know,' she said softly. 'Eat.'

He popped the pear slice into his mouth, easing the dryness within. Evelyn poured the wine.

He reached for the simple cup and looked over at her. 'I did want to . . . apologise. For . . . defiling you.'

'Defiling?' Evelyn frowned at him. 'What are you—?' She paused, then her face cleared. 'You mean the kiss?'

Orrin nodded. 'I soiled—'

'Oh, please.' Evelyn looked at him, amused. 'I'm no fresh-faced virgin, disgraced by your touch.' She held out a slice of bread. 'Besides, I had just tried to kill you.'

'Not very well.' Orrin took the food.

They ate in silence, lost in their own thoughts. Once the food was finished, Evelyn rose to go.

'Will you be there, Priestess?'

Evelyn raised an eyebrow. 'My name is Evelyn.'

Orrin turned in his chair and looked into her eyes. There was a hint of sparkle there, and of challenge. Something seized in his chest as he realised that he'd never get to meet that challenge. 'So it is,' he said slowly. 'Will you be there, Evelyn?'

Evelyn's face grew rueful. 'I will. The Chosen wishes to thank me publicly for my efforts. Although I did nothing in comparison to the sacrifices of others.'

Orrin smiled. 'It will please me to see you honoured. Perhaps you will honour a condemned man with a smile?'

Evelyn looked at him, her face etched with sorrow. 'No, Orrin. I do not think I will smile again for quite some time.'

Orrin's heart lurched within him, but he forced his face into a snarl. 'Do not waste your time on one such as me, Priestess. You'll be the only one to mourn, and more fool you for doing so.'

Calmly, Evelyn picked up the tray. 'I'm just as capable of foolish things as any other.' With that, she turned and left.

Orrin Blackhart cursed every god he knew for bringing Lady High Priestess Evelyn into his last hours before his execution.

Evelyn headed for the kitchens.

She could have handed the tray off to any servant she passed, but they were all busy with tasks of their own, preparing for the coronation of the Chosen. Besides, walking to the kitchen gave her a few moments to gather her thoughts.

It had been days since she'd seen Blackhart . . . Orrin. She'd been swept into the battle plans as soon as she had returned, and there hadn't been a moment's pause until they'd triumphed. But now, in this time before the Chosen's coronation, her thoughts had returned to the condemned man.

Blackhart, Scourge of Palins. His fate was sealed and the list of his crimes was being prepared, to be read out before he was sentenced. The entire kingdom would rejoice.

But not she.

Evelyn tried to tell herself that it was her background as a priestess that made her think of this death as a waste. That she regretted that he'd have no chance to redeem his soul in this life. But that wasn't really true, was it? There was something about him . . .

She shook herself back to reality. She had far more to think about than a condemned prisoner. The private dinner with the Chosen last night had proved that her work here was not yet done. No, in point of fact, it had not yet really started.

During the planning, the scheming, all preparing for this moment, it had occurred to Evelyn that it would take time to restore Palins to its former glory; time and hard work. And those efforts had to start right away – the Chosen could not waste a moment in her tasks. If her throne was to be secure, if they were to succeed, then she had to serve her kingdom's needs.

And Palins needed everything.

Evelyn nodded once or twice to the people she passed, but she didn't really see them. In her mind's eye she was seeing the countryside, the wasteland that was Athelbryght. Farentell's empty farms and villages. What little she'd seen of the Black Hills hadn't been good, either.

The Chosen's rebellion had taken all of the spring and most of the summer. Once winter hit, there would be shortages. If food and livestock could be gleaned from those areas, and whatever supplies the Regent had hoarded – if those were rationed, they might see the winter through. But making it through to the next harvest would be another matter. Hunger and hardship would drain the will and support of the people, support the Chosen still needed.

Evelyn sighed. Sometimes it seemed that no matter how many problems you solved, more came to take their place. Harder issues, tougher goals. It would be nice to have a bit of peace, time to think, pray and meditate.

'Lady High Priestess.'

The call caught her off guard. She turned to see one of the castle guards coming towards her. 'Yes?'

'Your pardon, but the Lady Bethral asks that you spare her a moment.'

'Where is she?' Evelyn asked.

'In the Warder's office, Lady.'

The previous Warder of Edenrich had fallen in the last battle. Lady Bethral had been the obvious choice to protect the Chosen, and Edenrich itself, and she'd moved smoothly to take control of the castle and the city.

She'd already made the Warder's office her own: weapons on the walls, a battered table and chairs, worn and comfortable. In one of the windows, a cat lay sleeping. It was one of the ugliest cats Evelyn had ever seen, with watery yellow eyes, its fur sticking out every which way, black and brown and yellow and a mottled kind of green. A tail so bedraggled as to be an embarrassment. The creature opened one eye, then closed it, completely indifferent to her presence.

Bethral was a warrior, a tall, lovely blonde with clear blue eyes. Lovely and deadly. And clearly not happy. She frowned as Evelyn walked into her office. 'I understand you fed the prisoner.'

'I did.' Evelyn walked in calmly and settled in one of the chairs. 'As he did, for me.' Evelyn arched an eyebrow. 'They wish him to starve?'

'They wish him dead, Lady,' Bethral answered softly. 'Some want him dead fast, some slow, but all want him dead.' Her blue eyes were focused on Evelyn's eyes. 'Not one voice is raised in his defence.'

'And I understand that,' Evelyn said, looking down at her hands, and at her ring. 'They are justified in their hatred.'

'And yet . . . ,' Bethral prodded.

Evelyn looked up. 'I am alive due to his mercy. I feel—'

'You are alive due to his needs,' Bethral cut her off. 'He needed you for the parley – and that is the full measure of his kindness.'

'He parleyed to save his men.' Evelyn kept her tone even. 'Doesn't that say something about him?'

'A day late and a copper short,' Bethral pointed out.

'One never knows what a copper might buy,' Evelyn replied.

Bethral flushed, and fell silent.

33

Evelyn sighed. 'I'm sorry. I—' She paused, unsure of what to say next. Everyone had heard the tale of the rescue of Ezren Silvertongue from the clutches of the Regent and his slavers. Many had heard of the abuse he had taken at their hands, and had seen the scars he bore. But few knew that Bethral had purchased him from the slavers for a single copper coin.

'You're a priestess,' Bethral said. 'A healer. The one kind soul who should feel mercy towards the man. I can't fault you for that.'

'His life is forfeit,' Evelyn said, 'but I can't help but think it a waste.'

'He may have surrendered himself for nothing. Reports say that the Black Hills are awash in Odium. Their legions are growing.'

'Someone is creating them.' Evelyn bit her lip. 'Hard on the people left there. Is that what you wanted to talk about? Are you taking a force in?'

Bethral shook her head. 'For now, the Odium are staying within the borders. We don't have men or supplies to waste trying to clean them out. First we see to our needs, and then we will deal with the Black Hills.' Bethral cleared her throat. 'No, I wanted to talk about—'

The door flew open and a young woman with brown hair, brown eyes, red leather gloves and special armour designed to display the birthmark of the Chosen entered the room. Her eyes lit up when she saw Evelyn.

Evelyn and Bethral rose from their chairs.

'Chosen,' Bethral said.

'Aunt Evie!' With a bound, the woman enveloped Evelyn in a hug.

SEVEN

Evelyn returned the hug, then set the girl back a bit. 'You are supposed to give us time to curtsey, Your Majesty.'

Gloriana tried to look contrite. 'I'll remember in public, Aunt Evie. I really will.'

Evelyn smiled at her. Gloriana was so young, with her warm brown eyes and brown hair cut shoulder-length. Evelyn had rescued her before the Regent's forces could slay her for bearing the birthmark of the Chosen. Gloriana had been raised by Lord Auxter and Lady Arent of Soccia, with Evelyn's help. They were not related by blood, but definitely by heart.

Lord Auxter had been killed while gathering the support of the High Barons for their cause. Lady Arent had come to Edenrich to support Gloriana. Though Arent bore her sorrow well, Evelyn felt sure she would want to return to her home in Soccia after the coronation.

Bethral gestured them both to their chairs. 'I thought you were meeting with the Chancellor, Chosen.'

Gloriana settled in the chair next to Evelyn's. 'Vembar is resting. He's pushing himself too hard. Lady Arent said that she would check on him, to make sure he did as he was told.' She turned to Evelyn. 'Isn't there anything you can do for him?'

Evelyn sat back in her chair. 'I cannot cure old age, Gloriana. But I will look in on him.'

'Thank you. We're going to review the coronation plans tonight, and rehearse the ceremony in the throne room.' Gloriana made a face. 'Vembar says that we should follow all the old traditions, but I am not sure I want oil poured on my hair.'

Bethral chuckled, and Evelyn smiled. 'There's a great deal of symbolism in the ritual, Gloriana. The anointing with holy oil is

35

important. The one thing the Regent never dared do was take part in the ceremony and swear the oaths of the sovereign.'

'The Archbishop wants the ceremony to take place in the church.'

'No,' Bethral said firmly. 'We have a hard enough task keeping you secure within the castle. There will be no procession, and the ceremony will take place in the throne room as planned.'

'Arent found some white silk and she's keeping the ladies of the Court in the sunroom, sewing like madwomen.' Gloriana grinned. 'They are making a design that will show off my birthmark.' She looked down at her gloves. 'What would Red say to that?'

'You are Red Gloves now, child.' Bethral's voice was firm. 'And on the morrow, you will be Queen Gloriana.'

Gloriana straightened in her chair. 'I know.' Her eyes were clear, her face composed. 'I have trained my entire life for this moment, and I will strive to serve my people and my kingdom.' Her face changed then, sadness flooding in. 'I just miss her. Uncle Josiah went after her. Do you think they will be all right?'

Bethral and Evelyn exchanged a look, then Bethral shrugged. 'Hard to say. Red is stubborn.'

'So is Josiah,' Evelyn reminded them both.

Gloriana sighed, and started to play with her hair. 'I asked Arent to be on the Council, but she said no.'

'She is of Soccia,' Evelyn reminded her. 'I suspect she will return there as soon as you are crowned.'

'She won't even let me thank her publicly. But you will be on the Council, won't you, Aunt Evie?' Gloriana asked anxiously. 'Vembar will be, and Ezren Storyteller.' She looked down at the floor. 'I can't lose everyone.'

'I will gladly serve you,' Evelyn said. 'As will the High Barons.'

A knock on the door and they all turned as a guard poked his head in. 'Your Majesty, the Lady Arent requests a moment of your time.'

Gloriana rose. 'I will see you both tonight at the rehearsal.' She smiled, her face alight with mischief. 'Aunt Evie, I have a surprise for you tomorrow.'

Evelyn raised an eyebrow. 'Don't you dare make me High Baroness of Farentell. We already talked about that.'

Gloriana laughed as she moved to the door. 'No, no, something better. You'll see.'

As the door closed, Bethral gave Evelyn a look. 'Farentell?'

'That bloodline is gone.' Evelyn sighed. 'There are none who can claim that barony, so it reverts back to the Crown. Gloriana is going to have to name a new baron or baroness, and my name was mentioned. I refused it. As did Arent. Vembar suggested that Gloriana wait for a while to try to find the best candidate, and she agreed.'

'Smart,' Bethral agreed. 'Gives her time to make a good choice and it dangles like a worm on a hook before the entire court.'

Evelyn laughed. 'You have an interesting view of Court intrigue.'

'A battle, like any other,' Bethral said as she stood and moved over to a chest against the wall. She took out a cloth sack with something heavy in it. 'I wanted to ask you about these.'

She poured the spell chains out onto the wooden table. The clatter caused the cat to wake and lift its head.

Evelyn shivered and pressed back into her chair. She remembered the feel of those things on her wrist, draining her powers. She wasn't sure she was fully recovered from their effects, and she knew the memory of her helplessness would be with her forever.

'I'm sorry, but I have to know.' Bethral sat back down. 'Would they help the Storyteller?'

'Contain his wild magic?' Evelyn's eyes went wide. 'I hadn't thought of that.'

Bethral shrugged. 'Mercenaries look for every advantage.' She tilted her head. 'Would it work?'

'I don't know,' Evelyn said.

Bethral picked up one of the manacles. 'Did you notice that the metals are different? The manacles don't match the chains.'

'No,' Evelyn said wryly, 'I was too terrified to notice much of anything.' She looked closer. The metals were different colours, and the chains seemed smoother. She sat forward and reached out, letting one finger brush the surface of the manacle. Even the faint touch brought the sapping effect. She didn't pull back, instead moving her finger along the chain. There was no effect once her skin left the manacle. 'The chain doesn't have the same effect.'

'Since High Baron Josiah left for Athelbryght, Silvertongue has managed fairly well,' Bethral said. She pulled the set towards her, and studied where the manacle and chain connected. 'He's been able to control his magic, and has stayed well away from your father.'

'Just as well,' Evelyn said dryly, 'since my father thinks he should kill Ezren.'

Bethral's eyes narrowed. 'He will not.'

Evelyn opened her mouth to issue a warning, then fell silent. Bethral had stepped between her father and Ezren the last time. Never mind that her father was Marlon, High Mage of Palins and of the Mages' Guild, one of – if not the – most powerful mages in the kingdom.

When the Chosen had been ambushed, Ezren had somehow been invested with mage power. Not true magic – no, Ezren had been filled with wild magic, a force no one could claim to control, much less understand. The Mages' Guild normally executed any mage foolish enough to try to wield that power; that is, if the wild magic didn't turn on the mage first, and fry his flesh off his bones – and the bones of any near him.

Ezren had been essential to the Chosen's cause. Marlon eventually agreed to allow him to live, and had even taught him some basic controls. But Marlon considered Ezren a danger, and it wouldn't take much to convince him to change his decision.

Evelyn didn't blame Ezren for avoiding her father. She'd been doing it herself, although her reason was simpler. She just didn't want to argue with him.

'Could they hurt the Storyteller?' Bethral asked.

Pulled from her thoughts, Evelyn gave her a blank look.

'The chains,' Bethral prompted.

'I really don't know,' Evelyn said. 'Wild magic is not predictable.' She gave Bethral a sceptical look. 'Will he even agree to wear chains again? You know how badly his wrists are scarred.'

Bethral looked away. 'Ezren Storyteller is deeply involved with the plans for the coronation. There hasn't been a moment he could spare to speak with me.'

'Ah.' Evelyn sighed inwardly. Something had happened between those two, something during the ambush. They weren't talking. She didn't know what or how, and hadn't had time to pry, but—

'I wouldn't blame him if he refused them in their current state,' Bethral continued. 'But Onza is here in the castle.'

'Auxter's mage-smith?' Evelyn considered that fact. 'He's one of the few who could modify the chains without destroying their power.'

'Then I'll have him use the castle forge to strike the chains,' Bethral said. 'If the manacles are still empowered—'

'I'll give them to Ezren tonight' – Evelyn rose – 'before the rehearsal.'

'Don't mention my name.' Bethral rose as well. 'He'll refuse them if you do.'

'Very well,' Evelyn said. She'd see what she could do about their relationship after the coronation. She walked to the door, then paused. 'Bethral . . . the execution tomorrow. Who—?'

Bethral gave her a long, steady look for a moment, then spoke. 'By my hand, Lady High Priestess. I've a block prepared, and a sharp axe. I'll make it quick and clean, I promise.'

Evelyn's mouth went dry, but she managed a nod of thanks as she went out the door.

Vembar of Edenrich, the Queen's Chancellor, wiggled his toes under the bedding and enjoyed the heat of the warming stone the servants had tucked in at the foot of the bed. He leaned back against the thick pillows and tried very hard to resent that he'd been told to rest. The truth was, he needed a respite. That was the worst part of growing old, losing one's strength of body. Not of will, though. Certainly not of will. He pulled his hands from beneath the blankets and looked at them in the firelight. How had they grown so weathered? Wrinkled, spotted, stiff – when had they lost their strength?

Still, though he was old, he wasn't dead yet. And on the morrow, Gloriana, his beloved student, would take the throne as the Chosen of Palins. And he'd serve her as long as there was breath in his body. Vembar took a deep breath. He'd a few years left. And there was so much to do to put the kingdom right again.

So much that was wrong. Here in the quiet of his room, he could see clearly the problems that would soon have to be dealt with. The release and restoration of the slaves. The need to secure the food supply, the need to get able-bodied men and women into the fields, to restore their prosperity. Farentell had to be rebuilt, and then there was the problem of the Black Hills.

Vembar had seen the reports that the Odium were ravaging the countryside. They would be hard pressed to—

He sighed, took a deep breath and tried to relax. He was supposed to be resting, not worrying himself into a knot. Time enough to work. This night and the next day should be focused on Gloriana. Already the vultures of the court were circling, looking for ways to insinuate themselves into her councils and favour. He'd have to keep an eye on the Archbishop especially.

The door of his chamber opened, and Lady Arent entered. He smiled at his old friend

'I thought I'd come to see if you are doing as you should. I'm glad to see you are resting,' Arent said.

'Escaping the fervour, more like.' He gestured to a straight chair by the bed. 'Sit and talk to me.'

She left the door ajar, as was proper, and came to sit beside him. The firelight reflected on the angles of her face, made that much starker by her hair, pulled back in a tight bun. He'd known her for years, her and Auxter. Though many might see severity, Vembar knew her better than that. He could see her pain. 'How go the preparations?'

Arent grimaced as she sat. 'I set every one of the Court ladies to sewing a dress for Gloriana. Keep them busy. But there is only so much twittering I can tolerate.'

Vembar chuckled. 'Has the bickering started yet?'

'Oh, yes.' Arent rolled her eyes. 'They're all trying to figure out ranks and family honour for the procession and harassing the Herald. Thank the Lord and the Lady I'm not involved with that decision.'

'Tired?' Vembar asked gently.

Arent said nothing. She dropped her gaze to her lap.

'Gloriana said she'd offered a royal funeral for Auxter, after the coronation. She said that you declined the honour.'

'So many died.' Arent didn't look up. 'It doesn't seem right to

40

honour him over the other dead. Besides, he would have hated the idea.'

'I think you are right,' Vembar murmured. He paused for a moment, waiting.

There was a soft hitch in Arent's breath.

'It's quiet in here,' Vembar continued softly. 'It's dark and warm, and there is no one about. Tell me the truth, Arent.'

She didn't lift her head. 'My head knows he's gone, Vembar. But my heart . . . I keep thinking he's back at the farm, training the warriors down by the forge. When I return, he will want all the details . . .' Her voice trailed off, and then she looked up at him with tear-filled eyes.

Vembar pushed back the thick blankets, and swung his legs over the side of the bed. It took a moment to stand and pull down his nightshirt, but he managed it.

'Vembar,' Arent began to scold, but Vembar held up a hand. He walked slowly over to the door and managed to grasp the handle without leaning on the damn thing.

He looked out at his guardians. 'The Lady Arent and I are going to speak privately. We arc not to be disturbed.' He saw them nod in response as he shut the door and secured the lock.

'Vembar' – Arent moved to his side and offered her arm – 'what will they think?'

He took her arm and let her guide him back to the bed. He sat with a sigh of relief, and then pulled on her arm until she sat next to him.

'With any luck, they will think we are making mad, passionate love.' Vembar smiled at her.

Arent looked at him, her eyes wide with surprise.

Vembar raised his eyebrows, planted his feet on the floor, and pushed. The bed frame rocked back, gently squeaking.

Arent clapped a hand over her mouth, smothering her laugh.

Vembar waggled his eyebrows and let the bed ease back so it creaked again. 'It would help if you'd moan a little.'

Arent's body shook as she sat there, but then, as he'd known it would, the laughter turned to sobs. He put his arms around her shoulders as she buried her head in his chest and clung to him like a child.

Grief rose in his own throat. He held her and said nothing. There was nothing to say, no words he knew that would ease the grief. She'd weep, and then the needs of the day would press in and she'd dry her eyes and see to them.

But for now, he'd offer what comfort he could. He held her close and let her cry.

EIGHT

Orrin thought it fairly sparse as royal coronations go. He'd half expected to be dragged through the streets behind the Chosen as the last living enemy of the victor. Instead, they'd brought him down to the throne room fairly early and secured him in an antechamber. The double doors were open wide, giving him and his four guards a prime view of the ceremony.

The fact that the Lady Bethral could see into the room from her position beside the throne was not lost on him.

She knew her business. He'd been stripped down to tunic and trous, bare of foot and chained tight at the wrists. He was not uncomfortable, but he wasn't going anywhere. There was a leather belt around his waist, with a chain leading off to each of his four guards.

The stones of the floor were cold under his feet, but the throne room was hot, what with all the people crammed within. The Archbishop was looking flushed, wearing resplendent robes of gold and white and crimson. Orrin smiled grimly. That fat bastard had other reasons to sweat.

He didn't see the High Priestess.

Trumpets sounded a fanfare and there was a stir in the crowd. His guards craned their necks to see.

A young woman came into view, dressed in white and wearing red leather gloves. She approached the throne and knelt on the lowest step of the dais. A choir started to sing a hymn. Orrin narrowed his eyes.

That chit had defeated them?

She looked so young kneeling there, practically glowing in the white dress. He could see the birthmark, framed by the white silk. *That* was Red Gloves?

He didn't believe it.

Three people stepped forward then and Orrin's heart beat faster. The old man had to be Chancellor Vembar. Orrin

43

grunted in surprise to see him alive. Ezren Storyteller stood straight and tall, looking rather better than the last time he'd seen the man. But it was the lady in white and gold robes who drew his gaze.

Lady High Priestess Evelyn.

He caught his breath at the sight of her. She too stood straight and tall, shimmering in the radiance of the thousands of candles, her white and gold robes reflecting the light. Her hair was tied up, forming a white, thick glory about her head: every inch a perfect priestess of the Light. As she tucked her hands within her sleeves, Orrin caught a glimpse of her silver ring.

If, in fact, one answered for one's choices in life, Orrin Blackhart knew he was damned. But there was one thing he'd done right and well, and he was fiercely glad of it. He'd saved her. He didn't think it would count for much in the balance. But it mattered to him.

It hit him then, hit him hard. The striving was done; the battle, over. Death was here, waiting, and part of him welcomed the possibility of oblivion. It settled in his chest, an odd sense of peace. Let it be done, then. He was ready.

Oh, but to look on her. He stared, drinking in the sight, ignoring the prayers and the rituals, until he heard the Archbishop's ponderous tones. 'People of Palins, behold your Queen!'

A loud cheer filled the room, echoing over the crowd, as the young woman, crowned and anointed, sat upon the throne. But Blackhart had eyes for one thing only.

Evelyn's smile.

The room quieted and the young queen drew herself up to sit tall and straight on the throne. She raised her hands and started to remove her gloves. 'I am the Chosen, restored to the Throne of Palins. But Red Gloves is no name for a queen.' She held up her right hand and began to tug off the glove.

There was a gasp from the crowd, and then a buzz of talk as she took off the first glove and began on the second. 'From this day forth, I shall be known as Queen Gloriana.'

Another rousing cheer from the people crammed into every nook and cranny.

Gloriana held the gloves in her hand. 'But let it be known, far and wide, that these gloves shall ever sit beside the throne of Palins, to be taken up in times of defence and war. Ever shall the

Sovereign wear red gloves when she wields a sword in defence of her people.'

She placed the gloves on a small table set by the throne, probably just for that purpose. Orrin suspected that the idea was Silvertongue's.

The girl continued, 'This day marks a new beginning for Palins. But there is much work to be done before we can truly celebrate. So for this night, let us mourn our dead, hold our loved ones close and offer prayers of gratitude to the Lord of Light and the Lady of Laughter.'

The Archbishop shifted his weight, and drew Orrin's gaze. For the briefest of moments the man appeared displeased about something, but the look was gone in an instant.

'Next year, after we've worked together to restore our people's and our kingdom's prosperity, we will truly celebrate.'

That brought a rousing cheer. Oh, sure, promise a festival. Orrin snorted, and two of his guards turned grim faces towards him. 'Your time is coming, bastard,' one growled.

'Save me from your breath, then,' Orrin replied.

A blow rocked his head back and he tasted blood on his lips. The man had a hand raised for a second strike, but another grabbed his arm. 'Lady Bethral said no harm. She'll take your head with his.'

The man stepped back with a snarl and turned away to watch.

Orrin waited until the ringing in his ears cleared before he could focus. The new Queen seemed to be making appointments to her Council. He didn't really pay much attention until one name was called.

'Lady High Priestess Evelyn.'

That got his attention as Evelyn curtsied before the throne. Orrin's lips curved up slightly when he saw the small silver ring on her right hand.

'We offer you our formal thanks, Lady High Priestess Evelyn,' Gloriana said solemnly, 'for all your services to this throne and our people.'

Well, she had the stuffiness of a queen, that was certain.

Evelyn inclined her head with a smile. 'My Queen, I did little. Others did far more.'

Gloriana shook her head, her crown glittering in the candlelight. 'Your humility is refreshing, Lady High Priestess Evelyn.

You are the most powerful healer in the land, and you treat noble and peasant alike. Without your aid, many more would have perished.' Gloriana took a deep breath. 'For this, we grant you a boon from this throne. Ask anything of us that you wish, and it will be given.'

Orrin's breath caught. A priceless reward, that was certain. It caught everyone by surprise, if the silence in the throne room was any indication. Once again the Archbishop's face twitched. Orrin's eyes narrowed as he noticed that the fat little man looked almost green with envy, and the look he was giving Evelyn bordered on rude. Yet there was a hint of something else there, envy and . . . ?

'My thanks, my Queen. You are kindness itself.' Evelyn was speaking, and Orrin's eyes were pulled back to her. 'May I think on this?'

Gloriana laughed, and Orrin saw the formality melt from her face as she leaned forward. 'Aunt Evie, I know you too well. You will "forget" to ask.'

The entire crowd laughed, and Evelyn smiled and shrugged. 'For all that, my Queen, I beg to be allowed to contemplate your offer.'

'So it shall be, Lady High Priestess Evelyn.' The girl looked fairly pleased with herself, even as she grew regal again. 'Now our Council has been named, and the work must begin. Our first task is to abolish slavery and make reparations. Wherever possible, we shall return our people to their homes and restore their lives. Will you join with me, my people, to rebuild this land?'

The crowd exploded in a roar of approval.

The joy faded from the young Queen's face. 'But we must first deal with a more serious matter. Bring forth the prisoner.'

Evelyn felt the crowd around her shrink back, as if to avoid the stain as Orrin was brought forth in chains. One look at his lean frame, dressed all in black, and she lowered her gaze. There was no denying his guilt, but the sight saddened her. She caught a glimpse of his bare, pale feet against the stones.

'Blackhart.' Gloriana's voice was grim.

Evelyn's gaze returned to the man. Orrin stood tall and proud, and matched grimness for grimness. 'Chosen,' he said calmly.

'Warder, read the charges.' Gloriana met Blackhart's eyes as Bethral prepared to read out the charges against him.

Lady Bethral stepped forward, a large document in her hands. 'Orrin Blackhart, late of the Black Hills, hear now the death warrant brought against you by Her Gracious Majesty Gloriana of Palins.'

Evelyn looked down at the floor. She should rejoice that an enemy – a foul, evil man – was being brought to justice. So why did she remember the look of loyalty in his men's eyes when he'd won their freedom?

A movement caught her eye and she looked over at Ezren Storyteller. His eyes filled with concern, but she shook her head slightly. He gave her a wry look, then turned back to face the condemned man. She saw the slight edge of grey under the sleeve of his tunic. He'd been reluctant to wear the manacles, but she'd seen the relief in his eyes when he'd put them on. She wasn't sure it was a final solution, but it was helping him now.

She hadn't mentioned Bethral's name.

'For Orrin Blackhart did wilfully send assassins against the Good King Everard, Queen Rosalyn and Heir Apparent Hugh, and did cause their deaths. Further, he did wilfully send assassins against the Council of Palins as they sat in session, and caused the murders of the High Barons of—' Bethral's voice rolled over the heads of the crowd, reading out loud and clear the list of his offences.

Evelyn offered a silent prayer, for all those slain that fateful night.

'For Orrin Blackhart did wilfully make war upon the Baronies of Summerford and Athelbryght and Farentell, and caused whole towns, villages and farms to be set to the torch, murdering the innocents contained within, and offering the men, women and children to rape and slaughter.'

Evelyn had known that the evils committed by Blackhart were long and deep, but the list seemed to go on forever.

'For Orrin Blackhart did cause the Odium to be raised and sent forth against the High Barons, and caused wanton destruction of fields and farms, crops and livestock, to the detriment of the people and the Crown—'

Yet she'd seen something in those eyes, something beyond the

47

darkness. She glanced at him again, standing there in chains, Darkness personified.

And yet . . .

Gloriana would pronounce sentence, and he'd be executed. They'd end the ceremony and the real work would begin. She'd return to the business before her and her healing rounds among the poor. The Archbishop would probably corner her and suggest that her boon be used for the betterment of the Church. She'd—

Save him, a woman's voice whispered in her ear.

Evelyn's breath caught in her throat as her eyes went wide. Her entire body seemed to vibrate to the sound of that voice, like a bell that had been rung. She glanced around, but no one was near her, and no one else seemed to have heard. All eyes were on the prisoner, listening to the list of charges.

Save him.

The voice was powerful and compelling, and echoed in Evelyn's mind and heart. She'd never heard that voice before but she knew with all her heart who spoke. It could be no other than the Lady of Laughter.

For a heartbeat, she rejected the command. The man was guilty, he had done the things he was charged with . . . the anger of the Queen, the High Barons, the Council . . . the Archbishop . . . oh, especially the Archbishop. If she survived this, she'd be cleaning forsaken old shrines for years.

There was no reason to do this, no reason to assume that the man could be redeemed, if that was even poss—

Save him. There was laughter behind the words now, but it was clearly a command. Evelyn shivered. Part of her trembled at what she was about to do.

Part of her remembered hazel eyes, and rejoiced.

As you will, Lady. Evelyn prayed silently as she moved forward.

Orrin didn't see the priestess until she stood between him and the young Queen.

He'd been listening to the litany of his crimes, some of which he'd done, some of which he hadn't. Which was which didn't seem to matter: in for a copper, in for a gold. If there were Gods to be faced, he suspected their list would be more accurate.

But a swirl of white and gold robes brought him back, and he blinked as Evelyn stood there.

The Queen raised a hand and the Lady Warder went silent. 'Lady High Priestess Evelyn? What—'

'I wish to claim my boon, Your Majesty.'

Gloriana's face filled with confusion. 'This could not wait until—?'

He watched as the Priestess drew a deep breath and interrupted again, 'I claim this man, his horse, and his sword.' Her voice sounded odd as it spilled into the room.

And then he truly heard her words.

A storm erupted in his heart and his chains rattled as he clenched his fists. The crowd was murmuring and he could see the anger growing in their faces.

The Priestess stood still as the winds of shock and outrage swirled around her. Orrin could see the Queen's confusion, the horror on the faces of the High Barons gathered around her.

Evelyn stood unmoving, the quiet calm in the centre of the storm.

'Lady High Priestess, do not do this.' Orrin kept his voice low, a bare whisper. 'I am steeped in blood and death, and you waste your mercy on me.'

She'd heard him. Her head turned ever so slightly and he saw the barest flash of her blue eyes. But her back straightened, and with a slight shift she once again faced the throne. This time, her voice rang through the silent room. 'As my boon, I claim the life of Lord Orrin Blackhart of the Black Hills.'

NINE

'Lord no longer, if ever he was.' Gloriana had recovered her wits and looked grim. 'Condemned man, a creature of the darkest evil. Lady High Priestess Evelyn, I would urge you to withdraw your request. This man is a coldhearted killer, and—'

'The High Priestess has gone mad. Or been bewitched by Blackhart.' The Archbishop was turning purple and sputtering in his indignation.

A voice rose from the crowd and the Lord High Mage Marlon moved forward, his eyes glowing with the light of a spell. 'My daughter is not bewitched. Insanity, however, is still a possibility.'

Evelyn held her breath, suddenly afraid of what her father might do. With his powers, her father could kill Blackhart. And she and her father hadn't agreed on anything since she'd entered the priesthood.

The glow left Marlon's eyes, and he regarded her calmly, almost with . . . approval? He gave her a slow nod. Evelyn swallowed and nodded in return before turning her attention back to the throne.

Certainly it seemed a day of miracles.

Gloriana looked confused. Evelyn was fairly sure that she also saw a bit of relief in her brown eyes. It had not been easy for her, knowing that she'd have to condemn a man to execution in the first moments of her reign. 'Aunt Evie, are you certain? You have spoken before of starting a place of healing, of wishing for the land and the funds. Will you give up this dream for this man?'

Evelyn smiled at her. 'My Queen, all I know is that the Goddess is not done with this man, and that she does not wish him dead. She has a use for him yet.'

The muttering of the crowd grew as the Queen considered the problem. The Archbishop was sputtering and mumbling, bending to whisper in her ear. Evelyn made a mental note to watch the man's health. She'd already warned him about rich foods and his lack of exercise.

Blackhart was cursing too, under his breath, and calling Evelyn all kinds of names. She was just as thankful that the man was still in chains and that she was out of reach.

A sparkle caught her eye and Evelyn looked down at the ring on her hand, blazing in the light, its star as bright as she had ever seen. It seemed to offer comfort and she decided to take it as such, for no human face in the throne room offered any.

After what seemed an eternity, Queen Gloriana held up a hand and the room went silent. 'I grant your reward, Lady High Priestess, but I do not pardon this man.' Gloriana focused on the man in chains. 'Blackhart, you have your freedom. The nearest border is four days' hard ride from here. I grant you asylum for that time. After that, if you are found within the borders of this kingdom, I will have you answer for your crimes. Am I heard?'

Evelyn turned her head just enough to see Blackhart nod.

Gloriana's jaw worked, but she continued, 'The border. My men will give you your sword and your horse.' She gestured to the guards. 'See to it.'

Bethral moved to stand next to the foremost guard. 'Come.' She gave Evelyn a hooded glance and lowered her voice. 'Through the kitchens.'

That was a relief. If they'd released him in front of the crowd, it was certain he wouldn't make it out alive.

The guards pulled at the chains and Blackhart moved off, giving Evelyn a grim look . . .

'Hold.'

Vembar stood there, leaning on his cane and looked at Blackhart, appraising him. 'The Lady High Priestess Evelyn has won your life for you. Would you win a pardon as well?'

There was puzzled reaction from the nobles. Gloriana looked at Vembar, who leaned over and started to whisper in her ear. Gloriana held up a hand and the noise in the room subsided. Vembar continued to speak and Gloriana nodded at his words.

Blackhart looked in confusion at Evelyn, who shrugged.

Vembar straightened, and addressed the room. 'The lands of the Black Hills are now infested with the foul undead that Elanore created. We've driven them into the hills and mountains, but Palins has no spare men to pursue.' Vembar studied

Blackhart's face. 'You know the lands and the people. Cleanse those lands and the Queen will pardon you.'

Lord Fael of Summerford stepped from the crowd. 'This man brought an army filled with undead against my people, killing innocent townsfolk or taking them for his own foul purposes. How can you—?'

'Can you guard your borders and start to clear the monsters? Do you even know where to start?' Vembar asked quietly.

Lord Fael paused, considering. He puffed out a breath in frustration. 'No. With the losses we've had, I'll be hard-pressed to guard my settlements and farms as is.'

'We have a land to rebuild,' Vembar said simply. 'We cannot waste anything. Including this man's knowledge.'

'Lord Vembar has the right of it,' Gloriana said. 'Further, it seems to us that the people of the Black Hills should not suffer for the crimes of their leaders.' She focused on Blackhart. 'Would you do this?'

Blackhart's eyes narrowed. 'What will you supply me with?'

'Nothing,' Gloriana replied firmly. 'The Lady High Priestess claims the Lady of Laughter has a use for you. You have your sword and your horse and I've nothing else to spare. But cleanse the lands within a year of this date and you will have a Crown pardon.' The Queen straightened on her throne. 'It's that or banishment. Will you accept this charge?'

'I wish to claim a boon as well, at the end of my task,' Blackhart demanded.

Evelyn's mouth dropped open at that, as did the mouths of almost the entire Court.

'No,' Gloriana replied.

'Kill me, then.' Blackhart threw his head back. 'You can deal with the Odium.'

For the first time, Evelyn saw anger flash in Gloriana's eyes. The young Queen's face was neutral, but her voice cut through the air. 'I—'

Vembar's soft laugh interrupted. 'A pardon *and* a boon?' He shrugged, sharing a look with Gloriana. 'What harm, Your Majesty? I am almost certain that he will die in the attempt.'

Gloriana's eyes and lips narrowed, but she nodded her head in agreement. 'I agree. A pardon and a boon. But only if I am assured that the Black Hills have been cleansed of all of the Odium. Now, strike his chains and send him on his way.'

The chains clanked as his escort moved Blackhart off to the side and through the doors. Evelyn knew Bethral well enough that the chains would not come off until he was clear of the throne room. She had opened her mouth to ask leave to depart when the Archbishop stepped forward yet again, his face florid and swollen with outrage.

'Lady High Priestess' – The Archbishop's ponderous tones sounded through the throne room – 'you have made a mockery of the justice of the Lord of Light and the Queen's gratitude.' He gestured off to the side where two church honour guards stood. 'Return to the Church, there to hold yourself ready to answer for your actions this day.'

Well, she'd known that was coming.

Gloriana opened her mouth as if to protest, but Vembar shook his head slightly. She looked at him, then gave a small sigh. 'Lady High Priestess, you have our leave to depart.'

Evelyn curtsied and bowed her head. She hated to see the disappointment in Gloriana's eyes. She hoped the young Queen would understand. She would try to explain it to her.

As soon as she figured it out herself.

Orrin stood naked in the rain, numb, chilled, and uncertain why he still breathed.

His sword was in his hand, the blade reflecting the torchlight from the kitchen. His horse stood next to him, without so much as bit or bridle, never mind a saddle.

The guards had struck the chains under Lady Bethral's watchful eye and stripped him of his clothing. They left him standing in the empty courtyard, bare of foot on cold cobble-stones. So he stood, cold and wet, with a split lip and an empty heart.

He was in danger and well he knew it, but he felt oddly hollow, unable to move. Once the coronation was over, the streets would fill and many of those people would kill him first and beg pardon after.

Still, numb and chilled, he stood there.

A noise brought his head up and he saw the Lady High Priestess Evelyn emerge from the castle. Her eyes went wide, then narrowed as she crossed to him and stood there, solemn. 'I see the Queen kept to the letter of her word.'

Orrin glared at her. 'You threw away your dream for something of little value, Lady High Priestess. Be sure that you've thrown away the Queen's favour as well.'

'Then her favour is cheap and of little worth.' Evelyn tilted her head as she unclasped her cloak. With a quick movement, she flung the heavy white garment around his shoulders, securing the clasp at his throat. 'For I am satisfied with the reward I have received.'

Orrin felt her warmth as the fabric settled on his skin, bringing the faintest scent of incense with it. He looked into her blue eyes and watched as she reached out and softly touched the corner of his mouth. A brief tingle and the pain in his lip disappeared.

Evelyn lowered her hand, then looked around. 'Now come. Quickly.'

TEN

'Lady High Priestess?' Orrin asked as he wove his hand in his horse's mane and tugged.

'We need to get you out of here, before anyone sees you.' Evelyn started across the small courtyard. 'The Queen may have granted my boon, but until word is spread, there are those who will strike first and listen later. We need to find you some clothes and gear, not to mention some food and . . .' Evelyn flushed. 'I should have thought to ask for your gear. Or even better, a full pardon.'

Orrin frowned at her. 'Don't be so greedy.'

Her eyes flew wide and she laughed softly. 'Oh, now I am to be instructed in the virtues by Blackhart, Scourge of Palins. Who is to say that the Lady has no sense of humour?'

The sight of that smile made Orrin's heart jump in his throat. He fell into step with Evelyn, leading his horse by the mane. 'More irony than humour, Lady High Priestess. You're lucky the Queen didn't call for both our heads.'

Evelyn nodded, looking unconcerned. 'That's nothing to what the Archbishop will say.'

The rain was a soft mist and it was starting to cling to her hair and robes, setting them to sparkling in the torchlight. They didn't need to go far, for the church and the castle of Edenrich shared a back alleyway. In one gate, down a cobblestone lane and then through another gate that swung wide at Evelyn's knock.

'Evie?' said a deep voice. 'I'd thought you'd be at the crowning.'

'Cenwulf,' Evelyn said softly, 'I need your help.'

An older man with a limp moved into the light, letting them pass into the courtyard beyond. 'Lass, what poor man have you draped your cloak over this time? Let's be hoping this one doesn't have fleas.'

'No,' she replied with an impish look at Orrin, 'he's naked.'

Cenwulf squinted in the light. 'Naked? Does Fat Belly know what you are about?'

Orrin coughed.

'Cenwulf, we've talked about that name' – Evelyn rolled her eyes – 'but I've no time, we have to move quickly. Would you see to the horse?'

Cenwulf grunted as she headed towards the far building. 'What do you need in there, lass?'

'Never mind, Cenwulf,' Evelyn said over her shoulder. 'The less you know, the better. Hold the horse. We will be quick.'

Cenwulf's head jerked at that, but he said nothing. He gave Orrin a hard look.

Evelyn pulled Orrin along. 'Come.'

They entered a cellar door of the guardhouse that opened into a huge catacomb. Orrin looked around as he was pushed down into a hard wooden chair with a broken back that was close to the door. 'Sit here,' Evelyn said. She held up a hand and whispered softly. A golden light appeared, illuminating the area around them.

Orrin sucked in a breath. The floor of the room was covered with men sleeping on pallets. No, that wasn't right. The sheets . . . the shrouds . . . covered their faces. They weren't sleeping.

'What is this place?' he whispered.

'These are the war dead, not yet identified.' Evelyn's voice was a whisper as well. 'Warriors all, who fell in the battle. We keep them here, using spells to preserve them, until their kin can claim their bodies.' She left the light hanging in the air. 'Wait here.'

She disappeared into the darkness, then returned with a small, thin copper box as big as her hand.

She opened it on a hinge, revealing a candle stub on a clever mount that swung out. The entire box sat on its end. She lit the candle from a taper and the small flame flickered, reflected by the copper of the box.

'Keep under the cloak; it's damp in here. Let me see what I can find,' she said softly and disappeared once again, taking the magic light with her.

Orrin did as he was told, sitting there with her cloak wrapped around him. He was cold, so cold, as if the world had taken a step back from him, as if he were in a dark well with only the light of a small candle, and the world far away.

He could hear Evelyn moving about, but it seemed unreal, distant, as if in a dream. His vision narrowed to just a pinpoint of light.

Suddenly there was movement near him and a voice, deep and old. 'Lass, you best see to him.'

'Cenwulf?' Evelyn's voice drew nearer. 'Oh, no. I should have realised. Orrin? Can you hear me?'

Her face filled his vision and Orrin frowned, unable to explain why the concern in those blue eyes was so important.

'This one's looked on his own death, and walked back.'

'His hands are cold as ice.'

'I'll fetch kavage, lass.'

'Orrin!' Her voice called him back and he blinked. Evelyn was kneeling before him, holding his hands. Her hands were warm, and feeling started to return in his fingers.

She tucked his hands under the thick white cloak, then pressed her palms to the tops of his feet. The warmth they brought startled him. It bothered him that she would do that. It felt good, but oddly intimate.

The next he knew, Orrin had a warm mug in his hands and he was urged to drink. The warmth swept through him as he swallowed the bitter liquid. Evelyn, Lady High Priestess, was kneeling before him, pulling a pair of worn socks onto his feet.

'Evie,' was all he could manage.

She looked up, worry in her eyes. 'I didn't realise how cold you were. Drink that entire mug. I'm going to look for boots.'

With that, she was gone.

When Orrin looked up, the grizzled old man was standing there, looking at him with a neutral, tense expression.

'You know who I am.' Orrin knew that fact should worry him.

Cenwulf nodded. 'Drink.' He looked towards where Evelyn had disappeared. 'There's already people searching the streets for you. I've heard what she's done.'

He wasn't pulling out his weapon, so Orrin kept silent and drank.

'Cenwulf, I need some help.' Evelyn appeared, her arms full.

'We need to get him on his way as soon as possible.' She placed her burden by Orrin. 'Are you feeling better?'

Orrin nodded.

'That's true enough,' Cenwulf said softly. 'But Lady High Priestess, this is not right.'

Evelyn drew herself up at his formal tone. 'Cenwulf, the dead in this chamber are not separated into winners and losers, friend or foe. We only know they are our dead, and we honour them.' She looked back over her shoulder. 'You are right, in that I cannot speak for them. But I ask you this' – she turned back, her blue eyes blazing in the mage light – 'you fought men and Odium. Would you send any man to face his enemies naked?'

Cenwulf stood silent, then shook his head with a sigh. 'No. Not even such as he.'

Evelyn nodded, placed a pile of clothing on the floor by Orrin's feet and dropped a pair of boots in his lap. 'Here's trous that might fit, and a few tunics. Try them for size. Cenwulf, help me. Where are the old scabbards that we . . .' They both disappeared.

Orrin reached down for the trous and started to dress. They were worn thin in the seat and crotch, but they were still good enough. No holes. He pulled on the boots, then stomped his feet to check the fit. A bit small, but better than nothing.

Evelyn and Cenwulf appeared one after the other, adding to the pile, then disappearing again. Orrin was amazed. In no time, they had quite a bit of gear for him. Some cook pots and a tinderbox were added to the pile. There were a few daggers and an old crossbow that had seen better days. Cenwulf appeared with a worn scabbard and belt with the Goddess's holy symbols worked in white thread. Orrin grimaced at the irony of that as he sheathed his sword and strapped it on.

Then Cenwulf came out of the darkness bearing an old saddle and bridle, and Orrin shook his head in amazement.

'Don't get too excited. The leather's cracked,' Cenwulf growled.

Evelyn appeared behind him with a horse blanket and a bedroll of sorts. 'Worn but clean.' She frowned at the saddle. 'Weren't there saddlebags to go with that?'

There were. Cenwulf went out to saddle the horse while

Evelyn and Orrin packed the saddlebags with what they'd found. 'There's one more thing,' Evelyn said. 'A cloak.'

'I can't wear white,' Orrin grumbled, then regretted his harsh words. 'I just mean that—'

Evelyn emerged from the darkness with a bundle in her hands. 'What about this?' she asked as she pulled forth a cloak, bright red. She wrinkled her nose as she held it out. 'This might suit. It's heavy and warm, but it smells terrible.'

Orrin stood and took the cloak in his arms. 'You have never served under arms, Lady High Priestess. Were you an old campaigner, you'd recognise the value of this cape. The smell means it's made of ehat wool. It's waterproof because of the oil in the wool, but that is what smells so strong. Heavy and warm, it will serve me well.'

Evelyn smiled. 'That's good, then.' She tilted her head slightly. 'Besides, red suits you.'

A knock on the door, and Cenwulf put his head in. 'The horse is ready and it sounds like the ceremony is almost over. They're cheering.'

'I've no food here,' Evelyn said as she blew out the candle and picked up the box, closing it carefully. She tucked it into one of the saddlebags, then doused the mage light.

'You've done more than enough.' Orrin frowned. 'The Archbishop will not be pleased.'

Evelyn shrugged as she headed for the door.

Cenwulf snorted. 'As if he knows about this place. As if anyone will tell him.'

'Cenwulf,' Evelyn scolded as they emerged into the courtyard. The mist was heavier now. Orrin strapped the saddlebags on his warhorse, which turned his head to sniff at the pathetic bundle.

Gone was the warrior all in black. Orrin knew full well that he looked like a weary mercenary – an unsuccessful one, at that – with his gear all hodge-podge. Rain started to fall in earnest as Orrin mounted and wrapped the cloak around himself. He drew a deep breath as he gathered in the reins, facing a future he had not thought to have.

'Take this.' Evelyn put one hand on Orrin's leg and reached up with the other one to place her silver ring with the white star sapphire in his hand. 'I've no coin to give you. Sell this when you are in need.'

Orrin looked down into Evelyn's cold, wet face and shook his head. 'No. The help you have given me is more than enough. I have already cost you far too much, Lady High Priestess.'

Evelyn smiled up at him. 'It's worth a few silvers at best, but you will need it.' She curled Orrin's hand around the ring and then drew back as the horse shifted. 'You'd best be going. I'll open a portal to Swift's Port and you can ride to the border from there.'

'No.'

'No?'

'I'm not headed for the border. I'm headed to the Black Hills.'

ELEVEN

Evelyn's breath caught in her throat as she looked up, searching his face. 'You could not be so foolish as to try to cleanse those lands.'

Blackhart shrugged. 'To gain a pardon and a boon? I might.' The horse shifted again. Blackhart looked down at the silver ring and closed his hand around it. 'Do you know of a portal in the Black Hills?'

Evelyn tucked her hands into her sleeves and shivered. 'The only one that I know is the one where you seized me. And I didn't open that portal.' She considered the problem. 'There is a shrine to the Lady close to the border of Athelbryght and the Black Hills. I think the village name is Summerset.'

'I know that one. The folk there will not be pleased to see me.' Blackhart's eyes narrowed. 'But that would be better than the one close to the keep.' He straightened in the saddle and slid the ring onto his little finger. 'If you are willing . . .'

Evelyn looked up into his face. It was madness, of course. But Blackhart didn't look insane. The weariness she'd seen before was gone. Now there was a new determination in that face, a spark that hadn't been there before.

He looked down at her and for a moment she was lost in his hazel eyes. But the sounds of cheering from the castle reminded her of the urgency. She lowered her gaze and turned to face the inner courtyard. Maybe this was what the Lady of Laughter had in mind all along, even if it felt as if she were sending him to his death. She lifted her hand and started her spell.

'Best blindfold the horse, if he's not used to this,' Cenwulf said gruffly. She felt his movement, but kept her mind focused on the spell, on opening the portal between this place and the—

The familiar rush of power and a faint breeze on her skin told her that the portal was open. Experience allowed her to turn to look at Blackhart, even as a part of her mind stayed focused on the spell.

He was still mounted, and his horse was blindfolded. Cenwulf was tying off the cloth. 'Think he'll go for you?'

'He'll do well enough.' Blackhart patted the horse's neck, then focused on Evelyn. 'I don't know whether to curse you or bless you, Lady High Priestess.'

Evelyn flashed a smile. 'That's honest. Let me know which you decide on.'

He urged his horse forward a step, so that he looked down into her face.

Evelyn looked up as he drew closer. 'I wish you well, Orrin Blackhart.'

Blackhart leaned in the saddle, reached out his hand and stroked Evelyn's face. His fingers were cold on her cheek, but his eyes blazed bright. Without another word, he straightened. The big black steed stepped forward, and they disappeared into the portal.

The portal was closed, yet Lady Evelyn stood there, staring as if she could still see him.

Cenwulf frowned, worried. He'd known the lass a long time, and there was something odd about this. As if she cared for the man.

But no, that could not be. He wondered a bit at the 'pardon' for such a man as that, but he'd not ask Evie. Others would tell him the tale. Still . . . He moved to stand at her shoulder. 'That one has a long, hard road before him,' he said.

Evelyn nodded. 'They'll pursue him.'

'The Queen's men?' Cenwulf asked.

'And his own demons, I think.' Evelyn sighed. 'Well, the Lady of Laughter placed him on the road, but he has to walk it.'

'Aye.' Cenwulf lifted his head. 'Sounds like the ceremony is done. You best be getting to wherever Fat Belly told ya to be.'

Evelyn nodded, shivering slightly. Her hair was covered with droplets of water, lit by the torches in the courtyard. She turned to go, but Cenwulf laid a hand on her arm. 'You gave him your old red war-cloak, lass.'

Evie smiled and wrinkled her nose at him. 'I did, didn't I? Not likely I'll need it in the future.'

Cenwulf gave her a narrow look.

Evelyn moved then, shaking her head. 'Don't worry so, Cenwulf. Damp or dry will make no difference to the Archbishop.'

She walked towards the church proper, and Cenwulf watched her go before turning back to his duties. She'd made a muddle in her haste, digging through the piles. He'd set the place to rights, so no one would ask questions. He limped inside slowly, shaking his head at the slovenliness of the young.

And the foolishness of a woman.

Lord of Light, but Evelyn was a beauty.

Eidam, Archbishop of the Church of Palins, eased his bulk into the chair in his private audience chamber, glad to be off his aching feet. As befitted his rank, the chair was on a dais, gilded and ornate, with a cloth of state suspended over it. The chair was ample, designed to be comfortable for a man of his substance. Behind it, on a thick tapestry, was the sun, its rays extending to the far walls, gold on a field of red. Red and gold, fitting colours for the Lord of Light's representative and spokesman.

He sat back with a grunt of relief.

If the ceremony had taken place in the church, as was traditional, he'd have had a similar chair, close to the throne, for his comfort and ease. But instead he'd had to stand for hours by the throne, conducting the ceremony, waiting on the young Queen. It had been cursed hot and he'd sweated all through the ceremony, making his skin itch. They'd shown no consideration for a man of his rank and stature, which had done nothing to improve his temper.

Even as the pain in his feet eased, his loins stirred. He'd long fantasised about this: Evelyn on her knees before him, soft and malleable. Repentant. Willing.

Pity about the witnesses.

He darted a look around the room, at the brethren lining the walls. Pity. But this had to be done publicly, to reinforce his position both as the head of the Church and as an advisor to the young Queen. Lady High Priestess Evelyn had to be punished for her arrogance and disobedience.

He twitched his robes into place as the other members of the Order continued to file into the room to line the walls. Evelyn remained where she was, gazing down at the floor.

His anger flared. She'd best keep those lovely eyes on the floor.

But the anger was a mistake, because his stomach started cramping again. He'd gone for hours without food or drink. He gestured to his aide, who came forward with a goblet. Cow's milk. He wrinkled his nose and waved it away. 'Wine. Spiced and warmed.'

His aide frowned, but Eidam would have none of it, no matter what the healers might say. At the end of a long, hard day, a man deserved a bit of wine.

He turned back and glared at the woman on her knees in the centre of the room. He'd had an eye on Evelyn since she'd first entered the Order, with her white hair and pale blue eyes. Under those white robes, he was certain, there was a body equally pleasing.

She'd advanced within the Order on her own merits, he'd grant her that, and seemed a true daughter of the Church. He'd risen as well, and if his advancement had been based more on his politics than on his faith, well, that was just how things were done.

He'd seen many approach her over the years and be gently rebuffed. He'd decided to wait and watch, certain that when he rose to a position of prominence, she'd consider his suit for her hand an honour.

Now he'd come to discover that she'd had her own plans for advancement all along. The prophecy of the Chosen was nonsense, of course, but she'd made it happen, hadn't she? And all his well-laid plans with the Regent and Elanore had gone by the wayside when the Chosen had returned to claim the throne. Eidam narrowed his eyes at the thought of all the time he'd spent working his way into the confidence of the Regent.

His aide brought the wine in a jewelled goblet and Eidam gulped it. Spiced and warm, exactly as he'd ordered. It slid down his throat, such a comfort after a long day.

One had to be flexible, of course. It had been expedient and easy enough to welcome the Chosen within the city and recognise her as the claimant for the Throne. His quick action had solidified Gloriana's position and his – that is to say, the Church's – and that was all to the good.

But it would have been far better had Blackhart been silenced. Their dealings had never been direct, but one never knew. His past actions might not seem . . . appropriate . . . to the young Queen.

Eidam smacked his lips and set the goblet on the aide's tray.

High Priest Dominic finally came through the doors at the far end of the room and closed them behind him, signalling that all members of the Order were within. The tall half-elf strode forward as Eidam twitched his hand to indicate a place at his side. Tall, straight, his long black hair flowing loose over his back, Dominic gave Evelyn a troubled glance as he crossed the floor. There was another who'd been rebuffed but who still hungered. Eidam recognised the signs.

Dominic came and stood next to him. The room grew silent.

'Lady High Priestess Evelyn,' Eidam began, drawing a deep breath to help cool his rage.

Evelyn lifted her head and looked him in the eye. There was no sorrow there, no repentance.

The Archbishop gripped the arms of his chair and leaned forward, keeping his voice low and reasonable.

'Our order is one of service and obedience. Obedience to the will of the Lord of Light, whose energies direct our days and our nights and order our lives. Obedience to the will of those set above us. We seek no greater glory than service.'

She opened her mouth as if to argue with him. He raised a hand, cutting her off.

'You have taken much upon yourself, Lady, without consulting with your superiors. You have sought to bring glory to yourself, raise yourself up in the eyes of the Kingdom.'

Evelyn's blue eyes flashed, but she lowered her gaze and said nothing.

'Your intentions may have been the best and we will admit that the end result for Palins may be a positive outcome – but at the peril of your vows to the Lord of Light and to your immortal soul.'

Eidam reached for his goblet, took another gulp and settled farther back in his chair. He was still angry, but his rage was contained, his voice low and moderate. Everyone in the room was focused on his words. Satisfied, he continued, 'This moral corruption is evident in your use of the boon before the Court this day. A wonderful gift from a grateful sovereign and you use it to release an enemy of this land, a foul villain now free to go his way and work his evil on our people. With a horse and a sword, no less. I'm surprised you didn't ask that he be awarded lands and power as well. A seat on the Council, perhaps?' Eidam leaned forward. 'Or perhaps your motivations are less than pure, eh? He is comely. You were his prisoner. Have you broken your vows of chastity as well?'

Her cheeks were splotched with colour now, and Eidam knew it wasn't a maidenly blush. Evelyn was furious, but her voice was calm. 'No, Holy One.'

Eidam leaned back. 'Now the Kingdom is at peace, with a new Queen on the throne. Challenges lie ahead, and much work needs to be done. But we feel that, for the sake of your spiritual well-being, you need a time of retreat. Meditation, prayer, rest, along with hard physical work. It clears the mind and does wonders for the body as well.'

'We will grant you this respite,' he continued, 'to contemplate your actions and to see the error of your ways. There is a shrine to the Lady on Farentell's distant border that has been long neglected. Since you claim that the voice of our Lord's Consort directed you, you will honour her by restoring it with your labour. For the benefit of the wild animals and the most deter-mined of penitents.

'During this time, I forbid you the use of the portals. I forbid you the use of the sacred and secular magics that you wield. I forbid you to leave the boundaries of the shrine until such time as I see fit to summon you to my presence.'

'My Lord Archbishop' – Dominic raised his voice – 'do the usual exceptions apply?'

'Yes, yes.' Eidam was none too pleased at the interruption. 'I've a mage waiting to open the portal for her. Escort her there, Priest Dominic.'

Dominic bowed and went to Evelyn's side as she rose to her feet. The anger was still in her eyes, but that would fade. A few weeks, maybe a month and she'd be humbled and pliable enough.

Eidam watched in satisfaction as they left and the other

brethren filed out, talking among themselves. A good day's work.

His belly rumbled then. He burped, the spiced wine filling his mouth with a sour taste.

TWELVE

Blackhart grabbed a handful of hair, yanked the boy's head back and pressed his dagger into the boy's neck.

The weeks he'd spent gathering his men together, securing this one town, fortifying its walls, stuffing it full to the rafters with the surviving people of the Black Hills: all that work and effort and this little shit fell asleep on watch.

The boy's eyes flew wide open, still clouded with sleep. With a gasp, he reached up to grab Blackhart's arm. His leg kicked out, sending his quiver over on its side, spilling the arrows.

The wind caught Blackhart's red cloak and it flared out behind him. He stood, his knee braced against the boy's back, next to the arrow slit he'd been assigned.

Blackhart leaned down and put his lips to the boy's ear. 'The next time I find you sleeping on watch, I'll kill you. Understand?'

The boy's eyes got even bigger. He nodded slowly and swallowed hard, his throat moving under the blade.

Blackhart released him, letting him fall back in his haste to get away. Without another glance, Blackhart walked on, furious. He sheathed his dagger, growling under his breath as he stalked off, determined to check the wall for other slackers.

There was a snort from the shadows and Archer emerged from the darkness, falling in step beside him. 'We're not gonna have anyone left to stand watch, you keep scaring them like that.'

Blackhart stopped and sucked in a deep breath. The air was cool, with a taint of something foul. He looked out over the wooden wall, over the area they'd cleared between the wall and the woods. Poor Wareington, once a thriving town at the crossroads of the Black Hills. Now . . .

Blackhart gave Archer a glance. 'He's old enough to learn. And fear's a good teacher.'

'Aye,' – Archer gave him a nod – 'but I'm thinking a blade to the neck is a bit severe for a lad nodding off on his watch for the first time.'

'Better me than an Odium tearing out his heart,' Blackhart growled.

Archer straightened. 'I'll check the rest. You're overdue a meal and a bed.'

Blackhart grunted and turned to look along the wall. 'We should add a bit more height, a few more logs.'

Archer shrugged, stepping out to take a look. 'We can, but last I heard, Odium don't climb nothing. Considering we've only been at this three weeks, I'd say we were doing well.'

'We'll do better when the attacks stop,' Blackhart said.

'Were there injuries in the last one?' Archer asked.

'Nothing fatal,' Blackhart answered.

'Then it's my turn to stand watch,' Archer said firmly. He nodded towards a ladder that led down off the wall. 'Go get something to eat and catch some sleep. If the horn sounds, ignore it. I'll see to it.'

'What's the latest head count?' Blackhart asked.

'Dorne will know.' Archer wrinkled his nose. 'You step in something?'

Blackhart looked down at his boots. 'I think the boy shat himself.'

Archer stepped back. 'You might see to that, too. I'll check the watch.'

Blackhart snarled, but stomped off the wall and headed towards the centre of town, where the inn still stood tall.

Town. Blackhart snorted. Not much of one when they'd found it, that was certain. But it had been in better shape than any of the others and already had a wooden palisade, so it had been the easiest to defend. So town it was, because town it had to be.

Three weeks it had been now. Three weeks since he'd found Archer and a few of the others and started the campaign to clear the Odium. Three weeks since they'd gathered people here, in a strong, defensible position. There'd be no crops planted this year. Instead, Blackhart had them out gleaning the fields as best they could, with warriors watching over them every minute. Winter was coming, and they'd need the protection of the town and what food they could gather to survive the cold.

None too pleased, the folk he'd roused from every farm and croft he could find. They'd fought his decision to round them up, fought him on being told what to do and how to do it. But most saw reason once they were within the walls and not cowering in their farmsteads as Odium overran their lands, seeking out the living. There were some who didn't understand and spoke against his actions, but they were few and far between.

Not that Blackhart cared. He'd be the cruel bastard they feared, so long as they survived to curse him.

Three weeks. A good start, to his way of thinking.

Blackhart yanked open the door of the inn and stepped into a blast of heat and noise.

It made sense to cram people together, for warmth and safety. Every square yard of the inn held a body.

Men gathered in the inn to share the evening meal, discuss the defence of the walls and learn their assignments. The women were more spread out, caring for the children, both their own and those without parents.

The room went silent as he entered.

There was a scent of many bodies, roasting meat and fried white root. He moved into the room, ignoring the stares. Instead, he focused on one of the lasses serving the meal. 'Dorne?'

'With the children, Milord.' She gave him a calm look as she balanced platters. She'd been one of the first they'd 'rescued', and she'd grown used to his ways.

After a quick nod he headed up the stairs, taking them two at a time. The conversations started again up behind him.

'Rescue' some called it; others called it conscription. But with the living gathered inside this town, the attacks could be fought off without much loss of life. Or, worse, having the living dragged off to be used to make more of the monsters.

He moved up to the third floor. Here the common hall had been turned into a nursery. The children gathered here were orphans, brought together to make it easier for those who cared for them. All sizes and ages. The babes were tended by the elders who could be spared from the work. The children all helped, even the toddlers.

Blackhart had set two of the most experienced warriors here as well. There was little chance that the Odium would get this far, but he'd take no chances.

70

The guards gave him a nod as he came up the stairs.

'All's well?' he asked.

'Aye,' the far one answered, 'but a few of the older ones are asking for swords. They want to help.'

Blackhart paused at that. 'Worth training?'

'Might be.'

'Wooden daggers, then. Teach 'em the basics.' Blackhart sighed. 'And teach them about the Odium.'

'Bella will not be happy at that,' the younger one said.

Blackhart rolled his eyes. 'When is she ever?'

The guards both chuckled as Blackhart stepped within the hall.

The fireplace at the far end was lit, with the children clustered about. Dorne was seated on a stool, talking quietly. Probably telling them one of his parables.

Blackhart moved away from the door, ducking his head to stand between the beams. The room was dark, with no windows, but it was warm and dry and secure. A little darkness never hurt anyone.

Off to the side a few women sat, some with babes at the breast. Orrin knew that the mothers were passing the babes around, sharing their milk with the ones whose mothers had died. Other women were there as well, taking each child as it finished and putting it to the shoulder. One of the women rose and crossed to greet him with a babe on her shoulder and a glare in her eyes. 'Blackhart.'

'Bella.' Blackhart crossed his arms over his chest, preparing for battle. Bella had been in one of the first villages they'd come across, guarding a group of children who'd lost their parents. She'd been armed with a frying pan and not much else.

'Any deaths?' she asked as she adjusted the babe, making sure the rag was well placed before she started to pat its back.

'None,' Orrin replied.

She nodded, rocking the child slightly. 'Sidian and Reader brought in three more families this day.' Bella continued to pat the babe. 'Dorne has the details.'

'Good,' Blackhart grunted. 'Any more warriors?' He watched Dorne look his way and rise from his stool, to the dismay and protest of the young ones.

'No, but word is spreading of your promise,' Bella said softly.

Might as well get it over with. 'I'm told the older children are asking for swords.'

Bella gave him a resigned look. 'Aye.'

'We'll see to some training,' Blackhart said.

Bella sighed. 'With any luck, there will be more warriors in the next week.'

The babe on her shoulder burped, spitting up on the rag. Bella shifted him again, wiping his mouth. The babe stared at Blackhart, then his eyes started to drift shut as he yawned.

'Luck,' Blackhart snorted. 'Might as well pray too, for all the good it does.'

Dorne heard his words as he came closer. He was a small, dark man with olive skin and a paunch, dressed in black with a small silver brooch pinned to his tunic. He raised an eyebrow. 'And doesn't the Lady of Laughter bring us good fortune?'

Blackhart looked at the priest. 'So you believe. I, on the other hand, believe in making my own luck through work.'

'Of course.' Dorne took Blackhart's elbow, leading him back out the door. 'The Lady expects us to do our fair share. Come, there is venison stew tonight. Let me tell you of our newest recruits.'

Bella hummed to the sleeping baby and closed the door behind them.

Blackhart followed Dorne down the back stairs and into the inn's large kitchen. One of the kitchen maids was still working, and she dished up stew and bread, then left them alone.

'Three families, twenty total,' Dorne said. 'The men are farmers, only too glad to shelter here and willing to fight. All are healthy and only one has a babe in arms. Two of the lads are old enough to swing a sword.' Dorne tore at his bread and dipped it in the stew. 'We've housed them and got them food. They'd a few cattle and sheep with them, and wagons.'

'Wagons?' Blackhart scowled, talking around a mouthful. 'They were told to bring nothing with them. Things we have aplenty, but—'

'The wagons were filled with seed corn,' Dorne said with a smile. 'When we can plant—'

'*If* we can plant,' Blackhart growled.

'*When*, Orrin. With the aid of the Lady.' Dorne leaned back. 'Hasn't she already shown you her favour?'

Blackhart kept eating. He'd told the story, of course – had to, since Archer had thought he'd been raised from the dead when he'd appeared out of the dark. If this was to work, this second chance, he'd need an army to deal with the Odium. And where better to find it than among his own men?

'Some favour, Priest,' Blackhart said. 'A sword, a horse and a chance. Not much more than that.'

'A pardon for you, if you can do this,' Dorne reminded him, 'and a boon that allows you to keep the promise you made to them.'

Blackhart took a drink of ale. That was the one thing he had to offer. He'd passed the word as best he could. Any who would aid him, he would ask their pardon as his boon. They'd be free men, forgiven their actions and free to start new lives under a new baron. Free to use their real names and rebuild their lives.

'I am a priest of the Lady, sworn to her service,' Dorne said softly, touching the silver brooch shaped like a half-moon. 'I came to the Black Hills thinking to minister to people in despair. You, my lad, have given them the only hope they have.'

Blackhart looked down into his bowl. 'A thin chance, that.'

'A chance, nonetheless,' Dorne said firmly.

The rain was heavier when he finally left the inn. Blackhart drew the red cloak over his shoulders as he splashed through the muck towards the blacksmith's. He'd claimed the building as his own quarters. It was dry, and though it wasn't as warm as the inn, it was easier for men to report to him there. Nor were there busy ears about.

He mounted the stairs and looked about the small loft. A simple rope bed was there, with an old wooden bench nearby. Enough for his needs. The mattress was stuffed with straw and he'd heaped the blankets high.

A full stomach made him yawn; he'd sleep well this night. He dropped his cloak on the bed and sat on the bench to work his boots off his feet. With any luck, in another week or so they could stop hiding and start going on the attack. That suited him just fine.

Boots off, he started to remove his weapons, leaving them within easy reach. One of the first things he'd managed was a bigger pair of boots. His armour too, which was a bit better than that the Priestess had scrounged for him.

Blackhart had to shake his head. That Lady High Priestess had dared much for him, taking him into the morgue to sort through the leavings of the dead on his behalf. Amazing, really. He hoped that fat Archbishop hadn't been too harsh. Blackhart remembered her bright blue eyes and that laugh . . .

There was a sudden sense of warmth under his tunic and Blackhart smiled as he set aside his leathers. Leaning over, he rummaged in his saddlebags and pulled out the copper candle box. He opened the box and lit the small stub within. The flame flickered, then grew, reflecting warm light off the copper.

Carefully, he tugged on the leather cord around his neck. It came up easily, displaying the silver ring with the white star sapphire.

Blackhart placed the ring in his hand and stared at it.

A star gleamed on the surface of the stone, moving over its surface as he moved his hand. Mage had checked the damn thing and assured Orrin that it wasn't magic. But he knew different. The ring glowed, almost as Evelyn had glowed in the darkness of that cell. That damn bit of sparkle danced on the stone as if with a quiet joy.

Mage might not be able to see it, but Blackhart knew there was magic in the thing.

He couldn't sell it. Not that it was worth much, a silver ring with a flawed stone. But it made its owner seem closer, somehow. Blackhart had a fancy that the ring glowed when Evelyn was thinking of him, but it was a fancy and nothing more. Stupid, really. She'd said herself that she was sending him to his death.

Still, a man who redeemed himself and cleared an entire barony of Odium might be able to approach an archbishop and declare for the hand of a certain lady high priestess. After asking the lady herself, of course.

Blackhart snorted at himself. The entire idea was incredible, of course. Unlikely. Hopeless. Pathetic, actually. Not to mention damned near impossible. But so was the idea that he was still alive.

It was a dream, nothing more. Hell, not even that – the barest of hopes. There were months of fighting ahead, even if he could figure out where the damned Odium were coming from. If the people he was trying to save didn't rise up and kill him in his sleep.

Blackhart shook his head and blew out the candle. He was a fool, that was certain.

Still, he carefully put the cord over his head before he settled back onto the bed and pulled the red cloak over the blankets for extra warmth.

Even one such as he could dream.

THIRTEEN

Peace and quiet wear thin after a while.

Three weeks was more than enough as far as Evelyn was concerned.

She sighed, eased back on her aching knees and threw the scrub rag in the bucket. The white marble of the shrine of the Lady glistened under the afternoon sun. It was a good thing, since her own white robe was grey with dirt.

This particular shrine to the Lady of Laughter was an open affair, a shallow pool on a white marble base with two rows of four pillars each. At night, the pool was intended to reflect the stars and the moon, and the white marble had been chosen so that it gleamed in the moonlight.

Evelyn could also attest that it showed every smudge of dirt tracked onto it.

She rose off her throbbing knees, and picked up the bucket of dirty water. As lovely as the marble was, as patient as she was supposed to be, if one more penitent soul showed up with muddy feet, she just might scream.

Not that there had been a lot of penitents at this remote place. But so help her, just one more . . .

Stretching, she looked down the rough path that led up through the hills to the shrine. As far as she could see, there was no one on the path. Which meant that she'd have no visitors this night.

She turned to walk up the path to her shelter, bucket in hand, when a portal opened on the platform behind her.

She turned, raising an eyebrow. The Church delivered supplies once a week, usually by mule. The regular delivery was overdue. With any luck, this would be—

Dominic came through the portal, his long black hair whipping in the breeze. Head held high, he stepped into the pool.

Evelyn laughed. 'Dominic!'

Dominic looked down at his robes floating in the water around his ankles. 'Lovely.' He stuck his head back through the portal and she chuckled at the tongue-lashing she was sure he was giving some poor mage.

Dominic reemerged, his nose pinched in disapproval. He looked every inch the proud half-elf as he walked through the pool and stepped over its narrow rim. 'Apprentices,' he snorted, shaking out his wet sandals.

Evelyn smiled. 'It's not easy to learn to cast the spell, much less move a portal once it's in place.'

'So I am told.' Dominic's face relaxed as he looked at her. 'You look well, Evelyn.' He raised an eyebrow as he took in her robe and bucket. 'The unkempt scrubwoman disguise suits you.'

Evelyn snorted, and was about to reply when more people arrived. They were acolytes, the newest members of the Church. They were all laughing and giggling, their robes hiked up in their belts to avoid the water, their feet bare. They were all carrying parcels – her supplies, no doubt. With the awkwardness of youth, they splashed through the pool, then gathered to bow to their elders.

'Where do you want—?' Dominic asked

'The one at the very top of the path.' Evelyn gestured up the hill, and they started running up the rocky path towards her shelter.

'Have a care,' Dominic called after them. 'Slow down.'

They slowed a bit, but still jostled into each other as they disappeared with their loads.

'Come,' Dominic said as he started towards one of the benches. 'Sit with me.'

'You can stay?' Evelyn followed him up the path, taking care with the bucket.

'Not for long,' Dominic said softly, giving her a warning look. He kept moving, and raised his voice. 'Your father sent an apprentice who needs to practise holding a portal open.'

The acolytes piled out of her shelter, almost running down the path. The group gathered on the path and bowed to them again, their hands tucked in their sleeves.

'Did you break anything?' Dominic asked. As they shook their heads, he gave them a nod. 'Very well. Go and play.'

With laughter, they moved down the path and to the shrine.

Dominic sat on the bench. 'These children have been at their studies too long and need to run a bit. They also need experience with portals. So I have charge of them for the afternoon.'

Evelyn sat at the other end of the bench and placed her bucket down at her feet. 'They also make good witnesses.'

'Why, Lady High Priestess' – Dominic gave her a side-long look – 'that almost sounded cynical.'

The boys and girls had produced bean sacks that they started tossing back and forth, and through the portal. Evelyn saw it waver slightly as they dashed in and out, splashing through the pool. Their laughter was loud and joyous.

'Your father asked me to give you this.' Dominic handed her a small ceramic cylinder, corked at one end. 'He said you'd know what it was.'

Evelyn took it from his hand. She smiled to see the familiar container, but had other concerns. 'What news?' she asked softly as she tucked the cylinder in her robes.

'I'm forbidden to say.' Dominic looked straight ahead. 'I'm forbidden to give you any information. I was told that you are to concentrate on the condition of your soul and your vows to the Lord of Light, the Church and your superiors. I am not to dis-tract you with worldly matters.' He turned his head slightly, and looked at her. 'Fat Belly told me that himself.'

'Dominic!' Evelyn looked at him, eyes wide. 'You've never called him—'

'The man's an ass, a fat, bilious ass,' Dominic growled. 'But as much as I hate to admit it, he may have been right in one respect. You do look better, Evelyn.'

'Well, I confess that when I first got here, I seemed to sleep the days away,' Evelyn replied.

'Magic, both of the Gods and the secular, comes at a price,' Dominic pointed out. 'Not to mention the pressures of your plotting with the Chosen. Perhaps a retreat was in your best interest.'

'I could have rested in Edenrich,' Evelyn snapped, 'and still been available to the Queen, not to mention my regular duties.'

Dominic gave her a steady look.

Evelyn tightened her lips and looked away.

Dominic turned back to the children, hard at play, and raised his voice. 'Semeth, mind your robes!'

The lad stopped long enough to pull his robes back up through his belt before he rejoined the game. Dominic shook his head and gestured as if speaking about the boy. 'So I am forbidden to tell you that Fat Belly went to the castle for the first meeting of the Council, and presented himself in your place. And I'm forbidden to say that the Queen was upset that you were not available, but she courteously refused his offer, indicating that your place would be held until your return from your "retreat".'

'Did she?' Evelyn couldn't help a chuckle.

'His face went purple when the Queen and Vembar questioned him concerning the nature of your exhaustion and retreat,' Dominic said. 'They are pressuring him very subtly to recall you. I suspect that pressure will get stronger as the days go by. Queen Gloriana can be very insistent.'

'How is she doing?' Evelyn asked, keeping her eyes on the children.

'I am forbidden to tell you that she is doing very well.' Dominic tossed his head, letting his long black hair fall over his shoulders. 'Vembar is at her side constantly. He has looked ill, of late.'

'Ill?'

'More worn than sick,' Dominic said. 'Lady Arent has not yet left for her home. And Warder Bethral is watching for any trouble.' Dominic paused. 'And Ezren Storyteller.'

'Ezren?' Concerned, Evelyn darted a glance in Dominic's direction. Had the wild magic flared?

'He's crafting tales of the Chosen, and keeping the entire court enthralled.'

'He's telling stories?' Evelyn asked. 'Has his voice returned, then?'

'No, he rarely speaks in public. He writes them down.' Dominic brushed dirt from his white robes. 'I can't stay much longer.' He gave her a glance. 'Have you been visited by any priests of the Lady?'

That surprised Evelyn. Those who served the Lady were usually out on circuits, travelling between towns and shrines, the eyes and ears of the Church. 'No,' she said slowly. 'I haven't, come to think of it.'

'I haven't seen one in over a year.' Dominic rose from the

bench. 'There have been fewer and fewer reports. And Fat Belly is not upset, I assure you.'

Evelyn rose as well. 'Where are they?'

'I don't know.' Dominic turned and looked into her eyes. 'The Archbishop is supposed to be the leader of the Church of the Lord of Light and Lady of Laughter. But more and more, I've noticed that the Lady and her laughter are pushed to the side.'

'He called her "consort" when he banished me here,' Evelyn mused.

'Yes.' Dominic nodded. 'I'm not sure what is going on. But Fat Belly had best be careful. I may not walk in the Lady's service, but I respect her position at the Lord's side.'

'You asked because I heard her voice, didn't you?' Evelyn said softly.

'I believe you, Evelyn,' Dominic said, reaching out to stroke her cheek. 'I don't approve of what you did, nor do I understand your choice. But I do believe you.'

Evelyn smiled gratefully, but had to ask, 'Has anyone heard from—?'

'No.' Dominic dropped his hand, his eyes cold. 'Even if there was word, I'd not—'

One of the boys fell full-length in the pool, splashing water everywhere.

'Enough,' Dominic said loudly. 'It's time we were going.'

The lad stood, his robes dripping, and pulled back his wet hair. The others lined up, shoving each other and giggling, trying to get their heads bowed and their hands in their sleeves. Dominic gestured for them to precede him through the portal.

'Come again, if you can,' Evelyn urged.

Dominic paused. 'I doubt that will be permitted, Lady High Priestess.' He saw her face and softened. 'I'm sure the Queen will recall you shortly, Evelyn. Be patient.' With that, he stepped through the portal and vanished.

Evelyn heaved a sigh, looked at all the water splashed about and went to get her bucket.

Later . . . much later . . . after she'd mopped up the shrine and put away her supplies, she'd started a stew by the fire and climbed onto the flat roof of her shelter. From here, she could watch the sun as it sank slowly in the west.

There was no formal requirement that she maintain the regular invocations, but she'd always loved the peace that sunset prayers brought her. So she settled down, arranged her robes about her and started to compose herself for prayer.

She took a deep breath. The air was sweet and clean and the breeze was light. All too soon, the leaves would be turning, with winter close behind.

Where had the summer gone?

She smiled and closed her eyes.

Once her breathing slowed, once she'd emptied her mind of all worries and concerns, she opened her eyes and focused on the sun. The great orange orb was not yet touching the horizon. She began the formal chant, thanking the Lord of Light for the day and welcoming the stars, the gift of the Lady of Laughter.

The words flowed easily, out of long habit. She timed her chant so that the last word left her lips as the orb touched the horizon. Then, as tradition dictated, she sat silent, watched the sun set, and considered . . .

It wasn't personal gain that had motivated her to start the rebellion. It had been the deaths of the children born with the mark of the Chosen. It had been the small girl who had kicked off her blankets as Evelyn whisked her away to safety. Not to mention the despair in the lives of the common people that the Regent's rule had caused. It had been wrong, and once Evelyn had the support of Auxter and Arent, she'd decided to do something about it.

If she had gone to the Archbishop . . .

Evelyn drew another deep breath as the sun sank lower. She loved being a priestess, serving the Church, serving those who needed her skills. She'd taken her vows with an honest and open heart. The rituals, the magic, the structure – it was safe and secure. She'd made her choice many years ago and never once had doubted her decision.

But she'd ignored the part of her vows that required obedience. Obedience to authority, the Archbishop . . . and the Regent.

She'd changed an entire kingdom without asking a single soul for advice and counsel. She'd imposed her vision of what was right on nobles and peasants alike, without so much as a by-your-leave. And if she'd had aid, from within the kingdom and without, she knew full well that without her decision to support the cause, the Chosen would not now sit on the throne of Palins.

Perhaps she had taken too much upon herself. As much as it would be comforting to say that it had been the will of the Gods that she had succeeded, not once during the entire time had any voice spoken to her. Nor was she aware of any divine aid.

Except for the voice that bade her save one particular man.

The sun seemed to freeze in the sky. For a long moment Evelyn looked at her actions full in the face, trying to see them as the Archbishop did: as arrogant, as wrong, as disobedient, wilful, disrespectful . . .

The young queen drew herself up to sit tall and straight on the throne. She raised her hands and started to remove her gloves. 'I am the Chosen, restored to the Throne of Palins. But Red Gloves is no name for a queen.' She took off the first glove and began on the second. 'From this day forth, I shall be known as Queen Gloriana.'

Joy washed over Evelyn as she remembered Gloriana in that moment. Perhaps she had overstepped her bounds, but she'd done the right thing for Palins. And if that meant scrubbing shrines for a while, so be it.

The sun was sinking below the horizon. The sky was still lit, but the stars were starting to peep out.

Soon, Dominic had said. Well, she could be content with that. She yawned, and got to her feet. Enough woolgathering. She'd eat and then sleep well this night.

But she paused for a moment and held still, knowing full well that she was imagining things. That she was being very silly. No doubt Blackhart had long forgotten her. But she couldn't help herself.

She turned her head and looked to the north.

The Black Hills still glowed with the faint light of the setting sun. She could see their tall granite tops, stark against the sky. There were forests at their base, but at this distance they appeared as dark splotches of deeper grey against the mountains.

Once in a great while, if the sky was clear and the wind was right, she'd think she'd caught a glimpse of a red cloak gleaming like a star beneath the trees.

A star that could be seen only in just the right kind of light.

Foolishness, really. But she prayed to the Lady of Laughter to aid Orrin Blackhart in his quest. She'd probably never see him again, or would only receive news of his death. But here, alone, with only the stars and the Gods to witness, she could dream.

And with that, she was content.

FOURTEEN

A week later, Evelyn was no longer content and her patience had worn thin.

A week with no summons, no news, no word at all. At least the pilgrims had been fewer, but Evelyn was growing more and more concerned. There wasn't much to do other than clean, pray and worry.

She had the worrying part down to a fine skill. What was happening back in Edenrich? Why hadn't she heard anything from anyone?

And now, by the sacred flames, there was a small crowd of pilgrims coming up the path to the shrine. Evelyn's irritation outweighed her priestly concern for their spiritual wellbeing. There had to be twenty or thirty of them.

All with dirty shoes, no doubt.

Evelyn rose from her bench and hurried down to greet them at the edge of the shrine. They could just damn well take off their shoes before they stepped onto the white marble. Their adoration of the Lady would be no less if they were barefoot. One could only hope that their feet were a bit cleaner than their shoes.

She paused halfway down the path and scolded herself. Some attitude for a priestess to have, that was certain. She should worry more about their souls than their soles.

That made her snort at her own joke, at her impatience, at her frustrations. Wouldn't the Archbishop chide her for her misbehaviour, and rightly so?

She drew a deep breath and watched as the pilgrims advanced slowly. As they grew closer she could see that they seemed to move oddly, staggering as if wounded. She frowned, then continued towards the shrine, now truly concerned for their safety. They might have run into a wild animal, or even a monster of the human variety. She was under a binding as to her magic, but she could heal those with serious wounds, and even portal them to help if necessary. It would feel good to work a bit of magic, especially to meet another's need.

And if the portal was to the church in Edenrich, and if there happened to be a reason for her to help someone across, well surely there was no harm in that?

In a better frame of mind, she stepped up to the platform of the shrine and moved around the pool to the far edge, to stand between the two pillars. She assumed the proper demeanour of one of the priesthood, standing tall and straight, her hands pushed into her sleeves. She lifted her gaze to the sky for a moment and focused on the correct mental attitude for one charged with the spiritual guidance of questing souls.

Biting their heads off about the condition of their feet was not appropriate.

Evelyn suppressed a smile and lowered her gaze to focus on the pilgrims. The first of the group cleared the last turn and came steadily on, looking oddly . . . grey.

Bad food, maybe? But their clothes were tattered and torn, as if they'd been out in the open for some time. She had opened her mouth to greet them when she realised—

Odium. They were the undead, coming fast, faster than she thought they could move. Their faces were grey, with rotting skin hanging and white bone exposed in some places. Any hair was matted and filthy; any clothing hung in tatters from their frames. The stench wafted over Evelyn, causing her stomach to clench.

The first was on her before she finished her thought. It reached out long, claw-like hands, grabbing for her robes.

Fear surged over her. Odium fought tooth and claw, like wild animals. Even if they didn't tear your flesh apart, the wounds they caused festered.

Evelyn stepped back, her hands raised to ward it off, falling back into her old training without making a conscious effort. With a single word, she called the battle magic she'd not used in a decade.

And the magic responded. Fire burst from her hands, burning through the chest of the Odium before her. It fell at her feet, its legs still twitching as its skin curled black.

Another took its place. And another.

She moved back again, stepping into the pool, releasing a burst

85

of fire towards the ones in front. But they kept coming, threatening to swarm her. She swept the area before her with flame, trying to keep them back. If she could get to the far pillar, get her back to it, she might—

A sound came from behind. She ducked as an Odium reached for her hair, grabbing at her bun. The braid fell down her back. They were closing in. She pulled her fists in close, closed her eyes and used her fear to fuel her magic. The flames exploded out and around her.

'Where is it?' Blackhart snarled as he pulled himself up the rocky trail. 'You said—'

Archer followed along. 'Save your breath. The shrine's supposed to be up this goat track. Over the next ridge, maybe.'

Blackhart cursed. 'Goats are too smart to use a trail this bad.'

Archer ignored Blackhart's words, feeling the same frustration. But they'd been told by a shepherd a few miles back that this was the quickest way.

He paused for a moment to look back. The others were climbing as well, spread out on the trail. Sidian brought up the rear, his bald black head gleaming in the sun.

Blackhart had reached the steep crest and was waiting, pressed against the rocks. Archer did the same, crawling on his belly to reach Blackhart's side. Loose rock shifted under his body and tumbled down the path onto Mage's hands.

'Wait for the others,' Blackhart breathed. 'I saw a building, maybe two.'

Archer nodded, catching his breath, digging in his pouch for his bowstring.

Mage moved up, with the others following. They all took a moment, crouching low, catching their breath. Reader had his dagger out. Thomas and Timothy were pulling their shields off their backs and preparing their maces.

Mage recovered first. 'See anything?' he asked, quivering like a puppy.

Sidian grabbed his shoulder. 'Head down, youngling.'

'Haven't looked.' Blackhart glared at him. 'It could be that she's not there.'

A fireball burst from the other side of the ridge, a gust of sulfur and ash passing over them.

'I'm thinking that's her,' Archer said dryly.

Blackhart was already over the ridge and gone. Sidian, Reader, Thomas and Timothy scrambled after him.

Archer and Mage rose to their feet.

'Wish I could do that,' Mage said wistfully as the Priestess scorched another Odium.

'Ya do what ya can, kid.' Archer stood, bringing his bow to bear in one swift, strong movement, his entire focus on the targets below.

Blackhart was charging down the path, his red cloak streaming behind him. The others followed right on his heels, moving fast.

It was easy to see the Priestess, clad all in white. She was almost surrounded by Odium, so intent on the ones in front that she didn't see the others moving around the pool, reaching for her. Her hair had come out of its bun and the braid was swinging. One of the Odium reached—

Archer drew a breath, waiting—

'Evelyn!' Blackhart's shout rang out.

The Priestess's head snapped around, as did the Odium's. 'Orrin?' Her voice rose in astonishment.

Archer's focus was the Odium. At the slight shift of its head, his first shot took it in the eye.

The creature fell to its knees, grabbing at the arrow.

They'd been fighting Odium for weeks now and Archer had learned a thing or two. It wasn't that the things felt pain. An arrow to the chest or leg didn't really do much to them. But whatever magic powered those things still needed eyes to see and hands to grab.

They weren't easy shots to take, but Archer was patient.

Mage was next to him, chanting under his breath. Archer waited, nocking another arrow. Mage had a spell that let him move small objects at a distance. It might not have the explosive force of the Priestess's flames, but it had its uses.

'Far right,' Mage said in a distant voice.

Archer waited.

Suddenly, an Odium's head was jerked to look right at Archer, as if held tight, an unmoving target.

Archer put an arrow in each of its eyes as easily as he'd hit a barn.

As the Odium fell, Mage spoke again. 'Far left.'
Archer nocked another arrow.

Orrin plunged down the stone steps. 'Evelyn!'

He saw her turn, saw her surprise and saw the Odium behind her go down, Archer's arrow in its eye. He ran then, coming up behind one of the Odium trying to surround her. It was what was left of a woman, its rotting flesh and sagging breasts hanging from white bone. He swung his blade in a wide arc, aiming at the monster's neck.

The sword cut through flesh and bone in one blow and the head went flying. The body took one more step, then collapsed.

Reader ran past on his right and Sidian on the left. They both waded into the Odium, Reader darting in, using his speed and his dagger to hamstring any within reach. The Odium didn't feel pain, so their legs collapsed before they knew he was there.

Sidian followed behind. As each Odium fell, he swung his mace and crushed its skull.

Thomas and Timothy attacked, fending the creatures off with their shields and bringing their maces to bear. Two-on-one worked best, but Orrin waded in, shearing off hands with his blade, pressing through to Evelyn.

She stood now, her back pressed to a pillar, breathing hard, her glazed eyes wide with shock.

He placed himself in front of her, giving her a bit of breathing space, facing the Odium that remained. Taking a deep breath, ignoring the stench, he swung his sword with care, using the heavy blade to break the arms of the Odium as they reached out.

Briefly, he heard Evelyn shout something and fire burst out behind the Odium, clearing the back ranks. The heat washed over him and Orrin watched with grim pleasure as their rotting flesh crisped on their bones as they fell.

Within moments, all the Odium lay on the ground, some still twitching and trying to crawl.

They'd learned the hard way to make sure that the monsters were truly dead. The others walked through the field of battle, smashing skulls.

Archer and Mage were headed down from the ridge. Orrin wiped his blade and then sheathed it, turning to look at Evelyn.

She stood there, leaning against the pillar for support. 'Orrin?' She looked at him, her blue eyes dazed. 'Where—?'

He reached for her arm, to steady her as she swayed. He could feel her trembling under his fingers. 'Are you injured?' He stepped closer. 'Did they—?'

She reached out, pressing her hand against his chest. He drew her a bit closer, but she shook her head, her long braid hanging over her shoulder. 'Just drained of power. Give me a moment.'

'That's more than we have,' Orrin growled. 'We need to get you out of here.'

Her blue eyes focused on him, wide with surprise. 'I can't leave the shrine.'

'You must,' Orrin said. 'We've learned—'

'I can't,' Evelyn repeated impatiently as she looked around. 'Look at this mess. Those bodies need rites said over them and a decent burial.'

'Evelyn,' Orrin snapped.

'I'm bound to the shrine.' She lifted a shaky hand to her head, brushing back the loose hair from her face. 'I can't leave without the Archbishop's permission. I'm not even supposed to use magic, except that—' She gave him a weak smile. 'I could really use some kav. Would you like some? I've some stew by the fire and—'

Orrin hit her square on the jaw.

Evelyn's head snapped back, her eyes rolling up into her head. Orrin scooped her up as she collapsed, unconscious.

'Kav, my ass.' He slung her over his shoulder, grunting as he got her into position. 'Let's move.'

'Did she say something about food?' Reader asked.

'Gather her things and try to make it look like she fled in a hurry.' Orrin shifted his burden, settling her on his shoulder. 'Mage, keep her unconscious.'

'No problem.' Mage stepped forward. 'I don't want her frying my ass when she wakes up. She's not gonna be happy. I didn't bring any spell chains and I can't take the time to make—'

'Cast the damn spell.' Orrin's rough voice cut through the babble.

Mage blinked, jerked his head in a nod and reached out to touch the Priestess's head.

'So' – Archer was looking out over the valley, watching for threats – 'we're kidnapping her?'

'It's a rescue,' Orrin said as he continued up the path, Evelyn balanced on his shoulder. Sidian and Reader were already moving to follow his orders.

'Ah' – Archer's voice held silent laughter – 'I'm just a simple man of the land, but it sure looks like a kidnap—'

Orrin turned and glared.

Archer closed his mouth with a snap.

Orrin turned again and headed up the hill.

FIFTEEN

Evelyn awoke slowly to the sound of a morning lark's song. She was stretched out, on the ground, on a bedroll, cushioned with blankets. She didn't have to open her eyes to determine that. On patrol, most like. It was oh-so-familiar, sleeping on the ground. Didn't really bother her that much. There was a pillow for her head, and she was lying on her side. The scent of ehat wool surrounded her – her old red cloak, no doubt. Though the smell wasn't her favourite, it wasn't bad enough to make her want to face the dawn just yet.

She was warm and comfortable. There was stirring in the camp, and something was cooking on the fire. The smell of strong kav hung in the air, as well as the scent of fried bread. Her stomach rumbled in response. If they were lucky, there'd be a bit of pork fat in the pan for seasoning. On patrol, that was a real treat.

She frowned, thinking, unsure of the day, or which patrol she was on. But it didn't really matter. She relaxed, trying to sleep just a few minutes more. Sure enough, there was a footfall by her head, more than likely the watch commander about to—

She hadn't been on patrol in years.

Evelyn's eyes flew open and she jerked up, wide awake. The old red cloak slid from her shoulders as she sat up.

Blackhart stood over her, steaming mug in hand. 'Thought you could use some of this.'

She blinked at him, confused. 'Orrin?'

'The same, Lady High Priestess.' Blackhart squatted in front of her, giving her an almost apologetic look.

She sat up within the blankets, smoothing back her hair and looking around to get her bearings. They were under some pine trees, with a tiny fire. There were pots and pans by the fire, but no one else was in sight. She reached for the mug, trying to cover her disorientation.

Their fingers touched when she took the mug. His were calloused and strong under hers.

Her body flushed at the warmth of his skin and she looked up into his eyes with a bemused smile. His hazel eyes were on hers, caring but also worried. Her heart warmed to see him as she took a sip of kav. It was hot, dark and bitter, and blew away all the cobwebs.

'You hit me!'

Blackhart leaned back on his heels. 'I did. You were blithering.'

'I wasn't.' Evelyn frowned as she remembered the fight. 'Where—? How long—?'

Blackhart turned and reached for another mug. 'Three day's hard ride from the shrine, in the Black Hills.' He looked at her over the rim.

Evelyn took in the state of her clothes, her hair, the faint fuzzy taste on her tongue. 'A sleep spell.' Indignant, she sat up straight and glared at him. 'You used a sleep spell on me.'

'I've an apprentice mage with me.' Blackhart looked smug. 'After I hit you, he made sure you'd not awaken until I wanted you to. He said you'd not suffer thereby.'

Evelyn narrowed her eyes. 'Where is he?'

'Hiding,' Blackhart said. 'My men have seen what you can do, Lady High Priestess. They are not eager to have their eyebrows burned off.'

'What's to say that I won't?' Evelyn pointed out. 'You've kidnapped me, after all.'

'I *rescued* you,' Blackhart corrected her. 'Fine thing, to roast your hero alive.'

'My hero?' Evelyn sputtered, then laughed.

'Exactly.' Blackhart stood. 'And since I think the food is cooked . . . and if you promise not to hurt them, or give them some kind of crotch rot . . .' He tilted his head at her. 'We are all that stands between the Odium and the people of the Black Hills.'

'I won't hurt them,' Evelyn said quietly.

'Thank you.' Blackhart gave her an odd look and lowered his voice. 'I need your help, Evelyn.' He lifted his head and called out, 'It's safe. She won't hurt you.'

The pines stirred and six men emerged, gathering up their plates and mugs and settling by the fire.

Evelyn studied them as Blackhart made introductions. They nodded their heads as their names were called, but seemed more intent on their food than anything else.

The one named Archer had a mug in his hand but remained standing, watching over the area. She recognised the stance of a man on guard.

The smaller man brought her a plate of pan bread and refilled her mug with kav. 'I've seen you before, Reader.'

'Might could be, ma'am.' The man bobbed his head nervously as he moved back to the fire.

There was a huge, bald black man, his arms and face covered in decorative scars. His big white eyebrows rose as he gave her a nod and a smile. 'Sidian, Lady High Priestess.' His voice was deep as she'd expected, but he had an odd accent.

The youngest, the one she felt certain had to be the apprentice mage, kept trying to hide behind Sidian.

'I won't hurt you,' Evelyn repeated.

'Mage, settle down and eat,' Blackhart said. 'We need to get moving as quick as we can.' He nodded to the last two men. 'That's Thomas and Timothy.'

Those two, clearly brothers, settled by the fire and helped themselves to food.

Evelyn bit into the warm bread and chewed thoughtfully. They ate in silence. Blackhart moved to take Archer's place so that he could eat.

After the last of the kav had been poured, the men started to gather their things.

'There's a stream back in the trees,' Blackhart said. 'We're off as soon as we've broken camp. The town's not far. If we ride hard, we'll be there before sunset.'

'I've nothing—' Evelyn cut off her words when Blackhart dropped a saddlebag by her bedroll. She licked her fingers and opened it to find the few personal items and the spare clothes she'd had at the shrine.

She looked up at the man who stood there, looking down at her. She thought about her options for a moment, then stood, gathering up the saddlebag. Without a word, she handed the red cloak to Blackhart.

He took it from her and swept it over his shoulders.

'I'll just be a minute,' she said softly and faded back into the trees. The stream was close and there was a fallen tree where she could take care of basic needs. Once that was done, she knelt by the stream and washed quickly in the cold water.

She could leave. There was nothing stopping her from opening a portal and returning to the shrine, or to the church in Edenrich for that matter. That was what she should do, under the sanctions the Archbishop had placed on her. Not to mention the gift from her father. That was still tucked within her robes.

But her curiosity had the best of her. Blackhart was alive and had men working for him. What had he managed to accomplish? And why did he need her?

Evelyn sighed, using her robe to dry off. She braided her hair back up into its bun and gathered her things into the saddlebag. She was a prisoner, wasn't she? Unable to work magic, as the Archbishop had instructed. She'd have to go along with Blackhart, wouldn't she?

Rationalisations firmly in place, she walked back to the camp.

Once they were mounted, Orrin gestured for Archer to take the lead. Usually he rode in back, but Orrin wanted his sharp eyes at the front on this ride.

Archer raised an eyebrow and nodded as he urged his horse forward. The others fell in line and Blackhart took the rear.

He had to watch the prisoner, didn't he?

He grimaced as his horse headed down the path. What was he thinking? Yes, she had power. Yes, she might help them. But she'd already risked so much on his behalf. This was trouble, pure and simple. There was no way she—

'Orrin.'

He looked up and saw that she had waited for the road to widen as they emerged from the trees and then moved her horse alongside his.

'That shrine, where you found me, that was in Farentell.'

'Yes,' Blackhart said. The truth would come out at some point, so he might as well tell her now. 'Just on the edge of the old border.' He paused, giving her a hard look. 'Your punishment?'

Evelyn's cheeks flushed pale pink. 'Yes.' She frowned and looked him in the eyes. 'How did you know I was there? Only a few priests and the Archbishop knew.'

Blackhart faced forward. 'I've managed to gather more than a hundred men to aid me so far, about all that's left of the army of the Black Hills. We decided to round up every living man, woman and child and stuff them into walled towns with strict curfews and warriors walking the walls. It accomplishes two things. It protects the people—'

'And it "starves" whoever is creating the Odium,' Evelyn said. 'They need living prisoners to make more.'

'Right.' Blackhart shifted in his saddle as his horse set a steady walk. 'Once we'd cut off the source, we started attacking, whittling down the numbers of the undead.'

'How many?'

Blackhart raised an eyebrow. 'What?'

'How many people have you saved?' Evelyn pressed.

'Oh.' Blackhart paused, then shrugged. 'Didn't count them. Enough to stuff Wareington to the bursting point. Took us weeks to gather them together.'

'Weeks?' Evelyn asked. 'Didn't they understand—?'

'He doesn't always ask nice,' Sidian offered.

'Farm folk can be kinda thick, ma'am,' Reader added.

'I see.' Evelyn gave Blackhart an arched look.

Blackhart scowled at his men. 'This is a private conversation.'

'Oh, that it is,' Reader said, not turning around on his horse. 'There's none about to hear us.'

'So you forced people into the towns,' Evelyn concluded, a barely repressed laugh in her voice. 'I take it they weren't pleased.'

'Like herding cats,' Blackhart grumbled. 'A few saw the sense of it, but I had to insist with some others.'

'Once within the gates, most came to understand,' Sidian pointed out. 'They chafe at the restrictions, but there is always them that ignore the rules.'

Evelyn coughed. Blackhart was sure she was biting the inside of her cheek. 'But what does this have to do with how you found me?'

'As I was saying,' Blackhart growled, 'we cut off the source of new Odium and then started to try to wipe them out, clearing the countryside as we looked for more of the living. But lately it seems we've seen more and more Odium, in larger groups.'

'Maybe they are getting their victims from Summerford,'

Evelyn suggested. 'Or maybe Athelbryght.' Her tone was doubt-ful, even as she spoke.

'Ain't Athelbryght,' Archer spoke from the front. 'No one's moved back, leastways not along the border.'

'And Lord Fael has pulled his people back from the border areas and into fortified towns,' Blackhart added. 'He's not pur-suing the Odium like we are, but he's protecting the living.'

'I'm not sure what this has to do with me,' Evelyn pushed.

'We came across a large group of Odium headed for Farentell. We attacked, wiped them out and found this.' Blackhart fumbled in his belt pouch, cursed and drew his horse to a stop. 'Hold up, lads.'

The group came to a stop, with Archer and the others taking up watch all around them. Evelyn sidled her horse closer to Blackhart.

'Hurry up,' Archer said, scanning the fields around them. 'Don't like to sit for too long.'

Blackhart handed Evelyn a piece of folded leather and she spread it out to look at it. He watched her face as her eyes flickered over the crude pictures.

'I don't understand,' Evelyn said.

'This is how we found you.' Blackhart leaned over. 'This is the keep, and this is the main road to Farentell.' He ran his finger down to point to the branching. 'This is the road that branches off to your shrine. It's not the most direct route, but easy enough for an Odium to follow.'

Evelyn gave him a doubtful look. 'Odium are stupid. They are little more than corpses powered with magic. They barely follow spoken commands. They certainly don't read.'

Blackheart tapped the figure on the leather. 'Then explain this.'

Evelyn held the leather up and looked closer. Blackhart knew full well what she was seeing: the crude figure of a woman with white hair, white robes and pale blue eyes, standing before a shrine.

Evelyn puffed out a breath, then opened her mouth.

Blackhart cut her off. 'And don't try to tell me that there are other priestesses with white hair.'

Evelyn closed her mouth.

'And if you think you can explain it away, then explain this.' Blackhart turned to Reader. 'Show her.'

'Pulled this off the ones we searched back at the shrine.' Reader took out a second piece of leather and unfolded it to show Evelyn the same crude drawing.

'We need to get moving,' Archer insisted. 'We're wasting time. Argue once we're behind the walls.'

Blackhart plucked the map from Evelyn's hands. 'They were sent for you, Lady High Priestess.'

Evelyn looked at him with wide, startled eyes. He could lose himself in those light blue depths, but he looked away and crammed the leather back into his pouch.

Archer urged his horse forward and the others started to follow.

'I was repaying my debt.' Blackhart kept his voice low. 'Now I find out that you wield more than just healing powers and the magic of the Gods. Just what other secrets do you have, Lady High Priestess?'

SIXTEEN

Evelyn didn't say much for the rest of the ride, and Blackhart didn't press her. She was grateful, lost in her own thoughts.

To her knowledge, only the Archbishop, Dominic and a few others knew where she'd been sent. Oh, the room had been filled with people when her banishment had been pronounced, but she couldn't remember if the Archbishop had mentioned the specific shrine at that point.

Of much more concern were the Odium. Odium were supposed to be stupid: shuffling corpses powered by magic and a mage's will. They were foul and dangerous, but there was no sense within them.

Except that the Odium that had attacked her had moved faster than she'd thought possible. And they'd carried a map, albeit a crude one, easily read.

What would they have done with her?

A frisson of fear went up her spine. Whatever – whoever – was behind these things knew more about her than she did about them.

And they wanted her.

They reached the town walls just as the sun was setting.

The gates were opened wide enough for them to ride in, then shut behind them. The courtyard beyond was filled with people. In the confusion, Evelyn wasn't certain who was who, but she was grateful for the safety of high walls and to slide out of the saddle. They'd ridden hard the last few hours and she ached.

Blackhart appeared next to her with an older woman. 'Lady High Priestess, let me introduce Bella of Wareington. Bella is charged with our injured and the nursery.' Blackhart paused. 'She's a healer, Bella.' With that, he was gone.

'You're tired, Lady. Let me see to you,' Bella said, taking her saddlebag.

Evelyn reached for her arm. 'I'm a bit stiff, Bella, but naught that a bit of walking and standing won't cure. Do you have a need for a healer? For the babes?'

'Aye.' Bella's face filled with pain. 'We've a few warriors with infected wounds and some of the babes should be seen to. Nothing life-threatening, but—'

'Take me to the warriors first,' Evelyn said, straightening easily now that she knew she was needed.

'This way,' Bella said with a pleased smile.

Blackhart found her in the nursery hours later.

He'd seen to his men, checked the walls and the watch and had reports from the scouts. All was as well as could be, given the Odium in the countryside. They'd even found a few more families to bring within the walls.

This late, the nursery was bedded down, children sleeping on every inch of the floor, the women watching over them. Blackhart took care to move quietly as he entered. It wouldn't do to wake the children.

He found Evelyn by the fire, a babe in her arms.

She was cooing at the little one, rocking him gently. The firelight seemed to make her robes glow and set her hair ablaze with glory. But then Blackhart blinked and realised that she was glowing because she was working healing magic on the child.

Bella put her finger to her lips. Blackhart nodded and moved back to the door. 'What's she doing?' he asked softly.

'A healing on the little one,' Bella whispered. 'His mother died in childbirth and his bowels aren't—'

'Enough.' Orrin lifted a hand to cut her off.

Bella huffed at him. 'The Priestess said she could set it right and we might be able to get a bit more sustenance in him.'

Blackhart nodded, then looked at the beds near the fire. 'The others?'

'Nothing that serious,' Bella answered. 'Nothing to worry yourself over. We'd one with a bad rash on the bum, another with a croupy cough. She's looked the others over, just in case.' Bella pressed her hand on his arm. 'You've brought us a fine one, Lord Blackhart, that you have. She's already seen to some of the warriors with infected wounds.'

Blackhart shook his head, but Bella had already moved off to

99

check the sleeping children. He leaned against the wall in the shadows and watched.

The baby was naked, dark-skinned, with black curls that hugged his head. He was kicking his feet and gurgling at the Priestess.

Evelyn was smiling, whispering something as she rubbed the babe's belly with her free hand. The light seemed to spill from her, catching on the white and gold of her robes.

Blackhart's eyes narrowed. Hadn't she even changed? Bella was supposed to have seen to her.

Evelyn's lips stopped moving and the deeply sleeping babe's head lolled to one side. She handed the child to one of the women and rose from her seat by the fire. From across the room her eyes met his and a spark went down his spine. Blackhart caught his breath as she walked towards him.

'Haven't you eaten?' he asked harshly, trying to cover the emotion in his voice.

'I've had kav,' Evelyn said softly. 'I wanted to see to the babes first.'

'That was hours ago,' Blackhart snapped. He took her arm and pulled her out of the nursery, tugging her towards the stairs. 'You're no use to me drained of power and starved.'

Evelyn jerked her arm out of his grasp and gave him a cold look. 'I decide how to use my powers, Lord Blackhart. Healing babes is not a waste.'

Blackhart scowled. 'That's not what I—'

Evelyn brushed past him and went down the stairs. 'There's food in the kitchen, I take it?'

Blackhart cursed and followed her.

An older man stood before the hearth, stirring a large stewpot as Evelyn entered the kitchen. He turned and she caught her breath as she realised that he wore the traditional black robes of a priest of the Lady of Laughter.

Blackhart followed her in and stomped over to one of the long tables, claiming a bench for his own. 'Dorne, this is Evelyn, Lady High Priestess of Edenrich.' Blackhart grabbed a mug and a pitcher of kav. 'Dorne is our cook.'

'But you are a priest,' Evelyn said.

'What better way to a man's soul than through his stomach?'

Dorne smiled at Evelyn. 'What can I get for you, Lady High Priestess?'

Evelyn returned the man's smile, then focused on his silver brooch and counted the stars on its surface. Her eyes widened and she curtsied to the older man. 'I greet thee, Your—'

'Priest is more than enough of a title.' Dorne cut off her words and gestured towards the table. 'And Cook is an even better one, if you think my skills merit it. Let's get you something to eat, shall we?' He turned and frowned at Blackhart. 'There's a well and a washbasin out back, Blackhart. Use both, and take the Priestess with you.'

Blackhart drained his mug and gestured for Evelyn to precede him. There was indeed a well, and Blackhart pulled the first bucket.

'You do know that's a priest of the Lady who's cooking your meals?' Evelyn asked quietly. 'I've never seen that many stars on a brooch before; he must be of high rank.'

'What does that mean, in a land with barely enough people to fill this town? Besides, he's said that he has no magic,' Blackhart said bitterly. 'I value him more for his cooking and counsel than for any rank he might hold in a church. Especially yours.'

Evelyn plunged her arms in the bucket. 'Those who pledge to the Lady have their own rankings, even if the Archbishop is deemed the head of both churches.' She scrubbed her hands and face as best she could. 'And not all have magic. They each bring their own skills to the Order.'

'Here' – Archer appeared and handed her a bar of soap – 'thought you could use this.' He also had a towel draped over his shoulder. 'Figured Blackhart wouldn't think of it.'

Blackhart scowled as Evelyn seized the soap with glee and started lathering. 'Where have you been?'

'Talking to the new ones.' Archer leaned against the well. 'Figured you'd want the information fast, and I'd have a better chance of getting it from them without scaring them half to death.'

'And?' Blackhart demanded.

Archer handed the towel to Evelyn with a courtly flourish. 'And they've been hiding, travelling in daylight, trying to reach safety. They don't know much more than that.'

'Damn,' Blackhart grunted as he plunged his hands in the

bucket, splashing water everywhere. 'How am I going to put an end to the Odium if no one has any information?'

Archer smiled at Evelyn. 'Ignore him. He'll growl less once he's fed and bedded.'

Evelyn flushed.

'That's "been to bed", not "bedded",' Blackhart growled. 'Idiot.'

'I am a mere lad of the country, a simple man of the land,' Archer said. 'Your courtly ways are strange to me.' He presented his arm. 'Lady High Priestess?'

Evelyn took his arm and they strode back to the kitchen, leaving a cursing and soggy Blackhart behind.

Dorne had dished out bowls of rabbit stew and was cutting thick slices of brown bread for them at the table. Evelyn inhaled the aroma as she and Archer settled on the bench. 'That smells wonderful, Dorne.'

'As it should,' Dorne said. 'I've had it simmering most of the day, and some of the lads found a field of wild garlic yesterday and harvested the lot.'

Blackhart, walking in with the towel and soap, demanded, 'Did they set aside—?'

'Yes, yes, they set aside enough for the next planting, as you have ordered,' Dorne replied. 'Sit yourself. You'll be fit to talk to after you've eaten.' He fixed an eye on Archer. 'You'll wait till we've said the grace.'

Archer sheepishly put his spoon back in the bowl.

Dorne set down his knife and bowed his head. 'Lady of Laughter, we ask that you grace this meal with your joy. Remind us that our duties can be leavened with a sense of humour now and again with no loss of efficiency—'

Blackhart snorted.

'—and that a kind word makes a better goad than a pointed stick. Our thanks, gracious Lady of Laughter, and to the Lord of Light as well.'

Archer dug in, and Evelyn wasn't far behind. The stew tasted as good as it smelled. Blackhart didn't slack either, and Dorne settled down next to him on the bench with his own bowl. They all reached for bread, and there was silence as they ate.

Evelyn concentrated on the food. She'd been on simple rations for the last few weeks and the taste was pure pleasure. The rabbit was tender, and the garlic and bits of onion added to the savour.

Archer got up to refill his bowl and brought back fresh kav. Evelyn filled her mug again and sopped up the rest of the stew with a bit of bread. She sighed and noticed Dorne watching her. She smiled at him, warm and content. 'That was wonderful, Cook.'

He gave her a smile and a dignified nod. 'It's a pleasure to cook for one who appreciates a good meal.'

'I appreciate your cooking,' Archer protested.

'Bah,' Dorne scoffed. 'You'd eat anything. And the way you make kav is a sin against the Lady.'

Archer leaned back and belched. 'Needs to be strong, to keep a man going.'

Dorne rolled his eyes. 'Not so strong it eats through the mug.'

'Enough,' Blackhart said, leaning his elbows on the table. 'Tell me about the new families that came in. How many? Any warriors?'

Evelyn sat and listened as Archer gave Blackhart the details. The kitchen was warm and she felt tired, but in a good way. The babe had been a joy to work on, setting his little belly and bowels right. She'd check on him again, but she was willing to bet that he would thrive now that the colic had been cleared. She smiled, remembering his dark face and happy eyes.

'Evelyn?' Dorne said softly, his deep voice a quiet rumble in the warmth.

She looked at him with eyebrows raised.

'There is a tale told in Palins,' Dorne said, wrapping both hands around his mug, 'of a young mage and a king on a battle-field.'

Evelyn's eyes went wide-awake, her sleepiness gone.

Blackhart and Archer frowned, both looking at her and Dorne.

'In the story, the king was struck down in battle,' Dorne continued, his voice soothing. 'In the midst of the fighting, the mage leaped to cover the king's body with her own, calling on the Lord of Light and Lady of Laughter to save him.'

Evelyn couldn't look away from Dorne's warm brown eyes as he continued, 'The dead king rose to his feet, alive and well, and led his troops to victory. The mage rose as well and found her hair turned white by the holy power of the Gods as it flowed through her: mage no longer, but priestess by the Gods' own hands.'

He paused, and the only sound was the crackle of the fire.

'Was that you?' Dorne asked.

SEVENTEEN

'It was,' Evelyn whispered. 'But it wasn't quite like that,' she added softly.

'What?' Blackhart demanded. Archer thought he looked a bit like a man who'd thought he'd picked up a kitten and got a mountain cat instead.

'If I'd known that, I wouldn't have kidnapped ya.' Archer looked at Evelyn sitting there, pale and tired. 'Neither time.'

She gave him a wan smile. 'The story's not quite true,' Evelyn continued. She looked down at her mug. Blackhart was staring at her as if he'd never seen her before.

'The best stories aren't,' Dorne said.

'My father is a powerful mage, and my mother was a priestess, each a member of a noble house of Edenrich,' Evelyn said. 'I was raised in a home where magic was like breathing. I chose to become a battle mage, to my father's joy. But to honour my mother, I also learned a bit of healing and served for a time as an acolyte to the Church.'

'The red cloak' – Blackhart still looked a bit dazed – 'it was yours.'

'Everard was struck in that battle.' Evelyn closed her eyes. 'He took an arrow to the chest, and I watched in horror as he fell limp from his horse.' Her eyes opened, and she looked at the fire, but Archer knew full well she wasn't seeing the kitchen.

'I threw myself down beside him and started a healing chant my mother had taught me. Everard and I were friends, had been since we were children. My hands were covered with blood, and he was so still, so pale. I prayed – pouring all the magic, all my power, everything I had into the chant – as his guard formed around us.'

She sat silent for a moment. 'I've never been sure if he was dead, to be honest, but he was sorely wounded. I'd closed my eyes; there was a flare of light all about me, and I lost consciousness. When I awoke, there was a cheering, victorious army, and Everard smiling at me. My hair was white as snow and my head was pounding with a horrific headache.'

'Evelyn, Lady High Priestess,' Dorne said.

Evelyn nodded. 'I never claimed to have raised him from the dead, but that version of the story would not die. I'd been a minor acolyte up to that point, but the Church insisted that I become a full priestess. I had a leaning that way so I agreed. The King awarded me the title of Lady, and I entered the Order.'

'Entered? Or fled to?' Dorne asked.

Evelyn looked at him, then looked away. 'I've magic, both sacred and secular. The Church allows me to use them for the betterment of others.'

'That's not what I hear. Eidam sets limits on you, doesn't he? Your gifts must be reserved for the powerful, and not the healing of the sick and the poor?' Dorne's question had a definite edge to it. 'The most powerful healer in the land, who can raise even the dead, is not permitted to use her gifts on just anyone.'

Archer looked at Blackhart, who shrugged.

Evelyn frowned. 'I've worked hard to do good works among the less fortunate, but then the Chosen . . .' Her voice trailed off, and she put a hand to her head. 'I beg your pardon. I'm more tired then I realised. Is there somewhere I could—?'

Blackhart stood. 'I'll show you to your room.'

Evelyn nodded and followed him out of the kitchen. Archer watched them leave, then turned back to Dorne. He gave the man a questioning look.

Dorne stood, gathering dishes. 'Ever see battle magic used?'

'Not before I saw her fry Odium like a rabbit on a spit,' Archer said. 'It was impressive.'

Dorne nodded. 'Magical fire does horrible things to a person's body.' He turned and headed for the washbasins. 'Friend and foe alike.'

'What's that got to do with her raising the dead?' Archer asked, confused.

'Never mind,' Dorne said. 'And don't even think of sneaking out of here without doing dishes.'

Archer froze, right in the middle of doing just that.

'You eat, you wash,' Dorne growled, 'or you don't eat again.'

Archer sighed and turned back.

Evelyn followed Orrin into the large main room, then up the main staircase to the second floor. She sighed as she saw the stairs and reached out to grasp the railing to pull herself up. 'I didn't realise how big this inn is.'

'Wareington was a major crossroads at one point.' Orrin waited for her at the top of the steps. 'From here, you can take the main roads to Edenrich, the Keep of the Black Hills, Summerford and Athelbryght. This place was quite busy, in its day.' He walked ahead of her, down the hall to a set of double doors. 'People came for miles just to stay here.' He pushed open the door and stepped back to allow her to enter.

'Why did they—?' Evelyn stopped dead in the doorway.

The room was panelled in a dark wood. A fire crackled on the hearth, warming the room. There were a few chairs there, and a small table. The windows were shuttered, but even in the light of the fire, she could see the only other piece of furniture.

An enormous bed.

The bed was huge, spanning most of the room. It was a four-poster, with heavy curtains hanging from the rods. The mattress was easily big enough for an entire family. She couldn't imagine how many geese had given up their feathers to stuff the mattress. Light above, maybe an entire gaggle of the creatures, and a year to stuff it.

She stood in awe.

'Behold, Lady High Priestess. The Great Bed of Wareington.' Orrin spoke from behind her. 'An attraction for miles around. The innkeeper had it built as a lure for his trade, and charged handsomely for this room. Made a fine profit from it, I am sure.'

Evelyn stepped closer as Orrin lit a few candles on the mantelpiece. 'It's amazing.'

And it was. The bed was carved with flowers and animals that seemed to be playing in a garden paradise. One of them, a fierce lion on the footrest, looked odd. Evelyn took a closer look.

Someone had carved their initials on its nose.

Evelyn laughed out loud at the sight.

Orrin's chest clenched at the sound of her laughter.

Even exhausted, she was still so damned lovely in the light, running her fingers over the lion's face and laughing.

He'd done her a disservice, dragging her away from the shrine, bringing her here. He should have made her open a portal, shoved her through and waited until it closed to make sure she was safe. He should have torn the damn shrine down, so that fat bastard of an archbishop couldn't send her there again. He should have . . .

She looked at him, and smiled.

'There's more of that kind of thing all over the bed.' he said gruffly. 'People have been carving their names and initials for years. Especially on the headboard.' He looked away. 'It's easier to see in the daytime.'

Evelyn laughed again. 'Lady of Laughter, you could sleep six in that bed easily and still have room for more.'

In a flash, he pictured her naked on the bed, her white hair spread out like a glory over the pillows, filling his hand as he—

Orrin shuddered, forcing himself to speak. 'You'll sleep here. Your things are behind the screen, with water for bathing. You've but to call if you need anything else.'

'And tomorrow?' she asked. 'You said you need my help.'

'I've changed my mind,' Orrin said firmly. 'You'll go back to Edenrich, where it's safe. It was folly of the worst kind to bring you here.'

'But not folly to ride three days to rescue me,' Evelyn said.

Orrin's mouth went dry at the idea of her dead or injured or taken by those things. 'That was no folly. I paid my debt, that's all.'

'And once I was helpless, unconscious, how did you transport me?' she asked softly, moving closer to him.

'In my arms. None but mine.'

Evelyn stepped closer. He could smell her, the scent of her hair, the softness of her skin. He stepped back, but she followed, reaching to place a finger on his throat.

Orrin froze, feeling his pulse beat against her finger.

Evelyn looked at him, and then he felt a slight tug. She'd captured the leather cord that lay under his tunic and slowly pulled it clear of his shirt.

Her ring dangled from the leather, caught between them, the white star sapphire gleaming in the light.

He heard her breath catch in her throat. She stood there, not moving, the ring suspended between them.

'I couldn't sell it,' Orrin said softly.

'It's not worth a great deal,' Evelyn whispered back.

'It is to me.'

Her eyes crinkled at the corners as her lips curled in a soft smile. She tilted her head, moving to kiss him. He felt the heat of her, her warm breath on his cheek.

He stepped back, pulling the thong from her fingers. 'No.'

Evelyn looked at him, puzzled. 'But—'

Orrin felt ill. 'I am a bad man, stained with blood and darkness. You are' – his voice cracked – 'you are the opposite in every way. Why are you still here, Priestess?'

She lowered the cord, letting the ring rest on his chest. 'You kidnapped me.'

'I rescued you,' Orrin growled, suddenly angry. 'And you have at least one way of leaving any time you want. Open a portal. Jump on a horse.'

Evelyn looked at him with a smile and reached into her sleeve. She withdrew her hand and held it open. There on her palm was a small clay cylinder with a cork in the top.

'What is that?' he asked.

'A summon stick,' Evelyn said gravely. 'You open it and break the stick within, and it summons help. My father gave it to me.' She tucked her hand back in her sleeve.

'It opens a portal?'

'Probably. Knowing my father, it would open one in the church sanctuary.'

'Your father, the Lord High Mage of Palins.'

'Yes,' Evelyn said softly.

Orrin drew in a deep breath, looming over her, as dark and as threatening as he'd ever been with his men. 'Why are you still here?'

'The Archbishop forbade me—'

He spoke through a clenched jaw. 'Why. Are. You. Still. Here?'

Evelyn grew serious, looking at him intently. 'There's something between us, Orrin. I felt—'

'Sympathy,' Orrin lashed out. 'Or worse yet, pity for one—'

'Love.' She looked him in the eyes, steady and strong. 'Love isn't something that I can control, Orrin, even with the powers at my command. It's an emotion, a feeling, one that—'

'Love.' Orrin's heart clenched in his chest at the word, but he forced himself to scowl at her. 'Love is nothing. It can falter, it can die. Let it.'

Evelyn shook her head. 'I can't explain, but I—'

'No,' Orrin stalked to the door. 'I'll not stain you, Lady High Priestess.' He threw open the door. 'In the morning, I'm sending you back to Edenrich. Through a portal or tied to a horse – one way or another, you are leaving.' He slammed the door as he left and stomped off, muttering curses all the way down the hall.

'Loving you isn't a sin,' Evelyn said as the door slammed behind Orrin.

She loved him. A man who by all rights was an enemy of all she'd fought for. And yet here he was, struggling to put things right when he could just as easily mount up and ride away.

She stood in the silence of the room, listening as Orrin stomped down the hall, cursing.

She sighed, too tired to figure out the conversation they'd just had. She was fairly certain that she'd confessed her secret and been brutally rejected.

She was almost too tired to care.

For now, the Great Bed of Wareington was calling her. She yawned and went behind the screen to find her things. There was a bucket and a bowl and some washing cloths. She'd make quick work of it now and be more thorough in the morning. She yawned again, and poured the water into the basin. It swirled against the sides, then settled as she reached for the soap.

As she reached for the cloths, a face formed in the water. 'Evie!'

Startled, she dropped the soap, rocking the bowl. The water splashed and the face frowned as it peered around the floating bar.

'Evie! What in the name of all the hells do you think you are doing?'

EIGHTEEN

Evelyn reached out to steady the bowl as the face of her father peered up from the swirling water. 'Father.'

'Daughter.' Marlon's face was grim. 'Are you well? Where are you? I've been scrying for days . . .'

'Father, I'm sorry.' Evelyn looked down at the bowl with a rueful smile as she fished out the soap. 'I hadn't thought to send word.'

'Inconsiderate chit,' her father scolded, but she could see his relief. 'I assumed that if you needed me, you'd have broken the summon stick. Priest Dominic said that he couldn't find it when he reported that you'd been taken. Do you still have it?'

'I do,' Evelyn replied, 'but I—'

'Then tell me what is happening, Daughter!' her father sputtered, his jowls shaking. 'I've been so worried, I've not eaten a thing.'

Evelyn dragged the chair closer to the bowl. 'Well, Father, four days ago . . .' She launched into the explanation, grateful that her father listened without interruption.

'Blackhart, eh?' Marlon frowned. 'He's right about the Odium. Elanore's death should have meant their collapse.'

'Yes, Father.' Evelyn hesitated. 'I'd be grateful if the full story remained our secret.'

'Hah,' her father chuckled. 'Well, anything to poke the Archbishop in his squinty little eye. He's been taking quite a bit of abuse from the Queen since she got word that you were missing.'

'She learned that from you, I take it?'

'The Archbishop wasn't going to tell her, that was sure.' Marlon gave her a long look. 'I'll keep my tongue, but if you're dealing with the Odium, you understand that you will have to use battle magics.'

'I do,' Evelyn said, 'as long as it's against Odium.'

'I wish you'd worked with it more than you have. Control can be achieved only with practise, Daughter. There's nothing to be afraid of.'

'Tell that to those I burned on the battlefield,' Evelyn responded sharply.

'It's foolishness, of course, but I am proud of you. The Odium need to be dealt with, and I suspect Blackhart is one of the few who can. He will need your magic.'

Evelyn leaned forward. 'How is Gloriana?'

Her father barked out a laugh. 'You might have given that child a sense of humour, daughter. She is so serious, so intent on her duties. But she is fending off the sycophants, including Fat Belly, quite well. You started this mess, though, so you should be here dealing with it.'

'It will be a few days at most, Father.' Evelyn sighed, smoothing back her hair. 'Then I will return and face the consequences.'

'Kidnapped – as if that were possible.' Marlon sighed. 'You have the summon stick?'

'Yes, Father.'

'You'll be careful?'

'Yes, Father,' Evelyn repeated patiently.

Marlon peered up at her from the bowl. 'You're not so grown-up that I don't worry, Daughter. Get some sleep. You look terrible.'

'Father!' Evelyn remonstrated, but his image was gone in an instant.

She sighed, and started to wash.

In the morning, Dorne welcomed her into the kitchen and served her breakfast. 'Comfortable bed, eh?'

'It is that.' Evelyn took the bowl of hot cereal from him eagerly. 'Of course, I think bricks and rubble would have been comfortable last night, I was that weary.'

'They might have been at that.' Dorne took a pot of cereal off the fire. 'This is for the nursery. Watch the other kettles for me. Just move them off the fire if they start to steam.'

Evelyn nodded, her mouth full of food, as Dorne headed out the door. As soon as he'd left, the outside door opened and a man appeared, carrying a load of firewood. He paused, his worried eyes looking out through roughly cut hair. 'You're the Priestess, am I right?'

'I am.' Evelyn nodded.

The man walked to the fireplace and dropped the wood beside it. 'I'm Torren, Lady. Are you well?'

'Well enough,' Evelyn said with a smile.

Torren darted a look around, then took a step closer. 'That bastard, he ain't hurting you, is he?'

Evelyn swallowed, and looked into the man's eyes. He was clearly worried, and really frightened. 'No, Torren. I am fine.'

'Blackhart killed my family, Lady; they died in the keep.' Torren's words came out in a rush as his eyes darted around the room. 'I could get you out of here, Lady. There's a way, if you wanna escape.'

Evelyn shook her head and had opened her mouth to respond when Dorne came back into the room. 'Here, now, Torren. What are you doing?'

'Brought some firewood to fill the box.' Torren backed up a step or two. 'Like I was told.'

'That's good,' Dorne said. 'But there's more to be done, I'm sure. Be on your way.'

Torren gave him a resentful look, but left.

'He's afraid of Orrin,' Evelyn stated.

'Most are.' Dorne pulled out a bowl and started measuring out flour. 'They blame him for the Odium, for being driven from their farms.' Dorne shook his head. 'They face two enemies – the Odium and hunger, since they can't get into the fields. Blackhart has to take a strong hand with them in order to ensure their survival, and they resent it.'

Evelyn looked at her bowl, the cereal sitting like a lump in her stomach. 'He did do some terrible things, Priest Dorne. The Odium—'

'And are you so perfect, Lady High Priestess?' Dorne asked.

Evelyn went pale. 'No.' Her hands clenched under the table. 'I've done things that cost people their lives.'

'And not just the rebellion,' Dorne said. 'I was there, child. I know.'

'The battle magics, they . . . I lost control,' Evelyn whispered.

'Any magic that spreads out over a wide area is hard to contain, and the power therein doesn't discriminate. I know that, you know that, and I am sure your father told you that.'

'I—'

'Don't misunderstand me,' Dorne said, adding water to the bowl. 'I believe you entered the priestly order with an honest heart. But you were fleeing, Evelyn, fleeing from the magic.'

She stared at him, wide-eyed. 'Who are you?'

'A simple priest who seeks balance in life and in his obligations to the Lord of Light and the Lady of Laughter.' Dorne's dusty white hand touched his brooch. 'Old Gross Belly is just asking for a fall. He feels that the glory belongs only to the Lord, with no honour for the Lady or her ways.' Dorne snorted. 'He'll find out.'

'She spoke to me,' Evelyn said.

'Eh?' Dorne asked, a spoon poised over the bowl.

Evelyn took a deep breath, and told him what had happened during the coronation. 'I tried to tell the Archbishop, but—'

Dorne laughed. 'Oh, that must have sent his stomach cramping in pain.' He smiled at her. 'Have you told Blackhart this?'

'No, not in so many words,' Evelyn said, thinking back. 'I've told him She has a use for him.'

'The Lady works her will in strange ways, and her wishes aren't always easy to understand.' Dorne started to stir the contents of the bowl. 'I think Blackhart might benefit from—'

Orrin stormed into the kitchen. He glared at Evelyn. 'Why are you still here? I told you to leave.' He turned to Dorne. 'We're talking in the main room. We need you, Priest. And some kavage.'

Without another word, he stormed out.

Damned if she was leaving.

The shutters were open in the main room of the inn and daylight streamed in, reflecting off polished wood tables and floors. The place must have been something in its heyday, Evelyn mused as she carried in two pitchers of kavage. Dorne followed with mugs and another pitcher.

The room was filled with warriors and townsfolk. They greeted the kavage with smiles, reaching for the pitchers and mugs.

Orrin stood before the hearth, his hearth-band seated around him. Archer was there, as were Sidian and Reader. Thomas and Timothy gave her a nod as they reached for mugs. Evelyn ignored Orrin's glare as people shifted on a bench to make room for her. Dorne pulled a chair from the kitchen and settled down into it, returning Orrin's look. 'So, what did you want me to hear?'

'Reports,' Orrin said. 'Vilbok has news from Ralan.'

One of the men rose from his seat. He had the look of one who'd lost weight from a recent illness. His stool slid back on the floor as he stood. 'Is this the Priestess?'

'Lady High Priestess Evelyn, let me make you known to Vilbok.' Orrin scowled at the interruption. 'He's aided me in organising the townsfolk.' He glared at Vilbok. 'The Lady is my prisoner, and under my protection. Make that known, Vilbok.'

The poor man had been about to bow to her, but now he seemed confused. Evelyn gave him a smile.

Vilbok gave her a nervous smile, darted a glance at Orrin, and bowed before speaking. 'As far as Ralan and his scouts can tell, the area between here and the keep has been cleared, at least along the main roads. Now the problem is that large groups of Odium are emerging from the keep, headed here.'

'Looking for fresh meat,' Sidian said.

Vilbok winced.

Orrin nodded. 'Anything else?'

Vilbok looked around at the other townsfolk. He wet his lips, then started talking quickly. 'Folk have been talking. We've been wondering what your plans are for the land, once you've taken the keep.'

'Plans?' Orrin asked.

'For when you're the High Baron.' Vilbok looked nervously at him, then at the others. 'Isn't that why—'

'No.' Orrin's voice was harsh. 'I won't be the High Baron. If there's nothing else . . . ?' His tone implied there'd better not be.

'No, no . . .' Vilbok took up his cloak. 'My thanks.' He bobbed his head towards Evelyn. 'The Lord of Light hold you safe, Lady.'

'And you as well.' Evelyn smiled at the confused man who trotted for the door, clearly glad to go. The other townsfolk filed out as well.

'And why not?' Archer asked as the door closed behind the last of them. 'Why not claim the keep and the land?' He dug in his belt pouch, then slapped something hard on the table. When he lifted his hand, Evelyn saw a gold ring with a blood-red stone, wobbling slightly. 'Who's gonna stop you?'

Evelyn looked into Orrin's face, and saw a look of pain pass over his features. But then it was gone, and he shook his head. 'No. Queen Gloriana offered me a pardon and a boon if these lands are cleared of Odium. And that boon buys any man who aids me a pardon as well. Best we take what's offered freely.'

Evelyn looked in her mug. That was why he had asked for a boon. A pardon would mean that the Queen's justice would not pursue them, allowing them to regain their status in the community.

Orrin picked up the ring and looked at it. 'I'll give this to the Queen when I return to tell her that we've succeeded.' He tucked the ring in his pouch. 'If we succeed.'

'We got a better chance of surviving the keep if she's along.' Mage gave Evelyn a grin. 'She can burn right through them things.'

'She's not going,' Orrin said.

'Yes, I am,' Evelyn said calmly. She picked up a pitcher. 'Kav, anyone?'

Suppressing his grin, Sidian handed her a mug. Orrin stood at the head of the table, glaring at everyone around him. Most ignored the heat of his gaze, but Mage shifted nervously on his stool.

'So you think they are coming from the keep?' Evelyn asked.

There was only angry silence from Orrin.

'Yes,' Sidian said, ignoring his leader. 'We're thinking that there's something in the depths of the keep that's creating the Odium and keeping them animated.'

'The Baroness had a workroom deep in the dungeon,' Archer added.

'Where I was held?' Evelyn shuddered.

'Beyond that,' Sidian said. 'Deeper, where only she was allowed. She and her . . . victims.'

'Wish we'd thought to check it out before we abandoned the keep,' Orrin said.

'We was busy trying to save our lives,' Archer reminded him.

'So when do we leave?' Evelyn asked.

Orrin slammed his hand down on the table. 'You are my prisoner and you are not going.'

'You rescued me,' Evelyn said calmly. 'And these people need my powers to save their lives.' She raised her head and gave Orrin a frosty look. 'I was sanctioned by the Archbishop and can use no magic to benefit myself. But there is no bar to aiding others in dire need.'

'Oh, there's a hair split down the centre,' Dorne muttered.

Evelyn ignored him. She looked Orrin right in the eye. 'If there's a chance – *any* chance – of stopping these creatures, then we have to take it.'

The horn sounded just then, and they all paused for a moment.

'Another attack,' Sidian said. 'If we do nothing—'

'They will wear us down,' Dorne said. 'You need to attack the problem at its source, Blackhart.'

'And it does no good to leave your best weapon safe in its sheath by the fire,' Thomas said softly.

The sound of running feet came to them and they looked towards the door as it opened. A guardsmen appeared, breathing hard. 'Lord Blackhart, there's a problem at the wall.'

Orrin straightened, and strode from the room without another word.

NINETEEN

Evelyn watched the door close behind Orrin. 'Was that a victory?'

'Close as he's gonna come to admitting defeat,' Archer said.

'Well, then' – Dorne stood – 'I'll get you more kavage and let you talk strategy. Blackhart will want to leave sooner rather than later.' He gathered the empty pitchers and disappeared into the kitchen.

Reader looked around, then leaned forward, gazing at Evelyn. 'Your pardon, Your Ladyship, but . . .' His voice trailed off respectfully.

Evelyn gave him a nod to continue.

'It's about you, Lady.'

'Yes?'

Reader gave the others a nervous glance, looking for support. 'Well, see, it's like this. We're going into the keep. The Black Keep. Made of black rock and all.' He kept talking when she stayed confused. 'At night. In the Black Keep at night, Lady.'

Sidian chuckled. 'He's trying to say that you are a shining beacon of hope, Lady.'

Confused, Evelyn looked at Archer.

He grinned. 'Ya glow. In those clothes, in the night – gonna give us away.'

Reader nodded. 'Blackhart, now, he won't tell ya, 'cause he likes it, Lady.'

'Likes what?' Evelyn said. 'My clothes?'

Reader shook his head. 'Likes your hair, Lady. And, well, begging your holy pardon, it is lovely, but—'

'Thank you,' Evelyn said.

'But deadly,' Reader said seriously. 'You see?'

'Yes,' Evelyn said slowly, 'I do.' She remembered all too well the Odium that had reached for her braid when she'd been attacked at the shrine.

'It's all that white.' Archer gave her a grin. 'You do tend to gleam. Begging your pardon, of course.'

'We can find ya some dark clothes, a different cloak,' Reader offered. 'And as to your hair, well, it is a glory, Ma'am.'

Each man nodded his agreement

'We might be able to hide it,' Reader said doubtfully. 'But—'

'It's what they're looking for,' Thomas said, 'long white hair.'

'Soot,' said Timothy. 'Darken it with soot.'

'That would work,' Sidian said. 'Might be able to tie the braid under her clothes.'

Evelyn shook her head. 'That's not good enough, is it? We all know what I need to do.'

Six pairs of stricken eyes looked at her, then darted glances at the door.

'Oh, ma'am,' Reader breathed, 'if the Odium don't kill us, he will.'

It took Orrin an hour to deal with the problem. The Odium were starting to attack the walls now, tearing at them, trying to breach their defences. He'd worked with the men to shore up the weak spot, and made new plans for dealing with Odium close to the walls. Archer was wrong; the damn things were going to start climbing the walls, and soon.

He'd known he needed to calm down, and so he'd taken a long walk along the wall, harassing the men on watch. Now he stood at one of the corners, looking out over the fields.

She was right, damn her.

If there was something in the dungeons that was creating those monsters, he was going to need her abilities. He couldn't afford to leave a weapon like that behind.

They'd harvested everything they could from the fields around the town. Orrin looked out over the stubble soon to be covered in snow. This was good land. Stony, true enough, but there was hunting and fishing. The mountains held their own treasures: gold, silver and gems. Whoever held the High Barony of the Black Hills would prosper, if he could stop the threat of the Odium.

He dug the gold ring out of his pouch. It sat on his gloved palm, the red stone warm in the light. It was a heavy ring, made to remind the wearer and all who saw it of the duties and the power of a high baron.

Or baroness.

Orrin's heart clenched in his chest.

Elanore had betrayed her oaths to the land and its people, and he had helped her. He'd forfeited any right to be considered a leader when he'd looked only to his own and not to the greater picture.

His hand closed over the ring. He had no right to claim it, but he could clean up the mess he'd created.

He'd need Evelyn's help to do it. He had no right to ask, but even less to refuse her aid. The Odium had to be stopped.

Blackhart gritted his teeth. It would have been easier if they'd just executed him right then and there in the throne room. A whack with the axe, and his head would have rolled on the floor. Much easier.

The wind picked up at that moment and carried with it the faint sound of a woman's mocking laughter.

Orrin sighed and tucked the ring back in his pouch, trying to convince himself to do what had to be done.

Reader looked up from his book. 'That's him coming.'

Archer turned from his arrow work and saw Sidian start to hustle Mage back through the kitchen door. Thomas and Timothy were right behind.

Reader jumped up, leaving his book on his chair. The small man wiped his palms on his pants as he darted to the door and jerked it open.

Blackhart stood in the doorway, silhouetted against the day. His eyes pierced the room. He looked at the other door, watching Timothy's back end disappear, then focused on Archer. 'Where is she?'

Archer jerked his head towards the main stairs.

Blackhart headed across the room and up the stairs, taking them two at a time.

'I'm finding someplace else to be,' Reader said, gathering up his book. 'You?'

Archer looked up from his tools and grinned. 'Nah. Not gonna miss this.'

*

Orrin threw open the door, striding into the room. 'Evelyn, we need—'

She wasn't there. There was a lad kneeling before the fire – short dark hair, dark clothes – tossing a long braid of white hair into the fire.

Furious, Orrin pulled his sword and crossed the room to grab the lad by the shoulder. He threw him to the ground, sword tip at his throat. 'Didn't I say she was under my protection? What have you—?'

Silver-blue eyes flashed up at him with a grin. 'Didn't recognise me, did you?'

He froze, standing there stupid. 'Evie? What—?' He raised his sword away from her neck.

'I cut my hair,' she said, smiling as she stood and brushed herself off. 'I guess it worked, eh?'

Orrin's breath caught in his throat. 'You *cut* it?'

'Of course. It was a danger.' Evelyn bent over, tucking the braid deeper into the coals. 'Sidian let me borrow his knife.'

Orrin glanced at the hearth where Sidian's knife, with its bone handle and odd stone blade, lay.

'I've seen one like it before, but I can't remember where.' Evelyn looked up at him. 'Orrin? Are you all right?'

Orrin just stared at her.

Her short hair framed her face, lying like a silky fringe on her skin. It gave her a soft sweetness that he hadn't seen in her before, in her formal attire. The dark clothing was form-fitting in ways that made his entire body pay close attention. Freed from her heavy white robes, she was lithe and lovely, her breasts straining against her tunic, her legs . . .

Orrin could only hope his tongue was still in his mouth. He sheathed his sword to give himself a moment to pull himself together. 'Your hair' – he swallowed hard – 'how did you darken . . . ?'

'I used soot, with a bit of oil. Sidian and Timothy suggested it.'

Sidian again. Orrin was going to kill the man.

Evelyn grimaced. 'It feels dirty, but it's safer this way.' She tilted her head. 'You can put your sword away, you know.'

He flushed and sheathed the blade, still stunned out of reckoning. 'Oh, Evie . . .'

Evelyn laughed, her eyes made brighter by the darkened hair.

She cupped his cheek with her palm. 'Oh, Orrin, it's just hair. It grows back, foolish man.'

She lifted herself on tiptoe, and kissed his open mouth.

Blackhart groaned, wrapped his arms around her and kissed her in return.

He felt like summer, like a warm summer day, hazy with heat and life. His hands moved over her, stroking her back as he claimed her mouth. Evelyn shivered under his touch, melting into him, feeling more through the thinner cloth of her dark clothing. She hungered for this, for his touch, for more.

His lips were warm and soft, and she opened hers under his assault, feeling his tongue touch hers. Her hands moved too, exploring the hard muscles of his back, moving lower to press him closer, feeling such a wave of desire flood over—

The door opened. Orrin broke the kiss, and stepped back.

'Oops,' Archer said, 'sorry.'

The door closed. A muffled voice came through. 'Just checking to see if anyone was dead.'

Orrin's glare at the door was murderous. 'One last chance, woman. Leave now. The Odium tried to get you once and now you are talking about walking in there like a lamb to the slaughter, licking the farmer's hand as he leads you to—'

Archer's muffled voice came through the door. 'If she ain't going, I ain't going. We got about a nothing chance of—'

With a snarl, Orrin took two steps, and wrenched the door open.

Archer's eyes widened a bit and he took a step back from the door.

'Get your ass away from this door and get the others down in the main room,' Orrin said. 'Spread out the gear, start making decisions. We need a plan.' He slammed the door shut.

Evelyn took a deep breath. 'You said it yourself. We'll never be rid of them if we don't attack the source. I'd rather do that than hide and wait for them to come.'

'Fool woman,' he whispered, his eyes grim.

She stared at him, reached out, but he took another step back and then another, his face stark and full of pain. 'I don't know what I was thinking,' he said roughly.

'Well, I do,' she growled, 'and I was thinking the same thing. Orrin, I—'

'No.' To her frustration, he shook his head, and took another step back towards the door. 'I can't – this isn't right.'

'Orrin' – Evelyn took a breath – 'I'm no virgin. My order is not celibate—'

'But you're chaste,' Orrin pointed out. 'You took a vow of chastity, right?'

Evelyn blushed. 'I . . . yes . . . but—'

'No, no – you don't see.' Orrin's chest heaved. 'I want you, by all the Gods I want you—'

A flush of pleasure washed over her at his words.

'But there is no future in it, between you and me.' Orrin raised his hands as if to ward her off. 'I'll not start something I can't . . .' He stopped, and swallowed hard. 'I'll not have that on my soul as well.'

'Why don't you let me worry about our souls,' Evelyn said. 'I—'

'What's one more vow broken, eh?' Orrin asked, his face stark with pain.

Stung, Evelyn stood silent.

'I'll take you with us,' Orrin said. 'It's what I have to do to have the best chance of winning through.' He walked towards the door, his face set. 'Besides, I doubt I could stop you even if I tried.' He opened the door, and gave her a haunted look. 'After that, I'll see you off, back to Edenrich. Back to your life, your Church, your friends. Far away from the likes of me.'

She opened her mouth to argue, but he cut her off. 'Come down to the main room. We need to start to prepare.'

With that, he was gone.

TWENTY

Evelyn walked down the stairs with some hesitation, but to her relief, Orrin wasn't in the main room.

It seemed that everyone else was.

Men spilled into the room, their arms filled with weapons, gear and supplies. Evelyn stayed on the bottom step for a moment, her hand on the railing, taking it all in.

Orrin's men were spread out, each at a table, emptying saddlebags and packs, spreading out all kinds of weapons and armour. They were asking questions, confirming orders and explaining their needs. More men arrived, but some left, each with a purpose in his step and a gleam in his eye. There was a sense of anticipation in the air that surprised her, given that Orrin had just been in such a rage.

Reader was closest, so she went to his side. He had a series of daggers spread out before him, a sharpening stone in his hand.

'You all seem in good spirits for men headed into peril,' she commented. 'Why so pleased?'

They all looked at her when she spoke and, for a moment, quiet fell as they stared at her, stunned.

Evelyn flushed a bit, putting her hand up to the back of her neck.

'Well, see, ma'am, it's like this.' Archer, at the next table, pulled a tangled rope out of a sack. 'We're going, that's true enough. And you're going with us.'

'And you ain't all white and glittering,' Reader said. 'And Blackhart's leading us.'

'We know the keep,' Sidian added. 'Know the land, so to say.'

Archer nodded. 'Gives us a bit of an edge. Not much, but some.'

Timothy and Thomas nodded as they spread out their gear, shaking out bedrolls.

'Odium are stupid,' Mage added. He had a cluster of papers in his hands, shuffling through them. 'We can't—'

'Get cocky.' Orrin's deep voice came from the door. He pushed past a man in the doorways, went to a clear table and dumped his saddlebags. 'You get cocky and we die.'

'Yes, sir.' Mage's shoulders slumped a bit as he turned back to his task.

'Besides,' Archer said, 'we've been holding them off. It's time to take the fight to them. Get this thing stopped. Finish it, one way or the other.'

A chorus of 'ayes' filled the room.

'It's a challenge,' Sidian added. 'A task worthy of our skills, to test our mettle.'

Evelyn walked over and offered him his blade, handle first. 'Thank you.'

'It did its work well?' Sidian asked.

'It did,' Evelyn confirmed. 'Sheared right through the braid.'

'Kind of you to offer it,' Orrin muttered.

'She was willing to make a sacrifice for us. It was right she use this blade.' Sidian bowed his head to Evelyn, took the knife and sheathed it.

'Pack enough food for three days,' Orrin said. 'Dried meat and hardtack. Water-skins, because the wells may have been fouled. No bedrolls, we'll take cloaks. Plan for tight quarters, fighting in hallways. Pack light.'

'Horses?' Timothy asked.

'We aren't taking horses,' Orrin said. 'Figure a day to get in, deal with what we find and get out. But we'll plan for three.'

'We're walking?' Thomas frowned.

Orrin shook his head. 'Evelyn will open a portal.'

'Wish *I* could,' Mage said with envy.

'It's not an easy spell to cast. There's very few who can do it,' Evelyn said. 'I'd be willing to teach you, once this is over.'

Mage's face lit up and he gave her a shy nod.

'Where she gonna open up a portal?' Archer asked.

A horn sounded. All heads turned and men could be heard headed for the wall, taking up their weapons.

Orrin returned to his task. 'The faster we leave, the faster that ends.'

The others returned to their work.

Dorne came into the room, carrying a sack and a handful of empty water-skins. 'I've dried meat and fruit and hard biscuits. There's plenty. If you've leaving in the morning, I can make honey bars tonight and have them ready for you.'

Archer grinned. 'I'll take all you can make.'

Dorne snorted as he left.

'Dorne, we need bandages,' Evelyn called out. 'And something to clean wounds with, if you have anything like that.'

He raised his hand to show he'd heard and bustled out.

'Here, Lady,' Timothy said to Evelyn as he handed her a pack. 'This is spare.'

Evelyn thanked him, and started to sort out the food into equal portions. 'Where do you want to go?' She repeated Archer's question.

Orrin stopped and stared down at the table. 'It has to be a shrine?'

'That works best.' Evelyn nodded. 'It's easier to hold the image in mind.'

'There's a shrine to the Lady in the keep,' Orrin said slowly. 'It was on the first floor. If we could go there . . .'

Evelyn gave him a doubtful look. 'I've never been there. I might be able to open a portal, based on a description, but it's tricky. And there's no way of knowing—'

'It can't have changed much since I saw it last,' Orrin said. 'No one used it. It might be a bit dusty—'

Reader cleared his throat. 'Might not be a good idea, sir.'

The others nodded.

'And why not?' Orrin asked.

Reader darted a guilty look at the kitchen door and lowered his voice. 'Might could be that things have changed in the room.'

Archer nodded. 'Might could be a bit desiccated.'

Evelyn exchanged a confused look with Orrin. 'Desicca—'

Sidian snorted. 'Desecrated?'

'That's it.' Archer looked satisfied.

Reader nodded. 'Might could be that, sir.'

Evelyn looked at them in horror. 'What did you do?'

Reader gave her a sheepish look. 'Not much to do, being in the keep and all, begging your pardon.'

Orrin covered his face with his hand. It took Evelyn a moment to realise that he was trying very hard not to laugh. 'What about that shrine in the village?'

'The one where you captured me?' Evelyn asked.

'Yes,' Orrin said, lowering his hand. His face was serious, but his eyes were bright. 'That's less than an hour from the keep, and—'

'I don't know,' Evelyn said. 'I only caught a glimpse before someone threw a bag over my head.'

'Er . . .' Orrin looked away.

'It was a clean bag,' Reader said. 'Made a point of that.'

'And hit me over the head,' Evelyn added.

'Just a tap,' Timothy offered.

'We was careful,' Thomas said. 'Gentle, even.'

'And clapped me in spell chains,' Evelyn pointed out.

'They were new ones,' Mage observed quietly. 'Made 'em myself.'

'And slung me over a horse on my stomach and hauled me to the keep and put me in the dungeon,' Evelyn finished.

There was no response to that.

Evelyn raised her gaze to the ceiling. 'I might be able to do it.' She lowered her eyes and gave them all a look. 'Or did you boys entertain yourselves there as well?'

'Nah, 'tis all in one piece,' Archer said. 'We started the looting at the tavern and never quite got around to it.'

That brought a strangled cough from Orrin. 'Well, thanks be for that mercy. So, we portal to the shrine, travel by foot, and go in through one of the hidden doors.'

Dorne came back in. He brought Evelyn a basket of cloths, and some jars and bottles. 'Take whatever you need.' Dorne headed back to the kitchen. 'I'd best see to my pots.' He paused in the doorway. 'And boys?'

They all turned to look at him.

'Anything you put wrong in the Lady's shrine will be put right again, once this is over. And by your own hands and the sweat of your own brows.'

The room was very quiet. Evelyn put her hand over her mouth.

'I'll be happy to supervise,' Dorne said.

He ducked back into the kitchen, ignoring their groans.

TWENTY-ONE

Later that evening, after the gear was packed and blades were sharpened, they sat and started to plan their route.

Orrin had taken some charcoal from the smithy, and they'd drawn a rough map on the stone hearth of the fireplace. This was more for Evelyn's benefit than anything else, since they all knew the place. They'd reviewed the path they'd take from the village to the walls of the keep, and how they'd enter the keep proper. It turned out that Reader had kept his set of keys. He shrugged. 'Ya never know when things might be useful.'

'So, we'll assume that the Odium are still standing watch in the places we put them.' Orrin said. 'There's a chance that they've moved, but our watch locations were good ones.'

Archer nodded, reached out and tapped a position by one of the towers on the inner wall. 'I'll take position here and wait.'

Orrin shook his head. 'I can't leave you there.'

Archer's face grew very still. 'Gotta cover the retreat.'

'I need you down there,' Orrin said quietly.

The silence between the two men grew. Evelyn gave Reader a questioning look.

'He don't like tight places,' Reader explained. 'Makes him sweat.'

''S'not that' – Archer hunched his shoulders – 'what good's an archer in them corridors?'

Orrin just looked at him.

Archer sighed. 'And I don't like tight places much.'

Orrin nodded. 'But you throw a dagger better than any man here.'

'No good hand ta hand,' Timothy said.

Evelyn's eyes opened in surprise. She expected Archer to object, but the man just shrugged his shoulders. 'Nah, he's right. Not much good at fighting close. Never have been.'

'We need to know each other's strengths and weaknesses.'

128

Orrin leaned back and took a mug of kav. 'Even if the truth hurts.'

Sidian laughed. 'I'm good with my weapons in a fight, but I need room to swing.'

'Decent with a bow,' Archer said.

Sidian smiled, his teeth gleaming against his dark skin, and gave Archer a nod of thanks.

'Timothy and Thomas are good with swords and shields, but better with pole arms.'

Timothy nudged Thomas. 'Long pointy sticks.' They both chuckled, as if at some private joke.

Archer wrinkled his nose. 'Can't throw for shit.'

'True, but the way they work together as a team is uncanny,' Orrin pointed out. 'I still think you are twins.' He pointed at the map of the dungeon. 'Where we can go two abreast, they are behind the front line. They attack, thrusting their spears of theirs between us, and do a good deal of damage.'

'Who takes the front?' Evelyn asked.

'Sidian and I.' Orrin turned his head to look at her. 'You'll walk with Mage, and Reader and Archer will bring up the rear.'

Reader nodded. 'I'm best with a dagger, and I'm fast. Can sometimes slide through and get behind them, sometimes. That lets me hamstring them and take them down.'

'He's good with locks too,' Sidian said. 'Hands like a lady.'

They all chuckled as Reader looked offended.

'That leaves me, ma'am,' Mage offered. 'I'm decent with spells. Not much with weapons, but I've been trying to practise.'

Evelyn tilted her head. 'You are an apprentice?'

Mage's face turned red. 'I was . . . I—'

Orrin interrupted. 'He's still an apprentice. His master mage was involved in the attack on Athelbryght, and he died. That's when I asked Mage to join my hearth-band.'

'Ah.' Evelyn said nothing more, but she suspected that meant Orrin had protected the lad from Elanore.

Mage gave her an envious look. 'Wish I knew more, but—'

'With what I've seen, you may be at journeyman level, if you were to be tested,' Evelyn said.

Mage sat up right. 'Really? But I still have to use paper to keep my spells.'

'You didn't at the shrine,' Archer said.

'And you were using what you can do to good effect,' Evelyn said firmly. 'I wouldn't have thought to use magic to hold Odium still and let Archer take his shots.'

They all turned and looked at her, and Evelyn realised it was her turn.

'I was trained as a battle mage, but I never mastered the ability to use my spells in an enclosed area. I also never really learned to rein in my emotions to develop the finer control of those powers.' Evelyn wet her lips. 'I can cast the priestly magics easily, and I am a powerful healer. But if I become too angry, or too frightened, I lose control.'

No one said anything, so Evelyn continued, 'Outside, I can wreak havoc. But inside, I'm going to have to be careful that the flames don't wash back over us.'

'Could you give some warning?' Sidian asked. 'Maybe we can cover our faces with shields or cloaks.'

Evelyn gave him a doubtful look. 'I can try.' She shifted in her chair, well aware of Orrin's scrutiny. 'I haven't used battle magic for a very long time, and the last time I did, people on my own side were badly burned by my magic.' She clutched her hands in her lap. 'I don't like hurting people.'

'They are not people,' Orrin said softly. 'They are bodies, just clay, that someone is using against us.'

'You did it at the shrine,' Mage said.

Evelyn nodded. 'I was terrified.'

'Those things give everyone the shivering fits,' Archer added.

'I've got an idea,' Mage said. 'Not sure if it's right, but . . .'

'Spit it out,' Archer said.

'I think those things might be sensitive to magic,' Mage said. 'I know they *are* magic, but I think that maybe they can sense magic being cast.' He looked around the group. 'I'm not sure. But I thought it best to say now—'

'And you were right, too.' Orrin gave him a nod. 'We will keep it in mind.'

Mage smiled, and Sidian clapped him on the back.

'One last thing,' Orrin added. 'We're going to wear the sigil of the Black Hills.'

They all shifted, uncomfortable.

'The Odium were trained not to attack anyone wearing the

sigil of the Black Hills,' Orrin insisted. 'We can't give up any advantage it might give us.'

'Wearing it can get us killed, if we run into any Queen's men,' Archer said quietly.

'Not once we accomplish this.' Orrin growled. 'I've sworn to you that I will use that reward to get a pardon for the men who aid me.'

'All of us?' Mage asked.

'All of you. That means the men we leave to guard the town, and any who offer us aid. Even the men who still guard their families' enclaves in the Hills – the ones that we can't get to, and I can only hope are still alive. A pardon for the army of the Black Hills.'

They all nodded, each in turn, as Orrin looked them in the eye.

'Enough of this, then. Get some sleep, because we'll leave at dawn.'

The men stood, stretched and left, leaving Orrin and Evelyn alone in the firelight.

Evelyn waited for the last footstep to fade before she turned to Orrin and opened her mouth, but Orrin cut her off with a gesture. 'Oh, no, Lady High Priestess. Not another word.'

TWENTY-TWO

'Don't even start,' Orrin growled, seeing the look in her eyes. 'We're not going to talk, discuss, or argue. Go up to your room.'

'I'll say just one thing, then I'll go.' Evelyn raised that lovely chin of hers and glared at him.

'Fine.' Orrin stood and walked towards the door. 'I'll go. Talk to the fire, because—'

'Loving you—'

Orrin stopped, his back to her.

'—caring for you is not a sin.' Evelyn's soft voice came from behind him. Her tone was firm and resolute.

He turned. 'Lady—'

'That doesn't mean that I condone your past, or that I'd support you now if you were still doing those things.' Evelyn stood. Her hands lifted in a familiar gesture, as if to tuck them into the long sleeves of robes she no longer wore. Instead, she wove her fingers together, and twisted them nervously. 'I – care – for the man standing before me.'

Hope blazed through his chest, and with one swift breath he crushed the emotion, trying to kill it.

Might as well have tried to stop his heart from beating.

She licked her lips and continued, 'I wanted to tell you before we leave in the morning. If we both survive, we can argue the rest for days on end.'

'We'll survive,' Orrin growled. 'And when we do, you're for Edenrich and I'm going to find a tavern where no one knows my name and get lost in a bottle for a month.'

'We'll see,' Evelyn responded. 'But for now, we'll be about the business. Agreed?'

Orrin gave her a hooded look, standing silent.

'Fine,' Evelyn sighed, and walked past him towards the stairs.

He turned his head to watch her go, fully intending to let her walk out—

But she brushed past him, and he caught a whiff of her sweet scent with just a touch of soot. He couldn't help himself. His hand reached out of its own accord.

He touched her shoulder as she walked past him.

Evelyn stopped, looking at his callused hand. She raised her face to his warm hazel eyes, giving him a puzzled look.

His mouth quirked in a rare smile and his hand slid along her shoulder, his fingers curling around the back of her neck.

Evelyn shivered. Without the weight of her braid, the skin there seemed extra sensitive. Or maybe it was just . . . him.

He pulled gently and she found herself facing him, her hands reaching for his waist. She lifted her face and closed her eyes, fully prepared for a demanding kiss.

Instead, she felt a gentle brush of his lips on hers: warm, dry, soft as a feather. With a sigh she leaned in as he explored her skin with the faintest of touches all over her cheeks and eyelids.

She brought her hands up then, to wrap around his shoulders, and his hands wrapped around her, rubbing her back. There was no demand, just a gentle gift. Dimly, lost in the pleasure of his touch, Evelyn understood he was telling her something he couldn't express with words.

Finally he stopped and hugged her tight, breathing in her ear. Before she could say anything, he stepped back, his eyes on the floor.

'Go, Evelyn.'

'Orrin—'

He lifted his head, his hazel eyes blazing. 'Lady, my head is so fucked up right now, that it little matters if I live or die on the morrow.' He stepped back from her. 'I've a town to see to and orders to give. Get to bed.'

Evelyn looked away and headed up the stairs.

'Evelyn,' Orrin said.

She paused, one foot on the steps, her hand on the railing.

Orrin stood there in the doorway, lit by the fire, his hazel eyes reflecting the firelight.

'Lock your chamber door,' he growled, then vanished into the night, pulling the door behind him.

She smiled then, her heart feeling oddly happy as she went up the stairs. She didn't lock her door.

But Orrin never came.

They gathered in the kitchen at dawn. There were no smiles this morning, no levity. Evelyn understood the change as they all started to focus on the task at hand.

Dorne had prepared a meal, and they ate quickly, drinking strong kav with their food.

There was some last-minute fussing with packs and gear, and Dorne handed out sweet nut bars for everyone to put in their packs. Then they silently walked to the well, to fill water-skins.

'Ready?' Orrin asked.

There were nods all about, but Dorne shook his head. 'Not quite.' He wiped his hands on his apron, then raised them up to the sky. 'Bless these warriors, Lord of Light and Lady of Laughter.'

Orrin rolled his eyes, but stood silent. The others bowed their heads respectfully, with some shuffling of feet. Evelyn bowed hers as well, but not before she noticed that Sidian had lifted his face to the sun, his eyes closed, his lips moving in his own prayer.

'Lord of Light, bless us with your light, to grace our paths and illuminate our ways. Lady of Laughter, bless us with your mirth, to bring our hearts comfort and strengthen our resolve for the task ahead.' Dorne's voice was firm as he finished, 'Praise be given.'

'Praise be given,' Evelyn echoed.

'Now, are we ready?' Orrin asked.

'Not quite,' Reader said. With a very serious look, he produced a small brown bottle.

'Not some of your gutrot,' Dorne said with a frown. 'Why not just cut your stomach out?'

'It's tradition,' Reader protested. He lifted the bottle and took a healthy swig. 'Whoosh, that's fine.' He coughed as he handed it to Sidian. 'I let it age a bit this time.'

Sidian tipped the bottle, then wiped his mouth. 'Oh, what, all of a day?'

Timothy and Thomas took their gulps, dancing a jig after they swallowed, making what Evelyn assumed were appreciative noises. Their eyes were watering as they handed the bottle to Mage.

'What's in it?' asked Evelyn.

Orrin shook his head. Dorne waved both his hands in negation. 'You don't want to know.'

'Only the finest of ingredients,' Reader said stoutly. 'I even washed the barrel.'

Mage took a swig, his face screwed up with anticipation. He couldn't speak, just handed the bottle to Archer, who accepted it with a nod and took two swallows.

He held the bottle out to Orrin with a smile. 'It's not quite got the kick of the last batch.'

Reader frowned. 'Must be the ageing.'

'Or the clean barrel,' Dorne observed.

Orrin reached for the bottle, but Evelyn beat him to it. Before she could have second thoughts, she took a careful sip.

She would have dropped the bottle if Orrin hadn't rescued it. Her eyes opened wide as she swallowed, the burn racing down her throat. She gasped as she started laughing, unable to form words.

Orrin started sputtering when he saw her reaction. There were smiles all around as she coughed.

'Reader, that is the gods-awfulest—' Evelyn shook her head as it hit her stomach, and burned.

'Why, thank ya.' Reader beamed.

Orrin gave the bottle back to Reader, who corked it and put it back in his pack. 'Now, are we ready?'

A change came over the group then. The levity was gone in an instant. Evelyn watched as their eyes hardened. Even Mage appeared to lose his youthfulness in his grim determination.

They looked each other over, and they all nodded.

'Very well,' Orrin said. 'Evelyn, if you would . . .'

Evelyn cleared her throat, closed her eyes and pictured the shrine in her mind, sending out her magic, seeking . . .

Her stomach burned and she shifted a bit. Hard to cast a spell with your stomach on fire. She took a breath, cleared her mind and . . . sought . . .

A shrine to the Lord, built of stone, with a painting of the rising sun over the keep. Just a glimpse, but it was enough. A glimpse, a direction, and with just the right . . .

She gestured, chanting under her breath . . .

'Wow,' Mage breathed.

Evelyn opened her eyes and saw the familiar oval with the

vague white curtains that seemed to move in the air. She concentrated, holding it open.

'Reader,' Orrin said.

The smaller man lowered himself to the ground and slowly put his face in the portal. He pulled it out and grinned back at them. Then he crawled forward, disappearing into the veil.

Orrin gave a nod and Sidian and Archer walked through, with Timothy and Thomas right behind.

'Wait for a signal,' Orrin said as he stepped through.

Evelyn held her breath, then let it out slowly before Orrin's hand appeared and gestured for them to come through. Mage gave her a look, then closed his eyes and stepped through.

Evelyn took a breath, and followed.

TWENTY-THREE

Archer's skin shivered as he stepped through the portal. Stepping into nothing and going to something was not the right way of things. But he cleared the magic with ease and brought his bow to bear as soon as he was through.

Sidian was crouched next to the door to the outside, scanning the street beyond. Timothy and Thomas pressed close behind him, holding their spears carefully. Reader was outside, tucked into a doorway, dagger at the ready.

Archer steadied his aim, and waited.

The sound of Blackhart's boot came from behind him. 'Clear?'

Sidian held up a hand, and Reader gave a nod.

Archer heard the rest of them come through, and then there was a sound like a cork being pulled from a bottle. Evelyn moved past him, with Mage and Blackhart close behind.

Blackhart signalled Reader to take the lead. The small man darted down the street, staying low. Sidian waited a breath, then flowed out the door. Timothy and Thomas followed after him.

Blackhart gestured, and Evelyn and Mage went next. Archer lowered his bow and brought up the rear, keeping an eye open.

They moved down empty streets at a trot, everyone alert to the least sound. Archer thought that was the spookiest part of it all, the quiet of the towns and villages they'd searched. And this one was no exception, dead quiet except for their footfalls.

Reader paused ahead and they all stopped where they were, tucking into doorways and such, trying to hide as best they could.

Archer caught movement from the corner of his eye and took a quick glance back.

Odium were behind them, moving into the shrine.

Archer caught Mage's attention and pointed back with his chin. Mage looked, and his eyes went wide as he jerked his head around to stare at Archer.

The Odium were still crowding into the door of the shrine.

Reader moved again. Archer gestured Mage on and continued moving himself, keeping careful watch behind.

They reached the edge of the village and crossed the main road to the pine woods beyond. Once they were under the boughs, deep within, Archer got Blackhart's attention and told him what he'd seen while the others caught their breath. 'They didn't follow,' Archer finished. 'Not that I saw.'

'We'll keep to the woods as long as we can,' Blackhart said. 'Ralan will be watching for us.'

'Should we stay in sight of the road?' Reader asked.

The others stood silent as Blackhart shook his head. 'No. We'll angle off. Ralan is running patrols along the woods closer to the walls. They'll find us.'

Reader gave a quick nod and headed out.

Fallen pine needles muffled their footsteps. Blackhart and Sidian took the lead now, keeping the pace quick.

Archer kept watch on their back trail, but there was no sign of trouble. He kept an eye on the Priestess too, but she was keeping up just fine.

He hoped he could do as well in those damn dungeon tunnels.

Archer growled at himself, and kept his focus on what he was doing. Later was later. Besides, the Odium would probably kill him dead long before he got to the tunnels, and wouldn't all that worrying be wasted then?

He focused on the task at hand, and tried to ignore the fear churning deep in his gut.

If only those tunnels weren't so damn narrow . . . and dark.

'You're all a sight braver then I am, that's the truth,' Ralan said. 'Not for blood or money would I go in there.'

His mounted scouts were bustling around them, seeing to their horses and tightening girths. They couldn't stay here long.

'There's no choice.' Blackhart shook his head.

'I know.' Ralan's gaze darted to the group under the trees. 'I just—'

Blackhart lowered his voice. 'We've got to get it stopped. And this is our best chance.'

Ralan shook his head. 'I know, Lord Blackhart. I know.'

None knew better, to Blackhart's way of thinking. Ralan's mounted scouts had kept watch over the keep for weeks now.

To Blackhart's relief, they'd passed through the pine woods without encountering any Odium. Ralan's men had spotted them as they'd emerged from the forest. From here they had a clear view of the first wall that surrounded the keep.

Ralan jerked his head towards the wall. 'The main gates are forced open, the doors pulled down. Once in a while we've seen Odium on the top of the second wall, as if they're patrolling, but it's not regular.' Ralan hesitated. 'I got an odd feeling that they do it only when someone thinks of it.'

Blackhart frowned.

Ralan shook his head. 'Don't ask me why I think that. More a gut feeling than anything else.' He drew a breath. 'The main gates are hanging on their hinges. The portcullis is bent and twisted. I've sent two groups to sweep the area between the two walls. So far, nothing.'

'You weren't supposed to go in,' Blackhart pointed out. 'Your job is to help us get in and keep the way clear so we can get out.'

'The faster you're in, the better,' Ralan said. 'The men just swept the area clear of the odd Odium. They didn't try to enter the keep proper. Horses can still outrun the monsters, and the damned things haven't learned to use the catapults.'

'Yet,' Blackhart pointed out.

Ralan's easy grin flashed. 'Always so optimistic, Lord. Ride double with my men,' he suggested. 'We can get you to the second wall fast, and drop you right at the base of that guard tower. We'll hold position and give you cover while you open the door.'

'Hard on the horses,' Blackhart said.

Ralan shrugged. 'They'll survive.'

'We'll do it your way,' Blackhart agreed. 'It's our best chance.'

'Oh, and don't bother with wearing the sigils.' Ralan grinned. 'The Odium will tear your throat out, either way.'

'Thanks,' Blackhart said.

'Anything to oblige.' Ralan's grin faded. 'How long do you want us to wait?' he asked.

Blackhart looked over his shoulder. His men were taking a break, eating and drinking before they continued. Evelyn sat in their midst, chewing on a piece of dried meat. She caught his gaze, and raised an eyebrow.

Blackhart turned back to Ralan. 'A full day. If we're not out by sunset tomorrow, pull your men back.'

'To Wareington?'

Blackhart shook his head. 'No. I mean all the way back. Get the people out of the Black Hills. I left orders that they make ready to flee.'

Ralan studied him.

Blackhart returned the look. 'Whatever is in there is powerful. We fail, you take the people and flee. Get word to Queen Gloriana that we failed.'

Ralan looked towards the wall. 'I'd rather drink to celebrate your success.'

'That would be my preference,' Blackhart said.

Ralan nodded. 'I'll see to it. Either way.'

Evelyn sat under the cover of the pines and watched Blackhart talk to the leader of the scouts.

The silence was oppressive here in the woods. There wasn't even a breeze to stir the branches. No birdcalls, no rustle in the undergrowth.

'This place reminds me of Athelbryght,' she said. 'So still. So quiet.'

'You know Athelbryght?' Thomas asked.

Evelyn nodded. 'Josiah is my cousin. I wish he was here now.'

'Lord Josiah?' Thomas asked. He exchanged a glance with his brother.

Timothy frowned. 'He's not a good fighter.'

'No.' Evelyn looked at the brothers, curious as to how they knew that. 'He can drain Odium of their magic, and they turn to dust.'

'Really?' Mage asked. 'How was he able to do that?'

'It was something that happened to him when Elanore attacked Athelbryght,' Evelyn said. 'We don't know for sure.'

'Huh.' Mage thought about that. 'The Baroness sent a lot of mages to Athelbryght. None of them came back.'

'Was that when your master was killed?' Evelyn asked.

Mage shook his head. 'My master was killed when there was a backlash of power through the linked mages, when the Baroness was hurt so bad.' He tilted his head. 'He drains Odium?'

'Let her eat,' Sidian chided. 'We've no time for what might have helped us.'

Evelyn nodded in answer to Mage's question as she worked off another bite of dried meat.

'Wonder if that had anything to do with the spell we use to make the chains,' Mage mused.

Evelyn looked at him closely. 'You mentioned that before, and I was going to ask you about it. You know how to make spell chains?'

Mage nodded. 'All the apprentices did. It's not so hard, once you know how to bind the spell to the iron.'

'I want to learn that one,' Evelyn said. 'We can teach each other, once this is over.'

Mage nodded. 'It's the waiting I hate.' He picked up a handful of dried pine needles and twisted them in his hand. 'Gets to me,' he said, 'the waiting.'

Evelyn nodded

'Eat something,' Sidian said. Reader nodded absently as he twisted a ring of keys in his hand, as if trying to memorise them. Timothy and Thomas had gone silent. They ate and drank methodically, as if doing a chore.

Mage stuffed his honey bar in his mouth, then looked over at Evelyn, his dark hair falling in his eyes. His cheeks bulging, he talked around his food. 'Can you teach me how you cast those flames?'

'You know how to light a candle,' Evelyn said softly.

'First thing they teach ya,' Mage stated.

'Well, you start that way, with that spark,' Evelyn explained. 'Except there's no wick to focus on. You just take the spark that you create, and throw it out, forcing more flame through it.'

Mage looked sceptical as he chewed. Once he swallowed, he pressed the point. 'Throw—'

'He's coming,' Reader said.

Orrin felt their stares as he walked over and knelt before them. Sidian handed him a water-skin. He drank deeply, then lowered the skin, noticing how the dappled sunlight streamed through the pines, lighting up Evelyn's lovely eyes. His stomach clenched as Archer handed him a sweet nut bar.

'We'll head out in a few minutes.' Blackhart looked at the food in his hand. 'We'll ride double with Ralan's men. They are going to take us through the main gate at a run, to the base of the guard tower. Reader?'

'Pretty sure it's this one.' Reader dangled a key.

'They'll drop us there, and give cover while we try to open it.'

He looked into all their faces then, from one to the other in turn. 'This is the last chance,' he added. 'Anyone wants out, now's the time—'

'Eat,' Evelyn said.

'Don't waste your breath,' Sidian agreed. Timothy and Thomas nodded, almost in unison.

'Or our time,' Archer said.

'Aye to that,' Reader agreed.

Blackhart took a deep breath, nodded, and bit into the bar.

They mounted up behind Ralan's men, and the horses started off at a trot, gaining speed as they headed for the road. Once there, they started to run, sweeping through the main gate. Evelyn had a brief glimpse of the massive wooden doors leaning drunkenly against the walls before they were past.

She pressed herself against the man in the saddle, holding on tight as the horse ran. They left the road, swerving off to sweep into the stretch of bare land between the walls. She scanned for Odium, but saw nothing.

The horses pounded the empty ground, galloping for all they were worth. The second wall of the keep loomed over them. They plunged into its shade, moving swiftly.

Blackhart was up behind Ralan, off to Evelyn's side. Even riding on the back of another man's horse, he seemed at ease. He turned his head as if sensing her gaze, and looked at her, his eyes strong and steady. The sight calmed her.

Faster than she'd thought possible they reached their goal. The horses pulled to a halt, rearing slightly. She grabbed the man's arm and slid to the ground quickly, stumbling a little as she found her footing. Blackhart swept up behind her, pulling her towards the wall, pressing her against the stones, out of the confusion of men and horses. He stood in front of her as the others gathered close.

The riders organised themselves. They faced their horses outwards, guarding their group. Evelyn couldn't see a door, but

Reader was facing the stones, pressing a key into a chink in the rocks. The keys jangled in his hands.

'On the right,' Ralan called.

Evelyn peered over Blackhart's shoulder. She could just make out a crowd of Odium stumbling towards them.

'On the left,' came a call. Her head jerked around to see another group coming, slowly but surely. The horses bunched around them, shielding them from the oncoming monsters.

'Reader,' Blackhart snapped.

'Workin' on it,' Reader said calmly as he tried another key.

Archer had his bow out. Mage was next to him. Sidian stood ready as well, and Timothy and Thomas were behind Reader, facing the door, their spears in hand.

'No magic,' Blackhart reminded her. 'Not unless . . .'

Evelyn nodded.

'Hold,' Ralan called to his men, 'wait for them.'

But even Evelyn could tell that the Odium would surround them soon, unless—

'Got it,' Reader said as the lock clicked. The stones swung in silently, letting out a draft of foul cold air. There was only darkness beyond. 'We can—'

An Odium lunged out of the darkness, and grabbed for Reader's throat.

TWENTY-FOUR

Before Evelyn could react, Reader jerked his head back and ducked down.

Timothy lunged over him, his spear plunging into the monster's chest. The point sank deep into its grey flesh. Thomas moved as well, his spear piercing the monster in the throat.

Reader scrambled to the side, letting them push it through the door and onto the floor beyond.

The Odium shrieked, flailing its arms. The brothers kept it pinned, their faces grim. Sidian stepped into the room, avoiding the creature's reach. He brought his mace down, crushing its skull with a wet thud.

Thomas jerked his weapon free. Timothy used his to push the corpse to the other side of the room.

'Clear,' Sidian said as he stepped farther into the room.

Reader was up and moving as Timothy pulled his spear free.

Orrin pushed Evelyn through the door, with Mage right behind. She couldn't see at first as her eyes adjusted to the darkness.

'Go,' Orrin barked to Ralan as he and Archer rushed in, slamming the door behind them. Darkness enveloped them, and the sound of running horses was cut off.

Archer swore, his voice tight. The only other sound was their ragged breathing.

'Wait,' Mage said.

Evelyn forced herself to swallow as she stood in the darkness. She heard a soft click, and light spilled from Mage's hand. He held up a small round copper lantern hanging from a chain, the top pricked with holes. The light grew a bit stronger, but it wasn't much more than a faint green glow.

'Magic?' she asked.

They all shook their heads as Sidian put a finger to his lips.

The room wasn't big. The pale green light illuminated a set of wooden stairs going up, and boxes and bales piled against the walls.

'Reader,' Orrin said.

Evelyn looked back to see that on this side there was an obvious door. Orrin was leaning against it, pressing it tight in its frame. Reader hurried over and inserted the large key and she heard the bolt click into place.

Orrin stepped away and they paused, listening. 'You hear anything?'

Reader pressed his ear to the frame. Then he shook his head.

Sidian had walked to another door in the far wall and was standing next to it. Timothy and Thomas moved behind him, taking up the same positions as before. Archer made for the steps, easing up quietly.

Evelyn stood in the centre of the room, feeling a bit foolish. They all seemed to know exactly what to do, and when. But she forced herself to relax. These men had worked together for years, and knew these grounds. Best she could do for now was stay out of their way.

Archer's voice floated down from the landing above. 'Nothing moving out there.'

Mage handed the chain of the ball to Evelyn and got a couple more out of his pack.

'Reader.' Orrin gestured towards the second door.

Sidian eased it open and Reader slid out. It took only a few breaths before Archer spoke. 'He's got it.'

They left quickly, Evelyn following Timothy out into the shaded courtyard. Their footsteps echoed against the stone walls. Evelyn risked a glance at the high towers above them, but saw no one.

They crowded into the entrance to the dungeons. Sidian closed the door firmly behind them. Once again Reader locked the door. It took a moment for Evelyn's eyes to adjust to the eerie green light that the small, round ball gave off. The air in here was cooler, and damp.

'What are these if they aren't magic?' Evelyn asked as Mage dug out yet another one and handed it to her.

'It's a kind of moss they use in the mines hereabout,' Mage said. 'No heat, and it's easy on the eyes. Gotta keep them watered just right, though. Too much, and—'

'Later,' Orrin said.

Mage clamped his mouth shut and handed out the remaining balls.

Reader and Sidian were already at the head of the stairs, peering down. Reader pulled his sword and disappeared into the darkness. Sidian followed, mace at the ready, with Timothy and Thomas right behind. They'd tied their lanterns to their belts, and the glowing lights showed a staircase spiralling down, the smooth walls damp and wet.

Mage slipped after them, and Evelyn took a step to follow when she heard a noise, a pained groan coming from Archer. The man stood there, his face stark in the dim light.

'Archer,' Orrin said from behind him.

Archer didn't move. His eyes were wide and staring.

Evelyn went towards him and his eyes met hers. He blinked, then lifted his lantern. It swayed from his trembling hand. 'I'm moving,' he said, his voice rough. 'Don't push a man.'

Orrin sighed, then shook his head. 'Stay here. Watch our backs.'

'You said—'

'Changed my mind.' Orrin moved towards the stairs. 'This is the only way out of the tunnels, Archer. Hold it.'

The tension went out of Archer's body and his shoulders sagged. 'Feel like I'm letting you down.'

'Only if this room's full of Odium when I get back.' Orrin signalled Evelyn to precede him.

Evelyn gave Archer a smile and started down the stairs.

No torches lit the narrow spiral staircase. Orrin tightened his grip on his sword as he brought up the rear, moving carefully. Reader knew this warren of tunnels, so it made sense to let him take the lead. Orrin was more concerned with what might come up behind them.

Evelyn moved before him, carrying one of the lanterns. He noticed that she didn't so much walk as float down, and her hips swayed within the confines of her trous.

He cleared his throat and brought his mind back to the task at hand.

They gathered at the bottom of the stairs. Five passages that led off from there, and Reader was peering down the one to the right, the one that led to Elanore's workroom.

'Archer's guarding the way out,' Orrin said as his foot left the steps.

Everyone nodded, accepting the change in plan.

'Doesn't smell right,' Sidian said. His voice seemed to fill the tunnel around them. 'Doesn't smell like them.'

Orrin took a deep breath, then let it out slowly. Sidian was right; it smelled like stone and dirt and damp, not the rot of walking corpses.

'You would think there would be more activity, if this was the source,' Evelyn said softly. 'You'd need a place to work, and' – she grimaced – 'a place to store your supplies.'

Reader gave Orrin a questioning look. 'Keep going?'

Orrin moved up beside him. 'Elanore came down here to experiment. She created Odium down here. It's where we start.'

Reader sheathed his sword, then pulled two daggers, bright and sharp in the light. 'Same order?'

Orrin nodded. 'Sidian and I will bring up the rear.'

Reader headed down the passage, the others right behind.

TWENTY-FIVE

They moved quickly, since this passage was wider and had fewer crossways to worry about. Orrin knew that it sloped down, then ran straight along for a while.

Reader was cautious, but he moved faster now. There was only the sound of their breathing in the darkness.

Orrin had kept track of their position, but it was still a surprise when they came to the wooden double doors of the workroom.

'Nothing,' he breathed, worried.

Sidian scowled and looked back the way they'd come, worry etched in the scars on his face. His bushy eyebrows were so close together that they looked like one brow.

Reader sheathed his weapons and studied the door. There was a lock on this one, and he was frowning.

'You can't have a key for this lock,' Orrin growled.

'Never could get my hands on one,' Reader agreed, as he reached in his pouch. 'But there's something wrong here. Don't know what.'

'Warded, maybe,' Mage said. 'If I cast . . .' He looked at Orrin for permission.

'Do it.'

Reader eased back and Mage stepped forward, mumbling under his breath. His eyes glowed for a moment and he nodded. 'Wards. Two. One inflicts pain, the other warns.' The lad frowned.

'What?' Evelyn whispered.

'They feel' – Mage bit his lip – 'I'd swear the Baroness cast these.'

'Probably before she hared off into Athelbryght and got herself killed,' Orrin said.

'No.' Mage shook his head. 'They feel fresh, as if—'

'Can you take them down?' Orrin demanded.

Mage nodded and reached out his hand, chanting softly.

Orrin returned to watching behind, trusting the lad to get the job done quickly.

'Done.' Mage moved back. 'The lock's still—'

Reader had two picks in his hand. 'That's my job.' He knelt before the door and started to work.

'Do you need more light?' Evelyn asked.

'Nah, Lady, it's more feeling than seeing.' Reader said. 'And I've a fair feel for these things.'

Orrin caught Sidian's eye. The only thing Reader liked better than books was a lock.

The lock clicked.

'That's got—' And Reader hissed, jerking his hand back, a thin needle sticking out of it.

Evelyn saw the needle shoot from the lock, saw Reader jerk his hand back and knew what had happened. The small man was slumping to the floor as she reached out and grabbed his wrist. The prayer of healing was half formed in her mind before she closed her eyes to pray.

Poison, swiftly moving, flowing with the blood, trying to reach the heart. She could see it, a line of black in the red. She placed her other hand on Reader's neck and started to pray.

Power flowed through her, stopping the black, cleansing the blood. She felt Reader's body trembling, felt him fighting to stay calm and still.

Dimly, she sensed movement about her, but she didn't waver in her work. Stop now, and Reader would die. She wasn't going to let that happen.

The poison was powerful, more powerful than the infections she'd dealt with in the past. It fought back, fleeing into the muscles, looking for a path to the heart. But Evelyn had seen that tactic before and burned it out with her magic, following it down every pathway, purging every last trace of the darkness from the healthy flesh.

When it was done, she opened her eyes and drew a long breath.

Reader looked back at her, dazed. 'Thank you, Lady.'

Evelyn nodded, rose to her feet and looked around. Timothy

and Thomas stood guard a few steps down the hall, facing away. Orrin was in the open doorway. He looked at Reader. 'Sloppy.'

Reader's eyes cleared. 'Sloppy? Who'd expect a poison trap after a magical one?' he asked as he scrambled up from the floor. His indignation faded as he peered over Orrin's shoulder. 'What's in there?'

Orrin snorted. 'Not what you'd expect.' He stepped back.

Reader saw it first and his mouth fell open.

The room was huge, and filled with treasure.

Mage stood in the centre, looking about with glowing eyes. 'No magic here.'

Reader darted in. Evelyn stepped into the doorway and moved close to Orrin, in awe of the wealth she saw before her.

Orrin chuckled, his breath on her ear. 'Look again.'

Evelyn glanced at him, then looked again. Mage and Sidian were moving around the room, searching, and she realised that she could see three of them. The room was big, and it was made to look bigger by the mirrors that leaned against the walls, reflecting the gold and silver objects displayed on tables and in open chests.

But it wasn't just gold and silver. The room was filled with bowls and plates and cups of various metals, shiny and glittery even in the soft green light of their lanterns. There were even a few chamber pots in the clutter.

'I think every glittery thing in the castle must be in here,' Orrin said softly. 'As if the Odium think a reflective surface means it's worth something.'

Evelyn nodded towards Reader, who was scooping a handful of gems from a chest and putting them in his pouch.

Orrin raised his eyebrows and shrugged.

Sidian held up a blue stone, showing it to Orrin. 'Prettiest sapphires I've ever seen.'

'I've seen prettier,' Orrin said. He lowered his head to Evelyn's ear and dropped his voice to a whisper. 'Like the sapphire blue of your eyes.'

Evelyn felt the heat flood her cheeks. She turned her head, but Orrin stepped outside the door. 'I'll take the watch, boys. Help yourselves, but go easy. We need to keep moving.'

Timothy and Thomas walked into the room and started to rummage around.

Mage pulled his attention away from the treasure. 'Where we going next?'

Orrin's voice floated back to them. 'If it's not here, it's in Elanore's private chambers. We need to go there.'

Mage groaned.

'Where are they?' Evelyn asked as she moved behind Orrin to help keep watch.

'In the West Tower.'

His men were smart enough not to load themselves down, taking only a pouch of gems each. Orrin gave them time to take what they wanted, then got them moving fast. He didn't know if the magic they'd used was enough to attract attention, but he wanted out of these tunnels.

He took the lead this time, moving deliberately, Timothy and Thomas at his back. He set a brisk pace and within minutes they were back at the base of the spiral stairs. No sign of Odium.

It worried him.

Elanore had used the workroom below to create the things. He remembered the people being herded down the stairs and dragged into that room. But what he recalled of the equipment she'd used – the tables, the bottles, the chains on the walls – nothing remained.

If they had to search the entire keep, they'd do it. The source had to be here.

He paused at the bottom step and pounded the pommel of his sword against the stone three times.

Three taps came from above.

'Go.' He gestured to Reader, who took the stairs fast, the others following. Orrin gave one last look into the darkness, waiting until the sounds faded before he turned and ran up to the top.

Archer was there, waiting. 'Well?'

'Nothing,' Orrin reported.

'Not a sound here,' Archer said. 'We headed into the keep?'

Orrin nodded. 'Stow the lanterns and let your eyes adjust to the light. We'll go as a group, across the courtyard and into the kitchens.'

It took only a moment to put the little ball lanterns away. A few adjustments, and then they were ready.

At Orrin's nod, Reader unlocked the door and threw it open.

As before, an Odium lunged from behind it and grabbed for Reader's throat.

As before, Reader jerked back and dropped to the ground.

As before, Timothy lunged over him, his spear plunging into the monster's chest. Once again, Thomas moved as well, his spear piercing the monster. Reader scrambled to the side, to let them push it through the door and onto the floor beyond.

But this time, there were more Odium behind the first, their hands stretching out over the first's shoulder. Reader scrabbled back on his hands and knees as they reached for him.

The weight of their bodies was too much to stop. Thomas went to his knees, bracing his spear against the weight. Timothy bore down, trying to press them back. 'Can't hold 'em,' he gasped as the haft of his spear bowed to the breaking point.

TWENTY-SIX

In an instant Orrin and Sidian brushed past Evelyn to the door. Orrin added his weight to Timothy's, grasping the spear and shoving. The Odium roared, unable to advance. They leaned forward, teeth bared, their powerful arms extended to grab the men.

Sidian stood over Thomas, wielding his mace, using his shield to press the Odium back.

Archer had taken a stance with his bow, cursing. Mage was focused, but Evelyn knew Archer didn't dare take a shot.

Reader had turned to face the stairs, guarding their backs.

'Evelyn,' Orrin said, 'now. Do it now.'

She hesitated, staring at the grey, empty faces of the Odium as they snarled and howled. Last time, she'd been terrified, but now . . . they looked so . . .

'They're not people.' Orrin's voice cracked as he strained to help Timothy. 'They're not—'

He was right. They were dead, undead, corpses walking through the use of perverted magic. She sucked in a deep breath, gathered her power and shouted three words.

The flames exploded behind the Odium, scorching the monsters outside. But the fire also lashed through the doorway. Everyone staggered back as heat and flame surged over them.

The Odium in the door fell, crisped and burnt. A new wave of the monsters started through the door, but Evelyn was prepared. She called the fire again – a pillar of fire now, that she fed with her anger and fear. The pillar danced around outside, engulfing the monsters, who fell, blackened, to the ground. She kept the flames raging, burning—

'Evie.' Orrin's voice was a whisper in her ear.

Her concentration broken, the flames collapsed. In the silence she stood, breathing hard from the effort, and looked into Orrin's approving eyes.

'Skies above,' Sidian said, lifting his hand to his face. 'Are my eyebrows gone?'

'Yeah.' Archer laughed nervously as Timothy helped Thomas up. 'Be glad it wasn't your face.'

Thomas nodded, putting his fingers to his face. His skin was reddened, as if he'd been out in the sun too long.

'We need to move,' Orrin said. 'Reader.'

Reader nodded and slid out the door, picking his way through the bodies.

'Sidian, I'm sorry.' Evelyn lifted her hands to his face. His skin was warm under her cold fingers. 'I didn't—'

Sidian chuckled as he urged her out the door. 'No need, Priestess. We were warned, yes?'

The smell outside was bad and Evelyn held her breath as they headed for the opposite door. They passed through the courtyard, then into the kitchens, unused and empty, and came into what had once been a dining hall.

'Nothing,' Orrin growled. 'I don't like this.'

'Ain't happy, either,' Archer said as they moved through the scattered wreckage of chairs and tables. 'Main or the servants' stairs?'

'Servants' stairs,' Orrin decided. 'Fast as we can.'

Archer nodded, and he and Reader headed for an entranceway beside the large hearth.

It was a spiral staircase, narrow and steep, designed to give the staff easy access and to be easily defendable. The stone was dark and cold, and smelled damp. The small shuttered windows let in enough light for them to see.

Evelyn kept the pace as they ascended the stairs quickly. But as she ran, she was conscious of being watched, as if the keep had awakened in some strange way. There was a feeling in the very air as if unseen eyes were now turned upon them, aware of their presence.

She caught a glimpse of Mage's face behind her and knew he felt it too.

The tight spiral carried them up the floors of the keep. Evelyn could see only Thomas in front of her and Mage behind, because of the curve of the stairs. But she knew that Reader was pausing at each landing, just long enough to make sure the way was clear.

One floor, then another. They continued up, until Thomas

154

stopped. Reader must have paused a few steps below the third landing.

She stopped, breathing hard, listening. Mage did the same behind her and she heard Orrin whisper a question below. Evelyn reached out and touched Thomas's arm. He looked back at her with a shrug, knowing no more than she.

Then a whisper came and Thomas nodded and bent down to her. 'Odium in the corridor ahead. Reader says move fast and we can get past 'em.'

Evelyn turned, but Mage was already passing the word down the stairs. He turned back and gave her a nod while digging in his pouch.

Thomas whispered something to his brother ahead of him and suddenly they were moving, faster than before. Evelyn ran behind Thomas, seeing the hallway pass in a blur, seeing the Odium turning to look.

Mage spoke behind her and she caught a glow of light from his hands. He threw a handful of the copper balls down the stairs behind him. They clattered and clanked as they fell. Mage flashed her a grin, but then his eyes went wide as Sidian and Orrin cursed below him. He urged her on, Sidian and Orrin close behind.

Evelyn grinned right back as she turned to run. With any luck the Odium would chase the balls down the stairs and ignore them. She reached the fourth landing and moved past that opening, only to run smack into Thomas's back. Mage pressed tight to her, Sidian and Orrin close behind.

'Odium – on the stairs above,' Evelyn heard Archer whisper.

'This way.' Orrin moved into the hallway.

Evelyn followed Mage and saw Orrin yank open a door to a small privy with a stone bench, a hole and a narrow window. She opened her mouth to protest, but Sidian never stopped, just stepped onto the seat and pressed himself against the wall. Mage scrambled in next, standing on the other side.

Orrin sat and pulled Evelyn into his lap as Archer came at a run. Orrin pulled her head close to his chest and ducked his head as Archer climbed up into the small window.

Timothy and Thomas pressed in, with Reader right behind, pulling the door closed and shooting the bolt.

They all froze, holding their breaths, listening.

After a long moment, Archer snorted. 'Oh, this is heroic.'

Evelyn pressed her face into Orrin's shoulder to stifle her laugh.

She felt wonderful in his arms.

Orrin was sure this was some new torture designed by the Gods to send his wits wandering. Evelyn filled his arms, her soft breasts pressed against his arm in ways that he wasn't going to think about. He put his head against the stone wall behind him, trying to think of Odium, of Sidian's breath, anything but the woman in his lap.

She pressed her face to his shoulder and he could tell she was trying not to laugh.

He was damned for all eternity, and then some.

Orrin drew in a long, deep breath and ignored the scent of her soot-filled hair.

Reader was on the floor between his knees, ear pressed to the door. 'Well?' Orrin asked quietly.

Reader sounded grim. 'They're out there.'

Evelyn was looking over Orrin's head. 'Archer, are you—?'

'I'm good,' Archer said. 'Long as I got a window, I'm good.'

'Anything outside?' Sidian asked softly.

Archer shifted in the casement. 'Nothing, far as I can see.'

'We can't stay here,' Orrin said.

'Not easy, fighting our way out of a privy,' Sidian observed.

'We wait until the hall clears a bit, then we go,' Orrin said.

'I've got a better idea,' Reader said. 'There's another way.'

Evelyn felt Orrin's arms tighten around her as he looked down at Reader. 'You can't be serious.'

'We go out this door, we'll fight every step of the way, up or down,' Reader said. 'There was more Odium coming down those stairs. We go out, there's less chance—'

'Out the window?' Mage squeaked.

'How about down the shit hole?' Thomas asked.

'We got rope,' Reader said softly. 'The stone's rough enough that I can climb freehand up to the next window and tie the rope off.'

'Rather take my chances on the stairs,' Timothy protested.

'Or in the hole,' Thomas muttered.

'The hole only leads down,' Orrin pointed out.

'Or,' Reader said, 'I go up alone and take a look.'

'No.' Orrin shook his head. His jaw clenched as he considered the options. Evelyn held her breath, waiting. 'That's the privy of the Lady's shrine up there, isn't it?'

Reader nodded.

Orrin sighed. 'Archer—'

'Ain't heights I got a problem with,' Archer whispered. 'Let's do it.'

Orrin craned his neck to look at the small window. 'Will Sidian fit?'

'I'll strip,' the huge black man said. 'Anyone got any grease?'

Both Mage and Reader reached for their packs.

Orrin hugged Evelyn closer as the men started to shift around them, carefully sheathing weapons and preparing for the climb. Sidian dug out a wicked iron hook and secured the rope to it.

Reader took off his boots and rubbed his hands dry on his trous. He removed his pack, weapons and cloak and tucked his tunic into his trous, tightening his belt. 'Ready.'

'Dagger?' Orrin suggested.

Reader shook his head. 'Don't want anything that might fall.' He stepped up on the seat and used Orrin's shoulder to reach the window.

Archer shifted slightly away from the window as Reader slipped the hook under his belt, letting the rope trail behind. Reader moved past him and out the window, his arms reaching above, searching for a handhold.

Evelyn looked away, tucking her face under Orrin's chin.

'He'll be fine,' Orrin whispered, his lips at her ear. She nodded, trying to believe, and when she looked up again Reader's foot was dangling in the window.

Archer fed out the rope, making sure it didn't catch on anything. The long strand wove back and forth as they sat in silence and waited.

Evelyn closed her eyes and wet her lips, forming a silent prayer. *'Please, Lord of Light, keep him—'*

'He's in.' Archer grabbed the rope and tied Reader's pack to it. The pack flew out the window as the rope was pulled up. Archer kept the end tight in one hand.

'Mage,' Orrin ordered.

The young man gulped, but he grabbed Archer's hand and climbed up into the casement. Evelyn saw the determination in his shoulders as he grabbed the rope and started to climb. The rope twisted about as he disappeared from view.

Sidian was removing his armour from his broad shoulders, revealing the scarring that covered his chest in swirling patterns. They seemed to move over his skin as his muscles flexed.

'Timothy.' Orrin pointed to him.

Timothy sighed and climbed up to the window. Archer took his long spear as Timothy grabbed the rope and started up, using both hands and feet. He was much slower than the others, but eventually his feet disappeared from view.

Thomas followed his brother as soon as Archer had handed up the first of the spears.

Orrin stood, setting Evelyn on her feet. 'You're next,' he said as he pulled his sword.

Evelyn nodded and climbed up to stand opposite Sidian. He had a jar of grease in his hand and was using a scrap of cloth to smear it over his arms and chest.

Evelyn looked at the window, then back at Sidian. He caught her look and shrugged. 'I'll fit,' he whispered, his white teeth gleaming against black skin. 'Might get scraped up, but I'll squirm through.'

Evelyn nodded and reached for a handhold to pull herself up into the window. Archer was kneeling in the window, reaching up, his arm extended to pass up the last spear. Without thinking, she brushed into Archer as she pulled herself up.

Archer jerked in surprise and lost the spear. He cursed under his breath as it started to drop and reached to catch it. His eyes went wide as he lost his balance, his fingers scrabbling at the stone. Evelyn watched in horror as he toppled backwards out the window.

TWENTY-SEVEN

With a cry, Evelyn threw herself over the ledge, reaching for Archer as he fell. Her lower body caught at the sill as her fingers grasped the hem of his trous. Her fingers closed in a fist and her arm took the full weight of his body as it slammed into the side of the keep.

They froze for a moment, Archer swinging upside down, his trous pulled tight. Evelyn drew a breath, preparing a spell to lift him, when her shoulder gave. She heard the sound, like a cork coming out of a bottle, then white-hot pain swept over her.

Unable to think, unable to focus, all she could do was clench her fist tighter in the cloth of Archer's trous. She reached with her good arm, to try to pull him up. But she felt herself slipping.

Lost in a cloud of pain, Evelyn felt someone's hands on her legs. She concentrated on breathing, then opened her eyes. Archer was dangling below her, his head curled up, his eyes wide with fright.

His trous slipped in her grasp as her fingers went numb.

Archer twisted then, trying to reach up to grab her arm. The movement made her gasp as her shoulder screamed in protest, the muscles tearing. She panted, blinking to keep the tears out of her eyes.

Firm hands locked on her waistband, but made no effort to pull. Instead, the rope dangled down, brushing her cheek.

Archer wrapped his hand around it and took hold, just as the fabric of his trous slipped from her fingers. Evelyn closed her eyes and moaned as the weight came off her shoulder.

'Lady?' Archer's voice was soft as he hung below her.

'Climb.' Blackhart's voice floated out to them. 'We've got her.'

Archer gave her a worried look, then headed up the rope.

Something tugged her tunic at the shoulders and Evelyn felt herself lifted and pulled back into the privy. Sidian had her, and lowered her to Blackhart's waiting arms.

She bit her lip, tasting blood, as he lowered her to the seat. No noise, she mustn't make any noise.

'Shoulder out of joint?' Blackhart whispered.

Evelyn nodded, bracing her arm with the other.

'Can you heal it?'

Evelyn shook her head. 'Has . . . to be . . . put in place. Pain. I can't—'

'Ease her forward,' Sidian said.

A moan escaped her as they shifted her. Evelyn let her head fall onto Blackhart's shoulder, resting it there. The agony was intense and she shivered, helpless.

Sidian eased in behind her on the seat and wrapped his arms around her, one over the good shoulder, the other around her waist. He tugged her back so that she was upright, held tight to his chest.

Blackhart took her elbow in one hand, bracing the other on her collarbone. He leaned close to her. 'Evelyn,' he said softly.

Evelyn struggled to lift her head, to focus on his face. He stood there patiently, his hazel eyes meeting hers. He had a wry expression on his face and she frowned, giving him a questioning look.

'Seems I'm always hurting you, Lady High Priestess.'

She shook her head. 'No, Orrin.' She drew in a shaky breath. 'That's not—'

Blackhart yanked on her arm, giving it a sharp twist. With a click, the joint slid back into place.

Agony flared. Her vision went black, bringing a blessed absence of pain and consciousness. For long, sweet moments she floated in bliss, free of pain.

'Evelyn,' a voice demanded.

The voice would hurt her, pull her back to the pain, and she honestly wasn't interested.

'Priestess,' the voice demanded again, urgent and loud.

There was a thump of a heartbeat in her ear and a pounding on a door, and Evelyn was fairly sure she'd slept past the dawn services. Wouldn't she be in trouble? But just a few more minutes . . .

'Wake up, Evie.' The voice sounded strained now. Pity, really. As much as she loved serving the Lord of Light, there were some mornings when you just wanted to sleep in—

Someone slapped her cheek. 'Now, Evelyn.'

Blackhart. She smiled then. Cradled in his arms, no doubt – alone, just the two of them in the . . . *privy*.

Her eyes flew open.

Sidian was close to her, his dark black face gleaming with sweat. He smiled when he saw that she was awake. 'Heal yourself, Priestess.'

'I can't,' Evelyn said. The joint was back in place, but the arm was stiff and sore. 'The Odium . . . they'll find—'

'They already have,' Blackhart growled.

Evelyn blinked, confused, until she realised that the pounding was coming from the door of the privy. Blackhart was braced, holding the handle, watching the bolt strain, his sword out before him. Something was trying to get in.

'Heal yourself and we'll get out of here,' Sidian said, tying his bundle of armour to the rope. His arms were still greased, his chest bare. 'There's not much time.'

'You can't climb a rope hurt,' Blackhart added. His voice softened. 'Focus, Evie. There's just us, in this moment. Take a breath and focus.'

Evelyn looked at him, at the worry in those hazel eyes. She put her hand under her tunic, feeling the heat of the abused muscles. She closed her eyes, took a breath and prayed. '*Hail, gracious Lord of the Sun and Sky, Giver of Light and Grantor of Health, I ask . . .*'

The tingle flooded her shoulder like warm sun on a cold day, easing the burn of the muscles and repairing the tears. She rarely needed to work a healing on herself, and the way her powers felt as they worked always surprised her.

The pounding on the door doubled and Blackhart gripped the handle with a grunt. The bolt was bending, the pressure on it growing. Evelyn stood then, climbing onto the seat, her arm restored.

Sidian was in front of the window, lifting his bundle out so it could be pulled up. He gave her a glance. 'Me first.'

Evelyn nodded.

The big man turned, easing his shoulders and chest through the hole. It was a tight fit. He backed up and tried again, one hand wound around in the rope, the other pressed against the wall as he blew out a breath and scraped through. Once his chest was free, he easily pulled himself up.

Evelyn looked back at Blackhart, still holding the door closed.

Blackhart glared at Evelyn. The door was going to give at any moment. But the stubborn woman ignored him, staring at the door.

'Move,' he growled as the door shifted outward. He sheathed his sword and pulled on the handle with both hands, forcing it back into its frame.

'No,' came her response. She stepped down and moved to the side, pressed against the wall. 'How will you—'

'Go.' Blackhart braced himself as the door shuddered.

'What's a bit more magic?' she asked.

He opened his mouth to snarl at her, but the door was pulled again, almost yanking the handle from his hand. The Odium wedged their grey fingers in the gap.

Evie's eyes got that unfocused look as she concentrated, looking through the gap at a spot in the corridor, crying out, summoning the fire.

He felt it first through the door as the wood grew hot beneath his body. Then heat and the smell of smouldering wood washed over him through the crack. The door slammed closed and they both froze, looking at one another.

Blackhart nodded towards the window.

Evelyn leaned forward and kissed him, her warm lips pressed to his.

Blackhart jerked his head back in surprise, but she was already scrambling for the seat, climbing up, reaching out for the rope and pulling it close. She stood in the window, gave him a glance, then started climbing, using both hands and feet.

Blackhart waited as her feet disappeared, waited for the assault on the door to begin again. But there was only silence, and the smell of burning flesh.

He leaped up on the seat and wasted no time climbing the rope.

Sidian was leaning out, watching for her. He grinned at her, reaching down to grab her tunic and haul her in the last few feet.

'Another privy,' Evelyn observed as she climbed in.

Archer was pressed to the wall, as if to keep track of it.

Evelyn gave him a guilty look. 'Archer, I'm sorry. I—'

'Moved fast enough to save my life,' Archer whispered. 'I owe you, Lady High Priestess. My own fault for being stupid.'

'You just figuring that out?' Blackhart snarled as he climbed in the window.

They all shifted around, making room as best they could. Sidian made a face as he put his armour back on, ignoring the grease. Reader was at the door, listening.

Blackhart hauled the rope up behind him. 'We need to move.'

'Where are we?' Evelyn asked softly.

'Priest's quarters, behind the Lady's shrine,' Sidian answered. 'There's a bedroom and a sitting room beyond, then two doors. One leads to the shrine; the other, to the servants' hall.'

'Let me guess,' Evelyn said. 'You looted that as well.'

'I wouldn't use the word "looted" so much as "stole",' Archer whispered. His eyes were still wide and he was breathing hard, but he got the words out.

'Through the door to the hall, then two doors to the left,' Blackhart said.

The others nodded, then Reader opened the door.

The room was clear. Evelyn had a brief glimpse of a bed and mattress overturned, and chests and wardrobes pulled open as they moved across the room, intent on their goal.

Reader listened briefly, then opened the door. They spilled through the door, into the shrine. Or what was left of it.

Evelyn drew in a breath at the battered walls and torn tapestries. Gold stars painted on the ceiling still glimmered in the soft light. But the reflecting pool in the centre of the room was filled with dark water, scum floating on the surface.

They moved around the pool, through the wreckage of smashed benches and chairs. There was something dark smeared on the walls, marring the pictures of the Lady of Laughter.

'Dorne is going to have your balls,' Blackhart said.

'Ain't lookin' forward to cleaning this up,' Archer mumbled.

Reader was at the door and they formed up around him, at the ready. He paused, then produced the key in his hand and knelt to unlock it. 'Can't hear a thing,' he whispered. 'But that don't mean—'

The door exploded into pieces, and the Odium were on them.

Reader was thrown back onto the floor. Timothy and Thomas surged forward with their spears. Sidian stepped around Evelyn, using his mace to crack Odium heads. Evelyn watched, trying to calm her breathing, ready to cast if necessary.

Then Thomas jerked back with a cry. One of the Odium had plunged a dagger into his chest.

'Weapons!' Sidian cried out a warning as he stepped over the fallen man. Thomas pulled himself backwards on the floor, the weapon still lodged in his chest. Mage reached down and dragged him clear, towards Evelyn.

She ignored the sounds of the fighting as she dropped to her knees. The dagger was high in the chest. There was little bleeding, but the dagger quivered with the beating of his heart. Thomas's eyes were wide and his breathing shallow.

Archer was at the doorway. He'd picked up Thomas's spear and was using it to hold the monsters at bay as Sidian wielded his mace and shield.

'Hold them,' Blackhart snarled.

Timothy grunted. Sidian brought his shield to bear and with Archer's help they started to press the Odium back. Mage had the edge of the door, ready to close it.

Evelyn was so intent on the man before her, she almost missed the faint splash behind her.

Odium were coming out of the pool.

Blackhart heard it too and whirled about to face the new threat. He stepped in front of her, pulling his blade. 'Behind us,' he cried.

Evelyn took a breath and half closed her eyes so that she could focus on summoning the power. She heard Blackhart's blade strike, heard the struggle at the door, heard Thomas panting, but ignored all of it in order to cast the fire at the enemy.

She opened her eyes, ready to cast—

They were children.

Children of all ages were coming up out of the water, dripping wet, horribly empty eyes in grey faces. They advanced on Blackhart, their hands out, reaching for him.

Blackhart raised his sword, but the blade hesitated, staying high over his head.

Evelyn's throat closed. Horrified, she scrabbled to her feet, away from the nightmare that advanced towards her. Thomas moaned, reaching out to grab her ankle, as if afraid she'd leave him.

Blackhart stepped away from the undead children, trying to brush them aside. But they clung with claws and teeth, hanging from his arms, fastening themselves to his legs . . .

'They ain't kids!' Mage was beside her, yelling at both of them.

Evelyn could hear the others struggling behind her, but she couldn't move, couldn't breathe.

'Too many,' Mage said, then glanced at Evelyn. His eyes were sympathetic, but then grew grim as he turned his attention back to the fight. He extended his hand and shouted three words, calling the fire.

His spell wasn't big, but it was hot and bright and it washed over the small heads as they emerged from the water. But the Odium were wet, soaked through, and though their flesh crisped, the water offered enough protection for them to swarm over Blackhart, their claw-like hands grabbing him, overwhelming him. Blackhart cursed as they pulled him down to the ground.

Evelyn heard his sword hit the stone floor, and she screamed his name. The magic came then, and she cast her fire over the monsters. Her fear fed the flames, and she struggled to keep them away from Blackhart. But there were so many she lost sight of him in the mass.

Mage pulled a dagger, but it was too little, too late. The Odium swarmed over them, clawing at tunic and trous, reaching for her outstretched hands. She stepped back, hearing the struggles of the others at the door, and gathered her will to burn these monsters to oblivion.

From behind, a body fell next to her. It was Timothy, his throat slashed open, his eyes wide.

Evelyn swept the flames closer, to try to stop the undead children. But they pressed forward, their wet clothes smouldering, their hair burning on their heads. One reached down and pulled the dagger from Thomas's chest.

Thomas screamed.

Something struck the back of her head. Evelyn staggered, but the pain and blackness swallowed her consciousness whole.

TWENTY-EIGHT

He was adrift in pain, darkness and despair. It was no less than he deserved. The agony grew, pain in his shoulders and arms. He didn't bother to cry out or call for aid. None would come.

It was the sound of movement around him that drew him back. He could barely open his eyes, crusted thickly with his own blood.

Orrin was in the throne room. In the keep. They were in the throne room.

That thought – the thought of his men more than any other – brought him back. His arms were chained above his head and he was hanging limp from the irons. He didn't move, just let himself hang from them as he struggled back to full consciousness.

Before him, two Odium held Reader between them and stripped him to the waist, throwing his armour on the ground. Reader's head hung down, his eyes were closed, but he still breathed.

There was a pile of weapons and armour already there. Orrin recognised his weapons, as well as those of the others. With grief, he saw that Thomas lay near his feet, face-up in a pool of glistening blood. Timothy's lifeless body was draped over Thomas's chest.

The bite of the manacles into his wrists was no more than he deserved, for having got such men killed.

Orrin watched as the Odium dropped Reader's armour and pack onto the pile. Reader's belt was tossed there as well. One end flopped on the floor, rattling the ring of keys.

The creatures heaved him onto a table set in the centre of the room and started strapping him down.

Orrin let his head loll to the side. Sidian was there, standing silent, in chains. He'd been stripped to the waist as well. He watched the Odium with a grim look on his face.

A moan came from Orrin's other side. Archer, from the sound of it.

There was something at the base of the opposite wall, but he couldn't focus well enough to tell who it was. But then he heard a soft moan and he knew.

He brought his feet under him at that point and stood, taking the pressure off his arms. They tingled with new pain, but he ignored that. 'Evie?'

A head lifted and he could just make out her blue eyes. Mage was next to her, sprawled on the floor. Orrin's gut twisted when he realised that their chains were those damned spell chains, attached to each wrist and running through the links on the walls.

'Orrin.' Evelyn's voice was a groan. 'Where—?' She lifted her head and looked around. 'Oh no, no.'

'Evie, are you hurt?'

'Children.' Evelyn's voice cracked. 'They used children.'

There was nothing to say to that.

Sidian pulled on his chains, testing their strength. Orrin did the same, but there was no give. 'How long have you been—?'

'In time to watch them bring Reader in and start stripping him,' Sidian said softly. 'Your head is still bleeding.'

'Mage.' Evelyn had managed to reach the young man, pulling his head into her lap. She was checking his arms and legs when he stirred, moaning.

Sidian twisted around, looking up at the wall where the chains were threaded through a ring. 'Odium can't be that good at stonework.'

'They aren't.' A soft voice echoed through the room. 'I used magic.'

The hairs on the back of Orrin's neck lifted. 'It can't be. You're—'

'Dead?' Elanore walked through the huge double doors with an escort of Odium. She paused in the light, looking as lovely as ever. Her red lips curved in a smile as she looked at Orrin fondly. 'Not so, my Lord Blackhart.'

She was dressed all in black, her bodice tight around her breasts, her skirts long and sweeping the floor. Orrin blinked, taking in the stunning perfection of her pale face.

She advanced, the Odium walking behind her in a crowd.

Men, women and children, all vacant-eyed and grey, following their mistress. A shiver went down Orrin's spine. A wave of cold, foul air swept over him as she drew near. He had to blink as his eyes watered from the stench.

Elanore stood before him, still amused. 'Orrin.'

'You're dead. They brought me your ring,' Orrin said. He focused on her face, flawless and serene.

'Do you still have it?' Elanore's voice sounded odd, as if distant somehow. 'I'd like it back.'

Orrin stared at her. 'The Chosen killed you.'

Elanore's perfect face screwed into an ugly grimace. 'That bitch with the red gloves. I'll suck her soul from her body after I've claimed what is mine.'

'Josiah is not yours.' Evelyn spoke from behind her.

Orrin watched as Elanore regained her composure. She laughed, a perfect laugh, artful in its perfection.

'Such a gift you bring, my Orrin. A high priestess of the Gods of Palins.' Elanore turned and walked over to where Evelyn lay in chains, glaring at her defiantly.

Orrin yanked on his chains. 'If you're alive, why send Odium against your own people? Why not summon me and—?'

'You don't look much like a priestess,' Elanore said, ignoring him. 'More like a street urchin. But I can taste your power.' She reached out to brush her fingers over Evelyn's hair. 'I've been looking for you.'

Evelyn jerked her head back. 'Why?'

'Portals.' Elanore turned back and smiled at Orrin. 'I haven't been able to learn that spell. Imagine being able to open a door to anywhere you've ever been. And you will teach me.'

'No. We'll stop you,' Evelyn said calmly. 'The Gods will not allow—'

'Gods.' Elanore laughed again. 'Did your precious Gods stop me before? Did they stop my Lord Blackhart from delivering the people of Farentell to my mercies? I used them all to create my Odium. Men, women' – Elanore looked back at Orrin – 'children.'

Evelyn was pale, her gaze on Orrin.

'You filthy, lying bitch.' Orrin threw himself against his chains. 'Never the children. Once we realised what you did down here, never, not once did we offer up a child. Evie, you have to believe—'

Evelyn's heart stopped beating.

Elanore chuckled again, looking down at her. 'Why should she believe you, when she has the evidence of her own eyes?' She gestured to the Odium. Evelyn couldn't help looking at the men, women and children. Walking corpses, she reminded herself. Who could feel no pain, had no awareness . . .

'It's the truth.' Archer's voice was little more than a croak. 'The adults, yeah, we gave them to you. We thought them the enemy, Priestess. We needed the Odium to protect our lands. But never the kids.'

'He herded them for me' – Elanore glanced at Evelyn, no doubt to see the impact of her words – 'like so many cattle. Down the tunnels to my workroom. Whole families at a time, chained to the walls, crying out for mercy, watching as I drained the children first.' She watched Evelyn closely, like a cat.

'You lie,' Evelyn said firmly. 'The Lady of Laughter spoke to me, telling me to save Orrin Blackhart. She would turn her face from him if what you say is true.'

Orrin's face was a mask of disbelief. Then he slumped in his chains with obvious relief.

'Pity.' Elanore turned away. 'I was enjoying his pain.' She turned, her skirts sweeping the floor as she stepped towards the table where Reader lay.

Evelyn took a breath then, once the stench retreated a bit. She watched Elanore move away, leaving a trail of something behind her on the floor. Evelyn's eyes widened as she realised they were bits of dried flesh.

'Odium,' Elanore said, 'a source of great power. Far greater than a human army.' She ran a hand over Reader's bare chest. The man gasped, as if in pain. 'What need have I for human warriors? Odium have no need to eat or sleep. As I grow more powerful, I control more and more from this distance.' She looked at Orrin. 'You will join them, Orrin. And you will obey. But let's start with this one, shall we?'

Elanore spread her hands wide and pressed them into Reader's chest. She started to chant vile words in a soft, gentle tone, almost like a lullaby.

And Reader started to scream.

Evelyn cried out and lowered her head to pray.

Elanore's chanting rose and fell in a soothing pattern, broken only by Reader's cries. Evelyn could hear him thrashing in his bonds, and the hoarse curses coming from Orrin and the others. Only the Odium stood silent and unmoving.

'Lady.' The whisper came from Mage, his head still in her lap.

'Mage.' Evelyn lowered her head. 'You're bleeding. Stay still and—'

'You must listen.' His voice quavered. 'The spell chains have a flaw.'

Elanore's voice was even, her chant continuing its pattern, unbroken by Reader's screams. Evelyn darted a look in her direction, then lowered her head to Mage's. 'A flaw?'

His eyes fluttered and he drew a few short breaths before he answered. 'Never got it right. They can take in only so much magic, and then they fall apart, Lady.'

Evelyn struggled to understand. 'What? How much—'

'Depends on how old they are,' Mage said. His hands shifted slightly as he felt the metal of the cuffs of her manacles. 'These have been around awhile. We might be able to burn through them.'

She had a thousand questions, but she wasn't going to waste any time. 'How?'

'Cast spells,' came the faint answer. 'Pour your power into them, and the metal will crumble like dried bread.' Mage flicked a glance at the Odium near them. 'But pour too much of your power into them and you risk death.' He struggled to sit up, leaning against her shoulder.

Evelyn glanced around the room. 'The Odium will sense—'

'She's using magic,' Mage whispered.

Evelyn bit her lip. Reader's cries were whimpers now as Elanore seemed almost to glow. 'We have to try. Elanore's made a mistake, Mage.'

He blinked at her, puzzled.

'The Lord of Light delivers justice to his people with a fair hand.' Evelyn shifted slightly, putting her hands over his manacles. 'But the Lady of Laughter delivers vengeance.' She looked at Orrin just as he lifted his head. She saw so much in his eyes. Shame. Horror. Repentance. Love. Desperation for a chance to set things right.

She'd call the magic and free him, even if it meant her own death.

'You save your strength, Mage. I'll deal with the chains. But you must promise me' – she grasped Mage's manacles tight – 'that you'll end this if I can't.'

'I swear,' Mage said. 'I've got an idea. Maybe I can use the draining spell against the Odium. But you have to get me free.'

Evelyn nodded and closed her eyes, trying to focus despite the suffering around her.

Orrin shouted a curse, trying to distract Elanore from her chanting. But the bitch kept going, her voice even and calm as Reader writhed in pain beneath her hands.

He risked a glance at Evelyn, sure that her eyes would be filled with disappointment, even hate for what he'd done. But she was sitting still, her eyes looking off in the distance, as if she were casting a spell.

Mage was struggling to sit up. Evelyn was covering his manacles with her hands.

Orrin's stomach twisted. Mage had told her about the chains.

He feared for her then, feared both she and Mage would burn themselves out. But it wasn't like he had an alternative to offer. And anything was better than watching her be tortured.

Sidian had pulled his chains so that one hand was higher than the other. He was rubbing his chest, still glistening with grease . . . and then rubbing his wrists. The manacles were tight enough that Orrin was certain he wouldn't have much luck, but it was worth a try.

Archer was stretching out his long legs, trying to shift the pile of weapons and gear so he could get to Reader's keys. His long foot was pale in the darkness as he strained; his face was even paler.

Orrin turned his attention to his own chains, pulling, trying to find a weak link. He pushed back the despair and grief and concentrated on finding a way to get free. It was all he could do, other than wait to die.

No. There was one thing more. Something he hadn't done since . . .

Orrin gritted his teeth. *Lady of Laughter* – he aimed a thought deep within as he tested his chains – *'laugh all you want, but here I am begging. She claims you saved me for your own reasons.'* He glanced at Evelyn, sitting there dirty, dressed in black, her hair filled with soot. *'I'll be damned if I know what they are, but I'll take whatever chance I get to redeem myself. But save them, Lady. I beg you. Please.'*

He wasn't sure if he said the last out loud, but the word seemed to echo in his heart.

There were no flashes of light, no signs from above, but he really didn't expect any.

Still, it couldn't hurt.

Archer sucked in a breath and froze, staring at the floor, as if turned to stone. Orrin glanced down.

Thomas's eyes were open, staring up at him.

TWENTY-NINE

She called the fire, and the fire answered.

She could feel the power within her, being pulled out of her by the manacles around her wrists. Every lesson she'd had as a child, every memory of her father working his spells – Evelyn used all of it, pulling from strength she didn't know she had.

It hurt, making her sick and dizzy, but still she focused, whispering the words, gathering her strength. She poured it all in, her rage and despair and fear, and used every bit of determination she possessed.

'*Lady of Laughter, hear my plea. Make me thy instrument of vengeance, Lady, for all this woman has done and will do. Give me help, Lady. Give me strength, Lady. Give me power, Lady. This I pray . . .*'

The magic rose within her and she channelled it through her fingers, guiding the power into the metal of their manacles.

Mage shifted next to her, trying to ease his pain. He was hurt, they all were. She needed more, needed . . .

She opened her eyes and looked at Orrin. He stood there, bare-chested, barefoot, helpless before his enemies, blood dripping down his face. He pulled at his chains, trying so hard . . .

She loved him, loved him more than she'd ever thought possible. Only the Gods knew if he'd ever return her love, even let her express it, but she despaired of having the chance to show him how she felt. Never would she feel his skin against hers, never lie with him on a soft bed, wrapped in his strong arms, feel him move within her body, know the joy of pleasure at his touch.

Her love fed the flames now.

'*Lady, let him have this chance, let him work free of his guilt, let it be here and now, let me . . . Lady of Laughter, please—*'

Her fingers suddenly sank into the metal of the manacles.

They crumbled away, leaving Evelyn and Mage both weak, gasping and free.

Orrin watched as Thomas blinked and tried to focus on him.

'Thomas,' Archer whispered, 'Reader's keys. They're—'

Thomas's head moved slightly. Then his hand appeared from under his brother's body and slid along the floor.

'Just a little more,' Archer said.

Orrin held his breath. Thomas's glassy stare revealed he wasn't long for this world. But his hand closed tightly around the end of the belt.

Sidian had seen and he rattled his chains to cover any noise. He was still trying to work the grease under his manacles, trying to pull his wrist through. He need not have bothered with the distraction. Elanore was chanting, absorbed in Reader's weak struggles.

Thomas jerked the belt. The end with the keys hit the wall by Archer's feet.

None of the Odium reacted.

'Good lad,' Orrin whispered.

Thomas's lip curled ever so slightly. He sighed and closed his eyes.

Archer grabbed the ring with his toes and lifted it to his hand in one swift move. Carefully, he tried the first key.

Orrin held his breath. There were so many keys, how could—

All the Odium started to turn towards Evelyn.

Orrin thrashed in his chains as the monsters moved in her direction. Archer cursed as he tried another key, and another. Sidian strained and cried out as one hand slid free of its manacle.

Mage scrambled up, shouting something. His hands seemed to glow with a sickly light. He lunged forward, dodged an Odium's claw-like hands, and touched its chest. Without so much as a whisper, the monster vanished in a puff of dust.

'It worked!' Mage looked at his hands in astonishment. 'I drained it!'

'Mage,' Orrin cried out a warning. Evelyn jumped up and yanked Mage back, out of the reach of another of the monsters.

Mage stood in front of her and started touching each creature as it got closer. The sickly light around his hands seemed to get brighter as Odium were destroyed. Mage had a grin on his face, but it disappeared as Elanore screamed in rage.

The cry was warning enough. Evelyn pulled Mage back to the floor, forcing his head down as Elanore raised her hand and swept a curtain of fire over both of them, holding it at a slight angle.

Flames washed over them as Elanore cast her fire at Mage, without regard for the Odium that stood between them. The monsters collapsed, blackened and crisped.

Evelyn kept her face to the stone, drawing cool air into her lungs. She watched as Elanore prepared to attack again and swept the fire over them once more as a shield to deflect the spell. 'I can't keep this up for long,' Evelyn said.

Mage shivered next to her. 'What's she doing?'

Elanore had stopped her casting. She stood there, her fists clenched at her sides and faced the door, as if concentrating on—

'The door,' Mage gasped. 'She's calling more.'

'I'll deal with her,' Evelyn said. 'You deal with the Odium. Can you—?'

A hoarse shout caught everyone's attention.

Orrin was free.

'Got it,' Archer said as his manacles swung open.

Orrin's breath caught as the flames rolled over Evelyn and Mage. He forced himself to hold still as Archer worked to free him. He saw Elanore focus on the door and knew what it meant. 'More Odium coming.'

'Hells,' Archer muttered as he finished and turned to Sidian.

Orrin didn't wait to hear the rest. With one step he swept his sword from the pile and leaped the bodies of his friends. He strode towards the bitch, the stone floor cold under his feet. With each stride he gained speed, charging across the room towards Elanore.

Sidian and Archer would see to the Odium.

He'd see the bitch dead.

Elanore broke off her chanting and stepped away from the

table. She faced him heads on; that perfect face smiled and laughed as he moved. She spread her arms wide, as if welcoming him as a lover.

Orrin screamed a battle cry and with a few more steps he plunged his blade into her chest, right through her heart. He ripped the blade free as he moved past and spun around, waiting to see her lifeless body collapse to the floor.

Elanore had turned as well. She stood, arms still wide, and laughed.

Orrin paused, his sword at the ready. But there was no wound in Elanore's chest, no blood. To his horror, she stepped closer, reaching out as if to stroke his cheek.

He stepped back, avoiding her hand. 'How?'

'Orrin,' Evelyn called out. She was struggling to stand, with Mage's help. 'She's an Odium.'

Elanore laughed again, stepping back and letting her skirts swirl as she moved to put the table between herself and Orrin. She trailed her fingernails over Reader's body. The man shuddered at her touch.

'How is that possible?' Orrin had his sword up, circling to keep the table between them.

'I felt myself dying, dearest Orrin,' Elanore said. 'Felt my life ebbing away as that bitch of a Chosen watched.' Elanore lifted her hand to her throat, caressing it. 'I couldn't let that happen. I used the magic, the spells, to bind myself to my body.' She drew her hand down, stroking her breasts. 'To make sure that I lived.'

Sidian and Archer were at the great doors of the throne room, struggling to hold back a mass of Odium. Orrin caught a glimpse of Mage limping up behind them, reaching over their shoulders, touching as many as he could. Mage was destroying them, but they were being overwhelmed.

'You didn't live,' Evelyn said, leaning against the wall with one hand. 'She's an abomination, Orrin.'

'Oh, such a precious little priestess.' Elanore paused. 'Destroying those chains cost you, didn't it? The shields cost you even more. Poor thing.'

'Not so weak I can't ask the Lady to show him what you are,' Evelyn spat. She raised her hand and gestured. 'See only the Truth, Orrin Blackhart.'

Elanore gasped and raised her hands, but she was too late. Orrin felt a tingle at the base of his skull, and he saw her as she truly was.

THIRTY

Orrin jerked back.

Elanore's skin was grey, her face half-burned away. Dead eyes were unseeing, lifeless. That pale white throat was slashed so deeply that he could see bone. Her dress hung in tatters, her flesh was stretched thin over bony fingers. The smell overcame him, the reek of rotting flesh.

His horror must have shown on his face, for Elanore howled.

'That's why you locked away the mirrors and bowls,' Evelyn said, moving closer. 'They'd show you the truth, wouldn't they? Metal is not fooled by magic.'

Orrin held his breath and eased over, trying to protect Evelyn.

Elanore howled again and lifted her hands. 'Die, die!' She threw long silver spikes of magic, aimed at his naked chest.

They were met by a wave of flames, and melted away.

Evelyn was beside him now, her hands before her, gesturing. He could hear her ragged breathing.

Elanore's monstrous face distorted in another scream. Again she threw the spikes of magic, and again Evelyn deflected them.

Again and again. Orrin stood, sword ready, but there was no chance to charge Elanore. He could almost see Evelyn weakening with each attack. He gripped his weapon, waiting for a chance.

Elanore stood before them, her disguise gone, laughing insanely as she threw her spells. But it seemed to Orrin that the spikes were smaller now, weaker.

Evelyn caught his eye with a sideways glance, then took a step back. Orrin moved with her instinctively, uncertain what she was trying to do.

Evelyn eased away again, as if retreating, and Elanore pressed her attack. Slowly they fell back and Elanore stepped out from behind the table and advanced on them.

Another spike of power, but Evelyn's flames were weakening. Orrin prepared to lunge forward. It was now or—

Elanore gestured and another spike appeared, flying towards his heart.

Evelyn stepped in front of him. With a soft grunt, she took the blow. The spike slammed into her chest and she collapsed to the floor.

Elanore shrieked her victory.

Orrin lunged forward and swung his blade for her neck.

With a gesture, she flung him against the wall, his blade clattering to the floor. 'It's not so easy, Orrin.' She advanced on him, her face still a hideous nightmare.

He scrambled for his blade and got to his feet, moving towards the throne, luring her away from Evelyn's body. Part of him howled with fear for Evelyn, but the other part lusted for nothing less than Elanore's death.

'I'll drain your friends as you watch, and have you as my prisoner,' Elanore gloated as she followed him. 'Then I'll take my Odium, and we'll—

Orrin stood, sword in front of him, and looked over her shoulder. 'I don't think so, bitch.'

'Neither do I,' said Mage from behind Elanore.

Elanore jerked around, seeing the apprentice for the first time.

Mage reached out, chanting his spell, the sickly glow still around his hands. But Elanore grabbed for his wrists, and laughed.

Mage jerked back, his eyes wide. 'No—'

'It can work both ways, apprentice,' Elanore rasped as she started her own chant, the same one she'd used on Reader. Mage struggled to break free, but she hung on tight.

Orrin reached out and grabbed her hair, yanking her head back. It twisted around in his hands, so that those eyes stared at him. The gash in her neck gaped wide.

Her chant was cut off in mid-word, a gurgle emerged from her throat.

Orrin stared down into her eyes.

Elanore released Mage and reached for Orrin's eyes with her claws.

Mage slammed his glowing hands down on her chest.

Elanore's mouth moved, and she let out a high-pitched squeal. She writhed in their grasp, her flesh tearing from the bone.

Mage's face twisted in a grimace, but he forced his hands deeper into her chest.

Elanore screamed, and dissolved into dust, her voice still echoing through the room.

Orrin and Mage stood there, silent. Then Mage fell to his knees, and started retching. Sidian and Archer stood by the door, breathing hard. The Odium were collapsing to the floor, nothing more than rotting corpses.

'Evelyn!' Orrin ran to her side, placing his sword on the floor as he pulled her into his arms.

Her eyes were closed, her thick white lashes pale on her cheek. Her breaths were shallow and faint. There was a burn mark through her tunic, and the skin beneath was red and blistered.

'Evie,' Orrin whispered, but there was no answer. She was broken – his bright perfect light – broken and dying in his arms.

He heard the clink of chains, and lifted his head. Mage was helping Reader off the table. Archer and Sidian were over by the brothers, checking Thomas.

'Evie,' Orrin whispered again, burying his face in her hair.

'I've no healing,' Mage said as he knelt down beside them.

'She's not long for it, that I know,' Orrin choked. 'Without help—'

'I wish I could portal' – Mage's voice broke – 'but I—'

Orrin jerked his head up. 'There's one chance.'

He freed one hand, and reached inside Evelyn's tunic. He pulled out the little drawstring bag, and then the tiny cylinder. He smashed it on the floor.

The summon stick lay in the shards.

He picked it up and broke it.

A portal formed in the room: white and glowing, with curtains that seemed to move in the breeze.

The others froze, and waited. Orrin cursed when no one came through, then he realised the problem.

He reached inside his tunic, caught the leather thong around his neck with a finger and pulled the white star sapphire ring free. The silver ring hung there, swaying, shining in the light.

He snapped the cord from around his neck and threw the ring through the portal.

It wasn't a breath before a man stepped through, one Orrin had seen before. The half-elf, the one with the long black hair.

He looked at the group with suspicion, but his eyes went wide at the sight of Evelyn.

'You are of the Church?' Orrin stood, taking up his precious burden.

'I am Dominic. What have you done to her?'

Orrin scowled. 'She's dying. Help her.'

Dominic placed his hand on Evelyn's chest and sucked in a breath. 'This is more than I can heal.'

'Take her,' Orrin urged. He transferred Evelyn into Dominic's arms. 'Take her, and go.'

Dominic raised one eyebrow in haughty disdain, taking in Orrin's state. 'We will take care of our own.'

Orrin looked down at Evelyn, resisting the urge to reach out and touch her pale face. 'Hurry.' He looked over at Thomas. 'There are others,'

Dominic turned towards the portal.

'Wait.' Orrin reached out. 'Tell her' – he paused, taking a breath – 'tell her—'

'I will tell her what she needs to know,' Dominic said. He turned, and disappeared through the portal.

The portal vanished.

There was a moment of silence. 'Bastard,' Archer growled.

Sidian frowned. 'Who was that?'

'A priest of the Church of Edenrich.' Orrin ran his fingers through his hair. 'That portal opened into the church of Edenrich.'

'Oh, that would have been a fine thing,' Archer said as he stood, 'us showing up there.'

'Thomas?' Orrin asked.

'Dead.' Archer scowled. 'Dead before that bastard arrived, I think. Still, he could have offered healing.'

'Not the way their minds work.' Orrin wiped the sweat off his face. 'Reader?'

'I'm alive,' Reader groaned. He slid off the table, with Archer's aid. 'But I almost wish I wasn't.' He gave Orrin a sharp look. 'You think that's it? That it's done?'

'I think so,' Orrin said. 'But it will take time to make sure the Odium are gone.'

'And them?' Archer asked, jerking his head towards where the portal had stood. 'Will they bring her back?'

'Doubt it,' Orrin growled.

Sidian rose from his knees then, brushing the dust off his hands. 'Let's be about it, then. We've work to do. Check the keep and the lands, and then head for Edenrich. You've a pardon to claim, and a boon.'

'Aye,' Orrin said. For the longest moment, he looked at the place where the portal had been. Then he shook his head at his own stupidity. 'You're right. There's work to be done.'

THIRTY-ONE

'So,' the Archbishop said as he bit into a pear, 'it has been thirty days or thereabouts, has it not?'

'Thirty days, Holy One,' Dominic said, watching the man's jowls jiggle as he chewed. He had to cast his eyes down from the sight. 'Thirty days since she was returned to us.'

'And she is healed?' the Archbishop asked as he lifted his wine glass, still chewing his fruit.

'Physically, yes, Holy One,' Dominic said as he watched the man wade back into his breakfast. 'The healers feel that they have done all they can.' Dominic paused. 'As to her gifts, they are uncertain as to when those will return.'

'And she obeys my strictures? She is under a discipline of silence and isolation?'

Yes, you fat bastard, Dominic thought. But he managed to restrain his tongue. 'She has not spoken, Your Grace, since your admonition.'

The Archbishop failed to notice Dominic's disdain as he shovelled his eggs into his mouth. 'Good,' he mumbled through his food. 'That is well.'

'The healers feel she would benefit from being able to leave her chamber,' Dominic said quietly. 'Perhaps some light duties—?'

'No,' the Archbishop said slowly. 'The Queen will insist on seeing her if she hears that Evelyn is well enough to leave her room.'

Dominic managed to stay silent over that comment.

'Evelyn is under discipline for her disobedience.' The Archbishop burped, raising his napkin to his lips. 'I have explained that to Queen Gloriana and her advisors.'

'We have not had a chance to hear her side of the story,' Dominic pointed out. 'Perhaps she had good reason to—'

'She was with that villain Blackhart. What more do we need

to know?' The Archbishop scowled. 'She has been too ill to press for details. I must know the extent of her sin before I can determine whether the restrictions should be lifted.' He leaned back in his chair, which creaked under his weight. Dominic had a brief hope it would break beneath him, but it held. 'In a day or two, I will meet with her privately. To hear her confession and offer spiritual guidance.'

The Archbishop's belly gave a loud rumble, and he grimaced as he reached for his spiced wine. 'In a few days, Dominic.'

Dominic deliberately waited for a moment until the Archbishop had a mouthful of wine. 'Blackhart is here in Edenrich.'

'What?' The Archbishop sputtered, spraying his white vestments with wine. 'Here?'

Dominic nodded. 'He has asked for an audience with the Queen, and his request has been granted. He will appear before the Queen tomorrow afternoon.'

'Damnation.' The Archbishop shifted in his chair, and Dominic heard him release gas. 'The nerve of that bastard.'

'He appeared at the doors of the church as well,' Dominic continued, taking care to breathe through his mouth. 'Early this morning. He asked to see Evelyn.'

'Under no circumstances!' the Archbishop bellowed.

'I had him sent away, Your Grace.' Dominic cut him off smoothly. 'But he may push the point before the Queen.'

'Why has he appeared?' the Archbishop demanded, mopping at his robes.

'I assume that he is here to claim his pardon, and his boon,' Dominic said. 'Certainly he owes thanks to the Lady High Priestess for whatever aid she rendered.'

The Archbishop heaved his chair back and pulled himself to his feet, muttering something under his breath. Dominic's nose twitched as the man moved off, but he bowed as required.

The Archbishop stopped and turned his head. 'We shall keep Evelyn here within the safety of these walls, for the sake of her immortal soul. This Blackhart will ask for his pardon and boon and disappear, and good riddance.'

Dominic raised his head. 'And if his boon is to ask for the Lady High Priestess?'

The Archbishop snarled, but it turned to a grimace as his

bowels rumbled again. He clutched his belly as the room echoed with his flatulence, and waddled off towards his privy.

Dominic left the room as quickly as dignity would allow.

That fat bastard. Dominic clenched his teeth as he strode through the corridors of the church. It had been thirty days since Evelyn had been returned to them, and not once had she been allowed to speak in her own defence or explain what had happened.

He'd been afraid that she'd die in his arms once he'd stepped through the portal. But though the other healers were not of Evie's strength, they'd been able to save her, and speed her healing. Physically, she was well. Still tired and prone to sleeping, but what else could she do? Isolated in her chamber, and unable to speak.

The Archbishop had even fought her father, who'd demanded to see his daughter. It wasn't until Marlon threatened to make the Archbishop's privates rot off that he'd been permitted to see her. Marlon had been content with a short visit, and hadn't yet pushed for another, but it was only a matter of time.

What worried Dominic more was the presence of Blackhart in the city.

Dominic reached the wide staircase that led to the private chambers of the High Priests. He started up, nodding to those he passed, careful not to let his concern show on his face. He'd seen the look in Blackhart's eyes when he'd surrendered Evelyn. Now, more than ever, he had to press his cause. Or risk losing her forever.

Evelyn sat in her chamber and listened to the echoes of the morning prayers die away.

Her chair was by the wall, near the bed, placed so that she could see outside. But today the window shutters were closed against the cold. Light filtered through the cracks, warming the stone floor by her feet.

She'd watched the light travel over the floor for many days now, ever since she'd felt well enough to leave her bed. Each day the sun rose and set, tracing a slightly different path on the floor by her feet.

She'd wondered if there was snow yet, but hadn't gathered the energy to walk across the room and open the shutters to look out.

The truth was that she didn't really care overmuch. It was cold in the room, but her heavy robes kept her warm and the servants kept the fire built high.

White robes with gold trim. The heavy robes of a high priestess of the Gods of Palins – new robes, since her old ones were lost. Evelyn contemplated the cloth as she sat. There were even gold threads on her slippers. She was the picture of perfection, her white hair just long enough to wrap up in a bun, a side-effect of the healing she'd received. There weren't even any scars from the wounds she'd taken.

She wasn't sure she deserved these robes.

Evelyn had tried to pray along with the Dawn Service, to greet the Lord of Light as he rose on his day's journey. But her lips would not form the words.

The silence seemed more appropriate, somehow. Much more fitting. It encompassed her sorrow. Magnified it.

Evelyn knew in her heart that she was committing a sin, wallowing in her pain like this. The fact that the Archbishop's dictates permitted her to do so made it no less an offence. But she couldn't bring herself to care.

Tears welled, and she was embarrassed by her weakness. Everyone had been so kind, healing her wounds, seeing to her needs. Her powers of magic had been drained so greatly that it was unlikely she would be wielding them anytime soon.

She had a dim memory of Gloriana at her bedside, with Vembar and Arent, urging her to rest and heal.

Her father had come to see her in the early days, when she'd been helpless as a kitten. He'd taken her hand and bent down and whispered in her ear. 'Quite an adventure you've had, Daughter. You get tired of these idiots and their stupid rules and restrictions, you let me know. There is always a place in the Mages' Guild for you.'

She'd teared up at his words and he'd fussed and left, leaving her to heal and to decide.

She wasn't sure where she belonged, anymore.

Dominic had been kinder still, waiting until she had regained some strength before telling her that Orrin had summoned the portal in order to have her healed, and to remove her from his presence.

Dominic had held out her ring and in gentle tones explained

that Orrin had returned it, indicating that her presence in his life was unwanted and unwelcome now that the task was complete. She hadn't wanted to believe. But there was the ring in Dominic's hand, the white surface glittering with its star.

She pulled her hands from her sleeves, and looked down at the ring. Dominic had softened the blow as best he could, but he'd passed on the message. Orrin Blackhart was done with the Lady High Priestess Evelyn.

Evelyn slipped her hand back into the warm sleeve, and closed her eyes. Perhaps it was for the best. She'd thought she'd understood that Orrin had done terrible things in the name of protecting his people, but the sight of those Odium . . . so many . . .

She stopped as tears spilled down onto the white robes and soaked into the cloth.

Still, she loved him. Even knowing all that he had done, the very worst of it, still she cared for him.

The time would come that she'd be forgiven her trespasses, and returned to the rhythm of life within the Church. She'd lose herself in daily prayers and quiet meditation – and healing, if the Gods allowed.

But she'd grieve this loss forever.

A soft knock, and her door opened. Evelyn smiled through her tears as Dominic came into the room, looking concerned.

Cenwulf stretched out his feet before the fire, and sighed. There'd be snow this night, his bones told him so. His watch was over, so he was free to sit in the barracks kitchen and warm himself. The others were either on watch or gathered in the main room, talking and throwing dice. Most were sleeping this cold night.

Cenwulf preferred the kitchen hearth, with its warm glow and quiet walls. He'd seek his bed in a moment, once he'd finished his kav. And dealt with the shadow that moved by the pantry door.

'You might as well join me,' Cenwulf growled. 'You're keeping me from my bed.'

The shadow stilled, then darkness stepped forward and the light revealed a handsome face and hazel eyes. The man was all in black, except for an old red cloak that fell from his shoulders.

'Last I saw of you, you were naked and shivering,' Cenwulf grunted, 'and in fear of the mob. No need for you to come back here, unless you're returning that cloak.'

Blackhart came to stand by the table. 'I've come for word of Evelyn. Have you seen her?'

Cenwulf looked into his cup. 'Fine job you did taking care of her.'

Blackhart stilled and Cenwulf saw anger flash through his eyes, then guilt.

'I can get no answers from the Court or the Church. So I came here, thinking you'd know.'

There was a pleading tone in the words that surprised Cenwulf. Never thought this man was one to beg. 'I've seen her. What's left of her.'

'What's left?' Blackhart planted his gloved hands on the table and loomed over Cenwulf. 'What's that mean?'

Cenwulf ignored the threat. 'She's well enough. They healed her body. But what's left is in pain. You can see it in her eyes.'

'Does she venture out?' Blackhart leaned forward.

Cenwulf shook his head. 'No, old Gross Belly has her isolated, and under discipline. She is silent and alone in her chambers. For the sake of her soul, you understand. Evelyn hasn't even been to Court, although the Queen asks often enough.' He glared at the younger man. 'The fight's gone out of her.'

'That doesn't sound like Evelyn.' Blackhart said.

'She's not arguing, not talking – I'm not sure she's even praying.' Cenwulf sighed. 'I think she's grieving, and to be honest, I thought she was grieving over you.'

Blackhart frowned. 'I need to see her. To talk to her.'

'She can't talk,' Cenwulf repeated. 'Gross Belly's put her under a command of silence. She ain't gonna be able to talk.'

'All she needs to do is listen,' Blackhart said.

The door from the main room opened. Blackhart stepped back into the shadows.

One of the guards walked in. 'Any bread and cheese left, Cenwulf? I'm hungry.'

'Cook will have your head, you raid his pantry,' Cenwulf said. He put his mug down and rose. 'I'm off to the privy, and then to bed.'

'Just a bite,' said the guard. 'Cook'll never miss it.'

'On your head be it, then.' Cenwulf opened the door to the yard and stepped into the cold. Blackhart slipped out behind him, as quiet as could be. Cenwulf closed the door behind them both.

'Thanks,' Blackhart said.

'I had to piss anyway,' Cenwulf said. He headed across the yard. 'There's not a chance in hell that they will let you see her.'

'I have to try,' Blackhart said.

Cenwulf stopped at the door to the privy. 'Why?'

Blackhart had moved, fading into the shadows of the small house, but he stopped and looked at Cenwulf. 'I . . . I have to—'

Cenwulf looked into the man's face, and for an instant he saw the truth. Whether or not Blackhart had admitted it to himself, Cenwulf knew what drove the man.

And he saw a hint of the cause of the pain in Evelyn's eyes.

Evelyn prepared for sleep, removing her heavy robes and laying them neatly folded in the press at the foot of her bed.

Dear Dominic. He'd been driven by kindness to offer for her hand, for pity of her. She'd shaken her head even as he'd spoken, but he'd told her that he wouldn't give up, wouldn't stop until he'd persuaded her. Such a dear friend.

She took a plain cotton shift from the press, and pulled it on over her head. The fire was banked and there was extra wood in the box. Her attendants had seen to her needs, then locked the door behind them.

She slipped beneath the blankets, shivering for a moment before the bedding began to warm. The shutters rattled in their frame. Winter must be on its way.

She'd try to sleep this night, instead of lying awake. In the morning, she'd try to pray again.

The shutters rattled once more, and the dead leaves of the ivy that framed the window rustled. She frowned. There was no sound of wind or storm. What—?

'Evie?'

THIRTY-TWO

Evelyn's heart leaped in her chest.

'Evie?'

It wasn't much more than a whisper, but it pulled her out from under the warm covers. She threw them off and darted to the window, her heart beating like a frightened bird. It was not true, of course; it couldn't be; she was ill, feverish . . .

Her fingers trembled so hard that she fumbled the latch, then finally was able to pull open the shutters and look out.

Orrin was hanging from the ivy by the side of the window, his face pale and anxious. 'Evie,' he breathed.

Evelyn braced her hands on the sill, leaned out and kissed him.

His lips were cold and still for just a moment. Then they came alive, warm and responsive, and Evelyn moaned as her entire body came alive too, vibrating with her need. She opened her mouth, letting her tongue dart out to taste him, and heard him groan in response.

A rustle of leaves and Orrin pressed her back, never breaking contact as he climbed over the sill. Evelyn reached out to wrap her arms around his neck, kissing him frantically, hugging him close. The sharp edges of his sword hilt pressed through her cotton shift, but she ignored the minor discomfort for the pure joy of having him in her arms.

Orrin broke the kiss long enough to secure the shutters behind him, then pulled her back into his arms and kissed her again, his gloved hands running over her back. Evelyn felt her knees go out from under her, but Orrin caught her and gently lowered her to the floor beneath the window, cradling her in his arms.

Evelyn released his mouth to scatter kisses over his face, to run her fingers through his hair. She couldn't believe he was there with her, and she shivered at the intensity of her feelings.

Orrin shifted, and brought his cloak around her, wrapping

both of them in its warmth. The familiar smell of ehat wool surrounded her, and she put her head on his shoulder and sighed.

'I was afraid you wouldn't want to see me,' Orrin whispered.

Evelyn lifted her head in surprise and looked at him, taking in the strain and exhaustion on his face. She opened her mouth, but Orrin placed a gloved finger over her lips. 'I know you aren't supposed to talk, so please, just listen.'

She closed her mouth and lifted her hand to touch his warm cheek. He reached up and covered her hand with his own. He closed his eyes and a shudder went through him. 'I was afraid I'd killed you. No one would tell me anything. At the Court, at the church, no one would say ' He opened his eyes, filled with worry. 'You are well? No lasting harm?' He looked her over, running his hand through her hair. 'Healthy? Healed?'

She nodded, her eyes bright. She slid her hand out and laid it on his chest, asking her own silent question.

'I'm fine,' Orrin said. 'Reader had the worst of it, but he's mending well.' He paused. 'Thomas and Timothy . . . they didn't make it, Evie.'

She closed her eyes and lowered her head to his shoulder.

'None of us could bear the thought of leaving them in the keep, so we buried them in the pines,' Orrin said.

Evelyn bit her lip, stifling a sob. She slipped her hand around Orrin's neck.

Orrin hugged her tight, placing his chin on the top of her head. 'Elanore is dead. The Odium are gone, cleansed from the land. They all collapsed when Elanore died.

'We spent a week spreading the word and checking the country-side, but all we found were corpses sprawled on the ground. They'd just fallen over when she died.'

Evelyn lifted her head and gave him a doubtful look.

'No, I know you've heard that before, but Mage made sure. He figured out how to use the spell that created those spell chains to drain the Odium. He used it on her, and all that was left was dust,' Orrin said. 'I'm sure of this.'

Evelyn tilted her head, then raised her eyebrows.

'The people are returning to their lands and reclaiming their farms.' Orrin looked over her head, a very satisfied expression on his face. 'It was slow, because we sent escorts with everyone, but so far there have been no problems. Before I left, I set up regular patrols and a watch in the town. They will do well until the Queen appoints the new high baron of the Black Hills.'

Evelyn smiled, her eyes filling again. Orrin looked at her with a frown. 'You're cold.' He stood then, pulling her to her feet. 'Will anyone come?'

She shook her head, and took his hand to lead him to the bed.

Orrin pulled his hand back. 'Let me build up the fire. Get into the bed and get warm. I'll take the chair.'

Evelyn frowned at his back, sensing hesitation on his part. She pulled the thick comforter off the bed, and sat on the floor next to him as he stoked the coals and added wood to the flames. He gave her a warm look, then settled beside her on the hearth rug. She took his hand in hers.

He looked down and smiled when he saw the silver ring on her finger. He rubbed the stone with his thumb. 'I thought you'd die, there in the throne room. I was so helpless, so paralysed with fear. It wasn't until Mage said something that I remembered the summon stick your father gave you.

'It tore me apart to let Dominic take you, but I had no choice. I asked him to explain, but he wasn't very' – Orrin paused – 'not very friendly. I can't say as I blame him, me standing there half-naked, and you broken and bleeding in my arms.'

Evelyn held up her hand and pointed at the ring.

'Your father didn't think that through very well. The portal opened fine, but they had no way of knowing what was on the other side. So I tossed the ring through the portal, to convince them it was safe. I—'

Anger boiled up in Evelyn's chest as she took in his words. Her ears roared with her rage that Dominic would deceive her so.

'Evie?'

Orrin's voice drew her back, his warm hands holding hers. He'd come to her, climbed the tower for her. Her joy almost burst from her chest, and her cheeks flushed.

Orrin reached out and brushed a strand of her hair behind her ear. 'I came to Edenrich as soon as I could, Evie. To claim my pardon, and the pardon for my men. But I wanted to see you, to make sure you were well, and to tell you . . . to explain . . .'

He looked away. 'About the Odium . . .'

*

Orrin drew a deep breath, grateful that Evelyn couldn't speak. It made this easier, somehow. He'd agonised over how to tell her, how to explain. He'd thought of avoiding this conversation, but he couldn't. He had to tell her the truth.

'Elanore was mad for power, and that didn't seem such a bad thing.' Orrin kept his gaze on the fire, holding Evelyn's hand in his own. 'She and the Regent came up with a plan, and I obeyed the orders of my Baroness. With Edenrich in chaos, Farentell fell like a soft plum in our hands.

'The Regent wanted the lands, Elanore wanted slaves to work the mines, and so the slave trade was born. Then Elanore decided to attack Athelbryght and Summerford at the same time. I argued with her, saying that to split our forces that way, on two borders, was madness. But she was the High Baroness, and would not be overruled. She said she had a weapon that we could wield that would assure our victory.

'That night, she ordered slaves delivered to her workroom in the dungeons, and the next morning Odium appeared: mindless creatures that could rip an opponent to pieces before our eyes.' Orrin wet his lips. 'I didn't see a person standing there. I saw a weapon. One I could use to achieve my Baroness's desires. And so I agreed. More slaves were delivered, and more Odium joined the ranks.'

Orrin shook his head. 'But the army of Summerford fought like madmen, and Wyethe came to their defence. The Odium had drawbacks as troops. I was forced to retreat, to save my men for another day.

'Elanore, using mages and men, managed to wipe Athelbryght out of existence. But the magic she used backlashed through her mages to her, and almost killed her. It scarred her face and mind. From that day forth, she created Odium every night, using our enemies as her source.'

He looked down and saw that his knuckles were white, so hard was he gripping Evelyn's hand. He released her at once, flexing his fingers and then forming a fist. 'Night after night, the slaves would be driven down into the dungeons and chained to the walls. No one stayed down there with Elanore, no one witnessed what she did. Each night, slaves went down. Each morning, Odium came up.'

Orrin rubbed his palms on his trous. 'After a while, our need for the Odium grew, but slaves were in short supply. So Elanore ordered that our own people be added to the lines that went down into the dungeons.

'I was trapped, Evelyn. I'd been so focused on my people, my lands, my Baroness. At least, that is what I told myself. But by the time I realised what we'd done, I knew that I was trapped between the needs of our people and the demands of the Baroness. If I'd confronted her, I'd have been added to the chains, and there'd be no one left who might be able to control her. But a part of my soul sickened and died every time I gave those orders.

'It wasn't until the day I met you, the moment you laughed in the depths of that prison, that I saw a glimmer of hope. Then, when word came that Elanore had been killed—'

He turned, then, to look at her, the Priestess of Light. She was sitting there, wrapped in the comforter, tears streaming down her face, her eyes filled with grief and pain.

It took him a moment to see that there was no condemnation there, no accusation; the grief and the pain were for him. He reached out for her hand, and she reached out as well, their hands meeting and clasping.

A sob rose then, from deep in his chest, an anguished cry. 'Oh, Evelyn, how can I ever atone—?'

She came up on her knees and pulled him to her breast, wrapping her arms around him, rocking him back and forth as he wept. All those people. There could never be forgiveness for his sins, for his actions. And yet, Evelyn's arms were around him, her tears on his hair. He reached out, wrapped his arms around her hips, and clung to her like a child.

She pulled him down then, to lie before the fire on the thin hearth rug, and covered them both with the comforter. Her fingers combed slowly through his hair. His head lay on her breast and he could hear the steady beat of her heart within.

Slowly, he calmed. His breathing returned to normal and he lifted his head. 'Evie.'

She gave him a sad smile, reached up with one hand and pulled his head down into a kiss.

He responded, lost in the heady rush of her mouth, the gentle scent of her skin. He explored for long moments, and Evelyn opened her mouth and shifted her legs, responding as she had during that first kiss, in the—

Orrin jerked his head away and scrambled to his feet. Evelyn looked up at him, her hair and shift dishevelled, her lips swollen from his kiss. 'No, Evelyn. I won't—'

She held up one finger and the tip began to glow, as if on fire.

Orrin took a step back.

Evelyn put her finger down on the hearthstone, and wrote, letting the fire trail behind her finger. *I know you, Orrin Blackhart.*

'No,' he said stubbornly, but she ignored him. She moved her hand again, tracing out the letters.

I know your heart, Orrin. You are not the man you were.

'I can never—'

I love you, Orrin Blackhart of the Black Hills.

She looked at him, at his face, so weary, so vulnerable. He wouldn't look at her, just stared at the blazing words on the hearth. 'I love you, Evelyn of Edenrich, Lady High Priestess of the Gods of Palins. I love you far too much to—'

She reached out, and wrote again, with broad strokes. *Orrin, don't be an idiot.*

THIRTY-THREE

Evelyn watched as Orrin choked on a laugh. 'Oh, I'm an idiot now, eh? Such romantic talk, Priestess. Sweeps me right off my feet, it does.'

Evelyn rose, letting the comforter fall to the floor.

Orrin's face went stern. He took a step back towards the window. 'I've said what I came to say. I'm glad to find you well, and more than grateful for your aid, Lady High Priestess.'

Evelyn took another step towards him.

Orrin stiffened, and bent to snatch up his sword and dagger. 'My men and I have decided to leave Palins once the pardons are official. Memories linger, and there are some with sharp blades who won't let a piece of parchment stop them.' He tied his scabbard back on his belt. 'Sidian has some ideas of where we can go to make our way in the world. He hasn't said where, but—'

Evelyn put her hand on his arm and looked up at him with a gentle tilt of her head. He froze, staring at her.

She moved her fingers down the sleeve of his tunic and slipped her hand into his. With a tug, she turned to lead him to the bed.

'No.' Orrin resisted her pull. 'No, Evelyn. Listen to me. I'll admit to breaking the rules to come here tonight, but that's on my head. I'll not be the cause of your expulsion from the—'

Evelyn tugged again.

'You love being a priestess,' Orrin said softly.

She stopped, and looked away.

'I saw you,' Orrin continued, 'back in Wareington, healing that babe. Don't try to tell me different. You love serving the powers above us, love aiding the people in any way you can.'

Evelyn's fingers tightened on his and she nodded without looking up.

'You've accomplished so much for Palins.' Orrin drew her towards him and wrapped his arms around her. 'I won't be the cause of your expulsion from the Order.' Orrin buried his face in

196

her white hair. 'I'd petition the Archbishop for your hand in marriage, but we both know that fat turd won't—'

Evelyn's head came up, her face open in surprise, her cheeks flushed. She mouthed the word *marriage*.

Orrin nodded. 'Yes, I would marry you if I could. But—'

Evelyn threw her arms around his neck, and kissed him.

Orrin groaned into her mouth, his arms encircled her, and he returned the kiss with a hunger that betrayed his true feelings.

Evelyn threw her head back, and Orrin's mouth trailed wet kisses down her throat. She put her hand out, and gestured. When he lifted his head, words were floating before him, gold and glowing. *Please, beloved. One night. Please.*

Orrin looked into Evelyn's pleading eyes, and knew he was doomed.

Another man, a good man, would walk away. Stride to the window and jump, for that matter. But he couldn't do it, not for the life of him.

'I'd have you in a bower, my lady, where the walls are covered in thick tapestries, with a warm fire and a featherbed covered in rose petals.'

She went up on her toes and kissed the corners of his eyes. The golden words swirled about them, repeating over and over, *Please, beloved. One night. Please.*

Orrin knew he couldn't leave if he wanted to, and in a bitter sweet way he wanted this as much as she did. One night in her arms. Sin or blessing, it was theirs to claim. This one night.

He unclasped his cloak and let it fall to the floor behind him.

Evelyn laughed, that pure, wonderful laugh of joy. The golden words popped in a glitter of dust, drifting down around them.

Orrin reached out to cover her mouth with his fingers. 'Hush, now, or you'll have the entire place at our door.' He hesitated. 'Is this what you truly want, Evelyn? There is so little time before dawn, and I—'

Her blue eyes sparkled. She opened her lips, and nipped at his fingers with her teeth.

He hardened swiftly, his entire body reacting to that touch. Evelyn drew closer, lifting her mouth to his, kissing him sweetly. She took his hand, and guided it to her breast. He ran his thumb over her nipple, a tiny peak under the cotton. She filled his hand perfectly.

His Evelyn, his beloved. For this one night . . . he'd see to her pleasure above all things.

She leaned into him, and he took her weight with ease, letting his mouth explore the soft skin behind her ear. Evelyn shivered, but he knew full well it wasn't the cold. It was the heat that lay between them.

Evelyn stepped back, and reached for his belt, but Orrin caught her hands. He moved back for a moment, breathing hard, looking at her flushed face and half-opened eyes in the firelight.

He knelt before her slowly, never losing eye contact. He reached out, and let his hands trail up the sides of her legs and over her hips, sliding the fabric of her shift to gather at her waist, exposing her.

Evelyn shivered again, reaching out to touch his hair. She shifted her stance, opening herself to him.

Orrin leaned in, and worshipped her with his mouth.

Evelyn cried out at the first gentle stroke of his tongue. Her hips jerked as she pressed his head in close with her hands. Orrin obliged, increasing the pressure, pulling her close, offering her nothing but pleasure.

Her sighs were soft, and Orrin curled his tongue to thrust deeper into her heat. Within a moment Evelyn shuddered, her knees giving way. Orrin reached up, cradled her, and eased her down onto the pile of bedding before the fire.

She lay there, dishevelled and dazed, her shift still pushed up around her hips.

Orrin stood, and looked down at her, pleased with his work. She stirred and smiled at him, then pulled her shift off over her head.

She was glorious, her breasts pale and perfect in the light. No scars marred them, to his relief. Every hair on her body was white, and it all caught the light and reflected it. It paralysed him for a moment, the idea that one such as she would allow him even to touch her with his rough, stained hands, much less . . .

She lifted a hand to him, with a pleading look.

Orrin swallowed hard. 'I've dreamed of you like this. Warm, and wanting me.' He started to remove his belt, lowering it to the floor, careful to leave the sword within reach. 'But in those dreams, you were stretched out on the Great Bed of Wareington.' He stripped off his tunic and threw it to the side. His boots were next and he placed them side by side near his sword. 'Cushioned in velvet and silk,' he whispered.

Evelyn stretched, lifting her arms over her head, pushing her breasts out, their nipples tight pink buds. He took a deep breath, enjoying the sight. 'It was all I could do not to enter your chamber that night.' Orrin stripped off his trous and added them to the pile.

Evelyn's eyes travelled over him and she smiled, clearly pleased. He took another deep breath, trying to maintain a bit of control. He reached down and offered his hand. 'Come to bed, lovely lady.'

She let him help her up and together they took up the comforter. The bed was not large, but they climbed in, skin on skin. Evelyn came into his arms with a sigh, her hair spread over his arm like a sheet of silk. He threw back the comforter so that it pooled at the bottom of the bed. Their shared fire was warmth enough.

He nuzzled her ear and she arched her neck, giving him access to that warm, sensitive skin. His hands started to move, exploring her softness and every curve. Following the line of her neck, he kissed her breasts, taking her nipples gently between his teeth and tugging. Evelyn's soft moans guided him and he listened to her body as he loved her.

Her hands weren't still, either. She reached to wrap her fingers around his length, her soft touch nearly sending him over the edge. But each time, she retreated, letting the passion build between them.

Orrin broke off his kisses for a moment, looking into her eyes. 'Evie, you're not . . . you told me before you aren't a virgin.'

She nodded, her hands on his chest. With a wicked look, she scratched lightly around his nipples.

'I want you to know—'

She arched an eyebrow.

'No, I'm not a virgin,' he said. 'But I want you to know . . . I need you to know . . .' He reached out and brushed her cheek with the back of his hand. 'I've done this before. But never with someone I loved.'

Her eyes lit up and she kissed him, bringing their bodies close together, skin against skin. For a brief moment, he was amazed at the difference it made. So much more than just physical caresses. He felt her love shine through their every move. Then he was lost, wrapped in her arms, no real thought other than their pleasure.

Finally, he was poised above her, trembling and ready, cradled between her hips. He nipped at her lips and she sought his with her own. As they kissed, he entered her moist folds.

Evelyn gasped into his mouth and he froze, trembling at the effort. 'Are you all right?'

She nodded, her eyes bright with tears, and then thrust her hips up. He gasped at the feel. Still he hesitated, uncertain.

Evelyn kissed him and used her hands to urge him on.

He did, slowly, carefully, until he was fully seated within. They both stopped then, their breathing ragged as their bodies fully joined.

'I never knew,' he whispered. 'I love you so much.'

Evelyn laughed in delight and flexed her muscles tight around him. He smiled then, loving her joy, and started a gentle rhythm that she matched. They danced then, on the edge of light, a gentle giving and taking, until they both fell, together, over the edge of forever.

THIRTY-FOUR

He woke to find her head on his shoulder, her hands running over his chest. He closed his eyes, enjoying her touch, content until he felt something wet on his skin.

Evelyn was crying.

He shifted then, careful to keep the bedding over them, and looked into her face. Her eyes were filled with pain and tears, her hands still moving, as if to try to memorise the feel of his skin.

She was trying to do just that.

His throat clenched tight, he leaned close to kiss her, the salt of her tears in his mouth. 'I'm always hurting you, Evie.'

She shook her head, denying his words, but he knew the truth. 'I can take the consequences of my actions,' he said, reaching out to cup her face, stroking his thumb over her cheek. 'But I can't bear your sorrow. I'm so sorry, love. Perhaps it's best that I—'

Evelyn's fingers stilled his mouth, her face filled with pain and anger. She kissed him, an act of comfort. He responded gently, not surprised when the heat began to build between them again.

Evelyn moved, rising above him, letting the blanket fall back off them.

His body responded swiftly, rising to meet her as she impaled herself on him. She leaned down, the tips of her hair brushing his face. He reached then, holding her hips, meeting her sharp movements as she rode him, denying his words, expressing her love. Evelyn was watching his face, waiting, and he willingly surrendered control to her. Just as he climaxed, she bore down on him and bit his shoulder, her teeth piercing the skin claiming him as he pulsed with pleasure.

His eyes half-open, he felt her shudder with her own release before melting back into his arms. He arranged them on the bed, cuddled together, her warm breath on his neck. As he reached for the comforter to cover them, he saw her expression, a mixture of satisfaction and shame. She reached out, her fingers tracing the bite mark.

He brushed her temple with his lips. 'You didn't hurt me. Close your eyes, Evelyn. I just want to lie here and hold you while I can.'

She nodded and drifted off to sleep, her hand on his chest. Orrin lay awake for a long time, listening to her breathe.

A knock at the door brought Evelyn bolt upright in bed. Orrin dived from under the blankets and grabbed for his sword.

'Lady High Priestess, it's Esie.' An older woman spoke at the door. 'The Archbishop wants to see you after the morning Council session. I'll be back in a bit with your breakfast and hot water for bathing.'

Orrin tossed her shift to her and grabbed for his trous. Evelyn scrambled from the bed, pulling the comforter up to cover the evidence of their loving.

Orrin was on the floor, pulling on his boots. 'An entire Church filled with early risers,' he grumbled as he yanked them on. 'There's a real drawback to worshipping a sun god.'

Ignoring him, Evelyn went to the window and opened the shutters carefully. There was no one in the yard.

Orrin stood, pulling on his tunic and gathering up his belt. 'Evie, beloved, I—'

She pulled off her ring and silently offered it to him.

He shook his head and wrapped her in his arms. 'No, love. Too many people would ask how I got it, or ask you where you lost it.'

He paused, listening, then grabbed her hand. 'Listen to me. When we kidnapped you that first time, remember? Evelyn, Elanore told us where you'd be and when. She told me the information came from the Archbishop.'

Her eyes went wide, but then they narrowed. It made sense. How else—

Orrin glanced at the door. 'Please, Evelyn, don't trust him.'

She kissed him desperately then, wanting forever but having only these last few precious minutes. She pulled him to the window, still kissing him, as the sounds increased outside her door.

Orrin broke the kiss, breathing hard. 'Evie, there is a way. A way we could be together.'

She gave him a questioning look.

He looked at her, then looked away. 'I could use my boon to ask for your hand.'

Hope flared in her heart for a moment, but then reality crashed in. She grabbed his arm, shaking her head.

'I know,' he said, looking at her with both defiance and shame. 'I promised my men, all my men, that I'd seek their pardons.' He took her hand and kissed it. 'Honour demands that I fulfil that promise, but honour be damned. I—'

A rattle of the door handle and Orrin was out the window, with barely a rustle of leaves to mark his passing. Evelyn quietly closed the shutters and latched them tight. With a heavy heart she smoothed her hair back and checked the room before turning calmly towards the door.

Orrin took care to keep as silent as he could as he climbed down the tower. The dying leaves trembled and rustled with every move.

It was still dark when he reached the top of the privy. He waited a bit, hanging from the ivy until he was certain it was empty. He stepped onto the roof and grabbed the parcel of armour and gear he'd left there. He swung off the slate tiles, dangled by one hand, then lightly fell to the cobblestones.

'Took you long enough,' a voice said from the shadows. Cenwulf limped out of the darkness. 'It was more than just talk you were doing.'

Orrin frowned. 'You've been in there all night?'

Cenwulf nodded. 'Told everyone I had the gripe. Must have been something I ate.'

'Thank you,' Orrin said.

'Come' – Cenwulf started to limp across the yard – 'I'll let you out the gate. No one back there this time of morning.'

Orrin followed, keeping an eye out for watchers. Cenwulf went to the gate and pulled the bolt.

'Cenwulf, thank you. Watch over her for me, will you?'

'I'll do that,' Cenwulf said. 'But just who am I protecting her from? You, maybe?'

'Don't trust the Archbishop any more than you trust me,' Orrin said.

'That's a given' – Cenwulf pulled the gate open – 'and actually, I might be willing to trust you a bit more.' He looked at Orrin as he scanned the alley. 'Where are you off to now?'

'My men are hiding outside the city, waiting,' Orrin said. 'I've an audience with the Queen this morning.'

'Have a care, until then.' Cenwulf said softly. 'There's those who would kill you on sight and beg forgiveness later.'

'I'll see to my own hide,' Orrin said grimly. 'I've a pardon to claim, and a choice to make.' He slipped through the gate, looking both ways.

'A choice?' Cenwulf asked, but the alley was empty. Orrin was gone.

Cenwulf closed the gate, throwing the bolt firmly in place.

THIRTY-FIVE

Orrin Blackhart had to grit his teeth as he handed his sword and dagger to the guard outside the throne room. His back itched at the idea, but none save her personal guard carried weapons in the Queen's presence.

He strode through the double doors, stalking through the crowd, which melted out of his path. This day's Court was for public petitions and requests, and the hallway was filled with people seeking audiences with the Queen or her advisors. The stares and whispers told him that word had spread of his appearance.

He'd taken care to wear his best this day, everything black, as suited his mood – except for the old red cloak that flared out behind as he moved. Evie's cloak. He wore it to remind himself of her love and her belief in his redemption.

Well, he might be redeemed in her eyes, but that didn't mean he was going to crawl and beg. He'd come to claim three things and he'd leave here with two of them.

But he did try to erase the scowl from his face and replace it with something a bit more pleasant.

The Queen's Herald had indicated that his was the first petition that would be called. Orrin suspected they weren't pleased to see him and wanted him gone as quickly as possible. Certainly that Lady Warder would not want the Scourge of Palins to linger anywhere close to her charge. Orrin had to give her credit for that. And truth be known, he didn't want to tarry any longer than necessary.

He walked into the throne room and admired its size. The last time he'd been in there he'd been more mindful of his chains than of his surroundings. It was impressive, to say the least.

The young Queen had made some changes. Light streamed through high windows. The throne was still in place, with a small table beside it where a pair of red gloves still lay. But they'd added chairs below the throne, apparently for her advisors. They probably appreciated it, especially when some windbag was presenting his case.

If those chairs were also between the Queen and a potential attacker, well so much the better. The Lady Warder Bethral had some sense, it appeared.

The sides of the room were lined with tables crowded with scribes. Orrin raised an eyebrow over that one. Apparently Queen Gloriana actually thought she'd get some work done in these sessions. He wished her well with that.

The Herald and his assistants were circulating through the crowd. Orrin caught the eye of one and was hustled into position as the guards started to enter the room.

The Herald tapped his staff on the floor three times. 'All hail Her Majesty, Gloriana, by the grace of the Lord of Light and the Lady of Laughter, Queen and Chosen of Palins.'

Everyone sank to one knee.

The advisors came in procession first, to stand in front of their chairs. Orrin recognised a few of them, including Ezren Silvertongue and Lord Fael of Summerford, and there were two others whose names he didn't know.

A fat man, clad in gaudy silken robes and leaning on a walking stick, appeared before one of the chairs. He stood there calmly, but Orrin could have sworn he hadn't walked in with the others. He wasn't the Archbishop, that was certain. This man had some intelligence behind his eyes. Besides, something about him reminded Orrin of Evelyn.

As if conscious of his gaze, the man turned his head, and his eyes narrowed as he met Orrin's gaze. A mage . . . with rank . . . was that Evelyn's father?

The Lady Warder also had a chair, the one closest to the throne. The tall blonde wore a sword and a dagger, and he caught her scanning the room for the placement of her guards.

Orrin stiffened at the sight of the Archbishop walking in, puffed with his own importance, two acolytes behind him.

Then came the Queen, with Vembar. The young girl had his arm and walked him to his chair, smiling at something he'd whispered to her. Vembar looked well, for a man of his age, although Orrin could see that the Queen's arm wasn't linked with his just for show.

206

The Queen settled Vembar in his chair and then mounted the dais and stood before her throne. With easy grace she sat, her advisors settling down a moment later as, with a great rustle of cloth, the entire room rose to its feet.

'Good morning,' Queen Gloriana said. 'My Lord Archbishop?'

The fat man struggled out of his chair and rose to address the crowd. 'Let us give thanks. Lord of Light, give us the benefit of your wisdom and guidance this day. Let justice be served on the wicked and the righteous be rewarded for their honour. Let any falsehoods be seen for what they are and truth be our only guide. Lord of Light, bless our Queen and our Kingdom with your holy light. Praise be given.'

'Praise be given,' the crowd responded.

'Lord Herald.' The Queen turned to him with a smile. 'What is the first order of business?'

The Herald stepped forward. 'Orrin Blackhart, late of the Black Hills, step forward and be heard.'

That drew a response from the crowd. A swell of voices rose behind him as Orrin stepped before the throne. His back itched fiercely, but he ignored it and bowed to the Queen.

'Blackhart' – the young girl had a frown on her face – 'I never thought to see you again.'

'Certainly not alive,' Vembar added, his eyes bright with curiosity. The man was leaning forward in his chair. 'What brings you here?'

'My Lord Vembar, you challenged me to rid the Black Hills of the Odium.' Orrin let his voice ring out over the room. 'I have done so, with the aid of the warriors of the Black Hills. I have come to claim my boon as was promised.'

'Pah,' the Archbishop scowled. 'How do we know that what you say is true, scum?'

Orrin fixed the man with a glare. 'As proof, I offer the ring of the late High Baroness Elanore. Also, the sworn statement of one Dorne, High Priest of the Lady of Laughter. Further,' Orrin added dryly, 'gems, from the vault of the Black Keep.'

One of the Herald's assistants came forward to take the items from him and brought them to the Lady Warder. Bethral opened the large leather bag and rummaged in it. She gave the lad a nod and he took the items to the Queen.

She removed the ring and a scroll from the bag and raised an eyebrow as she held up a large emerald to the light. She studied the ring for a moment, then carefully unrolled the scroll and read it over. 'If this is true, you have done a service to the kingdom and I will honour my word.'

The mage spoke up. 'Let me examine the scroll. I know Dorne's hand.'

'Take this to the Lord High Mage.' Queen Gloriana handed the scroll to one of the assistants.

Evelyn's father, then. Orrin flicked a glance over as the man unrolled the parchment and studied it.

'Gems can be stolen,' the Archbishop said, his jowls wobbling. 'This is no proof.'

'Lord Fael, what do you know of this?' the Queen enquired.

'There have been no attacks on my border for weeks,' Lord Fael said grudgingly. 'But that hardly means they are gone.'

'This is Dorne's hand and seal,' Marlon announced.

Orrin frowned at that. Marlon knew Dorne?

'There is a rumour that the Lady High Priestess Evelyn was involved in this,' Ezren Silvertongue spoke up. 'Is that true, Blackhart?'

'It is. Without her aid, we would be dead and your kingdom awash in monsters,' Orrin said.

'Nonsense,' the Archbishop sputtered. 'You kidnapped her from the shrine she was tending—'

'I rescued her, you fat fool, and she aided the people of the Black Hills with her magic,' Orrin growled.

'What is that of my daughter, Eidam?' Marlon asked. 'Let her speak for herself.'

Orrin darted a glance at Evelyn's father. Lord High Mage Marlon's eyes flicked over Orrin and seemed to recognise the red cloak on his back. He raised an eyebrow, but said nothing further.

'She's safe within the church, as you know, doing penance for the sake of her soul's salvation.' The Archbishop glared at Orrin. 'She broke the restrictions placed on her, and I—'

'How so, if this man kidnapped her?' Vembar asked.

The Archbishop shut up.

'It seems to me that we must hear from the Lady High Priestess herself,' Gloriana said. 'Send for her.'

'My Queen—' the Archbishop protested.

208

'Now,' Gloriana said.

For a moment, Orrin thought the Archbishop would refuse the royal command. But finally, with a sullen gesture, he sent one of the acolytes off at a trot.

'We will set this matter aside, Blackhart, until the Lady High Priestess appears.' Gloriana gestured, and Orrin gave a half-bow and stepped back

The Herald called the next matter, something to do with feral pigs roaming the common lands. Orrin listened with half an ear as he waited and watched.

If looks could kill, he was certain that the Archbishop would soon have his head on a pike. The man was clearly angry, his face flushing up.

Evie's father was also giving him the once-over, but there was no anger there. Only a keen interest that made Orrin nervous.

The Queen had moved on to another case. Orrin had to give her credit, she didn't hesitate in her decisions, and she was consulting with her advisors and actually appeared to listen to what they had to say.

A stir in the back of the room brought his head around. Orrin's throat closed when he caught sight of Evelyn, her head down, walking at the side of Priest Dominic.

She was dressed in the formal white robes of a high priestess, a glitter of white and gold. Orrin's heart leaped to see her. Part of him ached to hold her again, if only for a moment.

Dominic and Evelyn approached the throne together and bowed.

'Lady High Priestess Evelyn, we welcome you to our Court.' Gloriana sounded genuinely pleased. 'You are well, Lady?'

Evelyn looked up. She nodded, but said nothing.

Gloriana stared, a puzzled look on her face. 'Aunt Evie?'

'The Lady High Priestess is under a charge of silence as penance, Your Majesty.' Dominic's voice was matter-of-fact. 'She is forbidden to speak.'

Evelyn's father snorted, muttering something under his breath.

'Surely that can be suspended for this interview,' Vembar suggested.

'No,' the Archbishop stated. There was a long silence and he shifted in his chair. 'For the sake of her immortal soul and her vows to this Order.'

Vembar raised an eyebrow. 'She can nod her head?'

The Archbishop puffed out a breath. 'Yes, of course.'

'Lady High Priestess,' Gloriana said, 'Orrin Blackhart is here before us this day, to claim his boon. He claims that he and his men have cleared the Black Hills of the Odium. Were you with him, Lady?'

Evelyn nodded.

'Did you aid him, Lady?' Gloriana asked.

Evelyn nodded again.

'Are the Odium destroyed?'

Evelyn looked at Orrin. It hurt to see the pain in her eyes.

'The Lady High Priestess collapsed from her wounds before the battle ended, Your Majesty,' Orrin growled. 'She cannot say what she did not see. She would not lie to you.'

Evelyn looked at the Queen and nodded.

'You would, you bas—' the Archbishop growled, but the Queen's voice cut him off.

'We do not think so,' Gloriana said. 'We believe you, Orrin Blackhart. We will hold to our pledged word. What boon do you ask of us?'

THIRTY-SIX

Evelyn looked at Orrin, her heart torn in fear.

Orrin stared back at her, his eyes filled with pain and determination. He gave her a slight smile, so weary and tired that she almost cried out.

'Blackhart?' Gloriana spoke again. 'What boon do you ask of the Throne of Palins? Ask and it shall be given.'

'A pardon for the men of the Black Hills, Your Majesty.'

Relief and pride flooded through Evelyn, even as her eyes filled with tears.

Gloriana's eyes widened. 'You surprise me, Blackhart.'

Orrin gave her a wry smile. 'I've cleaned up a mess I helped create, Your Majesty, but only with the aid of the people of the Black Hills. It's only right that they not be punished for the sins of their leaders.'

'So be it,' Gloriana said. 'We shall have it proclaimed throughout the land of Palins as swiftly as may be done.'

'Priest Dominic, escort the Lady High Priestess Evelyn back to her chambers immediately,' the Archbishop directed. 'I will speak with you, Lady, upon my return.'

'My Lord Archbishop.' Orrin lifted a hand to interrupt. 'I ask you, before these witnesses, for the hand of Lady Evelyn in marriage.'

Evelyn jerked her head up, joy filling her heart.

Orrin looked at her solemnly as he continued, 'I have nothing to offer her but my heart.'

'Never!' The Archbishop struggled out of his chair. 'By the rules of our Order she cannot marry without my consent and I will never allow it. For one so perfect to be fouled by one so evil is an abomination.'

Orrin's hands clenched into fists. 'I'm not going to stop petitioning for her hand. I'll never stop.'

'Be damned, then, for you can pound on the door of the

church until your fists bleed. You will never get her. *Never*.' The Archbishop's face flushed, his hand clenched white on his staff.

'My daughter's a grown woman, with a mind and a heart of her own. She's free to make her own decisions,' Marlon said mildly.

Evelyn looked at her father, confused.

'Evelyn,' Orrin said.

She looked at him then. There was a large crowd of people behind him, all still as mice, their eyes glued to what was happening before them. But Evelyn was conscious only of Orrin's eyes, his face weary and resigned.

'Evelyn, my heart is yours, now and forever. Know that I will be the man of honour you expect me to be, now and until my dying day.' Orrin turned. 'Your Majesty.' He bowed, then backed towards the great doors through a silent crowd.

Evelyn's heart sank as she watched him stride away. The Archbishop was settling back in his chair, a smug look on his face. Dominic was next to her. She felt his hand on her elbow, ready to escort her back to the church, to days of prayer and meditation and rules and restrictions. A life she loved . . .

Didn't she?

Evelyn drew in a breath and looked at her father.

He was looking at her as well, but only with concern. No condemnation. Her life, her choice.

Once before, she'd made a choice and she'd chosen the safe way: a life in the priesthood, with its prayers and rules and safety. But now, with all that had happened . . .

She pulled her elbow from Dominic's grasp and straightened, throwing back her shoulders. Her eyes filled with tears and she cried out from the depth of her heart, over the noise and buzz of the crowd, 'Orrin!'

Orrin Blackhart stopped dead at the sound of Evelyn's voice. He turned, uncertain that he'd really heard her.

She was standing, her eyes bright with tears, in the empty space before the throne. Dominic stood next to her, an appalled look on his face. The look of shock was repeated on the faces of the Queen and those around her.

Dominic placed his hand on Evelyn's arm. 'Evie, please,' he said, his voice an anguished whisper. 'Don't do this.'

Evelyn didn't even look at him.

'OUTCAST!' thundered the Archbishop. His voice echoed off the stone walls. 'Outcast and excommunicate, woman. Say one more word and you are—'

Evelyn turned and faced the Archbishop. She reached up and undid the clasp of her white cloak. 'I, Evelyn of Edenrich, can no longer serve in the Order of the Church of the Lord of Light and Lady of Laughter.' She let the cloak fall to the floor. 'I cannot serve when its leader is a selfish, vain man who thinks more of his position and status than of his people.'

The Archbishop's face went white with rage. 'You cannot—'

Evelyn stripped off her heavy white gloves, letting them fall to the floor as he sputtered his outrage. She stepped out of her white and gold slippers and started to unbutton her overdress.

'Evie, don't do this.' Orrin said. His heart was pounding in his chest so hard, he was afraid it would leap out of his chest. 'Not for me. Don't—'

She turned away from the Archbishop and let the dress fall as well, until she stood there in her soft white tunic and underskirt. Her face was radiant, glowing with light. Orrin could not believe the joy that shone in her eyes.

Evelyn stepped over the pile of garments, her bare feet pale against the floor. She tugged off her ring and held it out to him, the white star sapphire blazing with light. 'I, Evelyn of Edenrich, in the eyes of those present and before the Lord and the Lady—'

'Who'll have nothing to do with you, whore,' the Archbishop thundered.

Dominic spun on his heel. 'Shut up, Fat Belly.'

Eidam gasped and sputtered.

Evelyn ignored them all. She took another step forward, holding out the ring. 'Before the Lord and the Lady, I ask you to be my husband and to have me to wife. For the labour of the day and the repose of the night, for the good and the bad, the joy and the sorrow, the light and the darkness within both our souls, Orrin Blackhart.'

He was struck dumb, his heart so full of hope he didn't dare breathe.

'I stand here, empty of hand, bereft of my titles and powers, with nothing to offer but my heart and this simple ring. I ask this of you, woman to man, heart to heart, body to body, soul to soul.'

Evelyn took another step and held out the ring. It trembled in the light, the star shimmering on the white stone. 'Orrin Black-hart, will you have me to wife?'

Orrin stepped towards her. He swallowed hard before he dared speak. 'I, Orrin' – his voice cracked – 'of the Black Hills, take you as wife and ask you to have me as husband. For the labour of the day and the repose of the night, for the good and the bad, the joy and the pain, the light and the—' His throat closed tight. He reached out and took the ring from her hand. 'The blackness of—' He swallowed. 'Evelyn, are you sure?'

She laughed, then, through her tears. 'Oh, yes. Please say yes, beloved.'

He reached out and she stepped into his arms. 'Oh, yes, Evie, yes. Heart to heart, body to body, soul to soul.' He buried his face in her hair. 'I love you so much.'

The entire crowd broke into cheers around them.

'Damned, both of you,' the Archbishop shouted, spitting his words, his face livid. 'Be damned for all eternity.' The crowd went quiet as his words echoed off the vaulted ceiling.

Orrin lifted his head and snarled. He shifted their bodies slightly, so that he was between Evelyn and the Archbishop.

The Court was shocked into silence and Gloriana was pale as a ghost.

'We should leave,' Evelyn whispered.

'Have a care.' Lord Mage Marlon spoke loud enough to be heard over the rant. 'A man your age should not—'

The Archbishop ignored him, lifting his staff and shaking it. 'Damned before the Gods and man. In the name of the Lord of Light and the Lady of Laughter, I curs—'

His words stopped suddenly as his face went white, beads of sweat on his forehead. An odd gurgle came from his throat.

'Your Grace?' Dominic stepped towards him. 'Perhaps you should sit down.'

The Archbishop seemed to collapse in on himself. With a groan, he leaned on the staff and wrapped an arm around his belly. He leaned forward and vomited on the floor.

Dominic danced back to avoid the splatter.

Archbishop Eidam swayed, then dropped to the floor to lie in his own spew. There was a brief moment of deep silence, and then the unconscious man drew a rasping breath.

For a moment, no one moved. 'See to him,' Dominic snapped.

The acolytes rushed over, their faces screwed up in disgust as they tried to pull the unconscious man off the floor.

Evelyn shivered as other guards ran forward to help to at least get the man upright.

Dominic looked at Evelyn.

Orrin felt her hesitate. 'If you want to try to help him, I won't argue,' Orrin said.

She gave him a grateful glance and walked over to where they'd managed to get the Archbishop back in his chair. Avoiding the mess, she stepped close to Dominic. They joined hands and Dominic's voice rang out. *'Hail, gracious Lord of the Sun and Sky, Giver of Light and Grantor of Health, we ask . . .'*

Evelyn bowed her head and closed her eyes. The room fell silent as all eyes focused on the healing.

With a shake of his head, Dominic broke off the words. Holding on to Evelyn's hand, he said something to her.

Evelyn's face was grim and she shook her head, pulling her hand away. She returned to Orrin's side and slid under his arm.

'My Queen,' Dominic said. 'I must return the Archbishop to the church. Quickly.'

'Did it help?' Orrin asked Evelyn quietly as the room filled with talk again.

'No,' she whispered. 'I renounced my vows and the power that goes with them. But the healing didn't flow for Dominic, either. I can't help but think that if he'd collapsed a few moments earlier, we might have been able to heal him.'

'I'd levitate him, but I'd be sure to strain something,' Marlon said over the noise.

'Perhaps a few more men,' Vembar suggested. 'And a cart from the stables.'

'Herald' – Queen Gloriana stood – 'let us clear the room so the Archbishop may be taken care of by his people.'

No one moved until the Herald stepped forward. Then people started filing out, abuzz with the news.

Orrin studied the mass of moving people, frowning. It was a fairly good bet that at least a few of them wanted him dead. His weapons were at the main doors, and though Evelyn still had her battle magics, she wouldn't want to use them here. If he could get her to Cenwulf, through that back alley . . .

Lady Bethral caught his attention.

The tall blonde woman was standing by one of the recessed doors, off to the side, behind the throne. She summoned him with a nod.

Orrin swept Evelyn out of the centre of the frenzy and towards the door as quickly as he could. Bethral held the door open for them, then pulled it closed.

Ezren Silvertongue stood there, a smile on his face. 'Come. I would hear more of this story.'

Orrin stiffened, but Ezren shook his head. 'You are welcome in my chambers, Orrin Blackhart.'

'My men are awaiting word,' Orrin said.

'As simple as sending a messenger,' Ezren responded. 'Come now, while they sort this all out.' His green eyes gleamed. 'Come and tell me everything.' He walked off, gesturing for them to follow.

Orrin leaned down to Evelyn's ear. 'Maybe not everything.'

She blushed and then laughed, a joyous sound.

THIRTY-SEVEN

Ezren Silvertongue's quarters had a fire burning bright and more chairs in one room than Orrin had ever seen.

He also had servants of every age and race. They came at his bidding and disappeared just as quickly at his rasped commands: 'Food and drink and shoes for Lady Evelyn.' He gave her a smile, his green eyes sparkling. 'Cannot have you barefoot, Lady.'

'Just Evelyn now, Ezren,' Evelyn reminded him gently as she sat, tucking her feet under her.

'That is not quite true, Lady,' he reminded her. 'The late King ennobled you as an honour quite separate from your status as a priestess.'

'An honour that fat idiot cannot take away from you, Daughter.' High Mage Marlon strode into the room, looking smug.

'Papa,' Evelyn launched herself out of the chair and into the man's arms. 'Oh, Papa.'

Marlon's arms wrapped around her in a massive hug. 'Evie.'

Ezren looked at Orrin and they stepped to another part of the room, giving Evelyn and her father a little privacy for a quiet conversation.

An older man entered the room, his hat in his hand. Orrin noticed his hands, rough and big-knuckled.

Ezren waved him over. 'This is Hew, one of my men. We need a message taken to Blackhart's men. Bring them here—'

'Not a good idea,' Orrin interrupted.

'Good point.' Ezren thought for a moment. 'The Flying Pig, then. Take them there and install them in rooms for tonight. I will send a message to have everything ready.' Ezren turned to Orrin. 'Where are they?'

'They're outside the city walls,' Orrin said. 'Near the mass graves, in the trees. There's a stand of birch off to the right of the road.'

Hew nodded. 'How shall I know them?'

'Sidian,' Orrin said, 'a big, tall man with black skin and scars all over his face, chest and arms. He'll be there, with three others.'

'How will they know me?' Hew asked.

Orrin took off his cloak. 'Wear this, and tell them the white-haired lady wishes to see them.'

'Easy enough.' Hew took the cloak and wrapped it in his own. 'I'll see it done, Lord Silvertongue.'

Ezren nodded. 'Take two others with you, just in case.'

Hew nodded and went out the door as servants arrived with food and drink. As they left, another group entered, including a young girl with shoulder-length brown hair and a glowing smile. 'Aunt Evie!'

Orrin almost didn't recognise the Queen without her regalia.

Evelyn and Gloriana came together in a hug, crying and laughing and talking all at the same time. Others came in as well: a thin woman with a severe, plain face, her hair pulled back tight, and Vembar, using a walking stick and leaning on Bethral's arm.

'Officially the Queen, upset by the events of the day, has taken to her chambers with a sick headache,' Ezren said softly. 'This is just an informal gathering of friends, to exchange a bit of gossip and laughter. There can be no celebrations when the Arch-bishop's health is in question.'

'Of course,' Orrin murmured.

Ezren moved to join the group by the fire, but Orrin Black-hart eased back from the group, letting the others claim the chairs, watching as Evelyn greeted her friends. He did not begrudge her this reunion, but he was not entirely comfortable.

Once Vembar was settled in a chair, Bethral looked at Orrin with what was clearly a warning. He noted that she had her weapons ready, and he suspected there were more guards outside the door. It wasn't that she thought he was a threat. She was making sure he knew she was protecting her charge. He under-stood, and gave her a nod to make the point.

A glass was held out to him and he was surprised to see the High Mage standing next to him, his own glass in hand. 'It seems you've won my daughter's hand.'

Orrin took the glass, not sure what to say.

'Just want you to know that I don't give two damns about your past. All I care is that you make her happy.' Marlon poured wine into both their glasses and drank deeply from his. 'Ahh,' he said with satisfaction. 'A good wine. Not up to Athelbryght's standards, but good nonetheless.' Marlon held his glass out towards the chatting women. 'Of course, if you don't make her happy, I will fry your balls off.'

Oddly enough, the straightforward threat of bodily harm made Orrin feel more comfortable. 'Of course.' Orrin took a sip of wine.

'So, when can I expect a grandchild?'

Orrin choked.

It seemed to take forever for Evelyn to tell the tale of their adventures, but once that was done, it took far longer to get caught up to date with events in Palins. Orrin had become comfortable enough to sit on the arm of her chair. He was still on edge, but he was very interested in the conversation.

'Edenrich is secure,' Vembar said. 'The citizens and warriors have accepted Gloriana as Chosen and Queen. And the Baronies are cooperating. It's the lands between that are a problem now. Farentell is awash with bandits and thieves. We run the risk of the Black Hills going the same way.'

Gloriana nodded. 'Bethral is leaving tomorrow, taking some of our warriors to Radaback's Rill. She's going to clear out a group of bandits who have been attacking travellers on the main road.'

'It won't take long.' Bethral spoke with quiet confidence. 'The Lord High Mage has offered to open a portal for me and my men. I figure to be back before sunset.'

'What of Athelbryght?' Evelyn asked. 'Have you heard from Josiah?'

They all laughed. Bethral answered. 'Oh, yes. The message was brief. They are together. Josiah claimed he had to sic his goats on Red to catch her.'

Evelyn darted a glance at Orrin, but he didn't seem to have caught the reference.

'But they have made it clear that they are not leaving Athelbryght anytime soon,' Arent added. 'There is too much work to be done there.' She looked down at the mug of kav in her hand. 'As I need to return to Soccia.'

'Arent' – Evelyn leaned forward – 'I couldn't attend Auxter's funeral. I grieve with you.'

'Thank you.' The woman's voice was steady, but Evelyn heard the tightness in her throat. 'I've stayed to help Gloriana, but I must return to my home.'

Gloriana reached over, taking the old woman's hand. 'I wish I could convince you to stay.'

Arent shook her head. 'You'll be fine. You have a good council and warriors to watch over you. Besides, we need to think about the other Cho—' Arent paused. 'The other children as well.'

Vembar cleared his throat and changed the subject. 'What will you do, Evelyn?'

'Couldn't they stay here?' Gloriana leaned forward in her chair.

'No,' Evelyn said firmly, 'I'm sorry, Gloriana, but we can't.' She looked at Orrin, who shrugged.

'My lady wife and I haven't had time to think that through.' He glanced at her thoughtfully. 'I'd like to see my men home again and gather a few things of my own. But after that . . .' Orrin frowned for a moment. 'Sidian, one of my men, had an idea that we'd go travelling, but he wasn't specific.'

'It doesn't matter where we go,' Evelyn said. 'As long as we are together, my lord husband.'

Orrin's face lit from within and he reached over and took her hand.

'Then consider this,' Vembar said. 'So far, we have no one to rule the Black Hills.' He held up a hand to forestall their comments. 'Oh, many have petitioned. But those we trust are needed where they are. And those who petition either aren't trusted or don't have the skills to rule a chicken roost, much less a barony.'

Gloriana spoke up. 'Before this, the Court was focused on Farentell. It's seen as a fruitful and valuable land. The Black Hills were thought of as a dangerous wilderness, filled with Odium and a people with a stubborn streak a mile long.'

'Not far from the truth,' Orrin said.

Vembar sighed. 'Now . . . emeralds big as goose eggs will have everyone and their brother petitioning for the land grant.'

'What of Lord Fael?' Evelyn asked. 'His lands abut the Hills. He could extend—'

'There is no love lost between Fael and the people of the Hills,' Orrin said. 'Even before the death of King Everard, they raided each other. Now, after the fighting, it will be that much worse. Fael would not be welcome.'

'You can't be thinking of Orrin,' Evelyn said. 'The other High Barons would—'

'Actually,' Vembar said, 'I was thinking of you.'

Orrin blinked. 'Evie?'

'Yes,' Vembar said. 'I thought of it as soon as she came back from the Hills. I waited, thinking that she'd recover and we'd discuss it when she returned to court.' He looked at everyone in the room. 'If you think it through, it's almost perfect.'

'Not as the Baroness,' Evelyn objected.

'No,' Vembar acknowledged. 'Given your position in the Church, I thought we could appoint you Guardian or Protector.'

'A temporary baroness?' Marlon chuckled. 'Until such time as you found a suitable candidate.'

'But what about Blackhart?' Gloriana asked. 'He's hated.' She glanced at him, a blush on her cheeks. 'Sorry.'

Evie's fingers clenched around his and Orrin just squeezed her hand in reassurance. 'Don't apologise,' he said to Gloriana. 'It's the truth and you need to take that into consideration.'

Ezren spoke up then, his voice cracking. 'He is naught but a husband and it is not like his heirs would inherit. It is a fine solution for the short term.'

'I don't know,' Evelyn said. 'We would need to consider.'

'And I would need to talk to my men,' Orrin said firmly. 'They have a say in this.' He looked around the room. 'But we leave in the morning. It will be safer.'

'I'll open a portal for you,' Marlon offered. 'I assume Evie's not up to that yet.'

Evelyn smiled ruefully. 'I can only manage the small magics right now.'

'It will return,' Marlon said. 'It takes time to recover from that kind of drain.'

'Very well,' Vembar said, then opened his mouth in a wide yawn. They all chuckled as he scowled. 'That's the hell of getting to my age. You run out of energy just when the party gets going.'

'No parties this night,' Arent said. 'We've talked the day and night away.' She went to Vembar's side. 'It's time for bed.'

'Is that an offer?' Vembar asked slyly.

Arent smiled. 'I could never keep up with a wild man like you, Vembar of Edenrich.'

Evelyn was pleased when they learned that Ezren had taken the liberty of having quarters prepared for them. 'As late as it is, there is no sense in trying to get to the inn where your men are,' Ezren told them. 'It is a small inner room, but has a solid door and a good bolt. Good enough for this night.'

Small by his standards, but larger than her chamber at the church. The bed was good-sized as well, with thick curtains. A fire burned in the hearth and she was glad to see that there was water for washing.

Orrin closed the door and bolted it. He turned and pressed his back to the wood with a sigh.

Evelyn went to the bed and sat on the edge. She watched with a smile as Orrin looked around, then knelt to check under the bed.

'Orrin,' she said.

He checked between the bed curtains and the wall.

'Orrin,' she said.

'I'd feel better if I had my weapons,' Orrin growled. 'But I doubt that would be allowed.'

'Orrin.'

'At least there are no windows,' Orrin answered. He stalked back to the door, to check the bolt. 'I—'

'My lord husband.' Evelyn lowered her voice to a growl.

Orrin's eyes went wide and his head whipped around.

Evie smiled and patted the bed next to her.

As Orrin took a step towards her, a knock interrupted.

Orrin cursed loudly. There was a pause, and a muffled voice spoke. 'May I have a moment?'

'Dominic?' Evelyn asked. She got off the bed and moved to sit on the bench at its foot.

Orrin unbolted the door. The half-elf stood there, still dressed in his formal robes. They were stained around the hem and down the front. The normally immaculate priest looked tired as well. As he walked in, Evelyn caught a whiff of the sick room about him.

Orrin glowered as he closed the door.

'The Archbishop?' Evelyn asked.

Dominic stood straight, for all his weariness. He folded his hands into his sleeves. 'Dying.'

Evelyn covered her mouth with her fingers. 'Dominic, are you certain?'

He nodded, his long black hair falling into his face. He raised a thin hand to put it back behind his ear. 'He can't speak, can't swallow, and seems to be in pain. None of our prayers have brought any healing, so we are using herbs to try to make him comfortable. Either the Gods have decided to call him to their side or—'

'He's offended the Gods themselves.' Evelyn finished his thought.

'Serves him right,' Orrin growled. 'And no, I won't apologise for saying so.'

'I won't ask you to,' Dominic said. 'It's I who should apologise.'

THIRTY-EIGHT

'I owe Evelyn an apology,' Dominic repeated. 'And you an explanation.'

'For what?' Orrin narrowed his eyes. He remembered all too well the look of disdain on the priest's face when he'd taken Evelyn through the portal.

'For making me think you had rejected me,' Evelyn replied, 'after using me to get what you wanted.'

Orrin took two fast steps towards Dominic, his hands forming fists.

Dominic raised his chin, as if to accept the blow.

'Don't, Orrin,' Evelyn said. 'It didn't—'

Orrin's blow hit the snooty elf's nose with a satisfying crunching sound and a spurt of blood. Dominic's head rocked back, but he took it silently. He raised his hands to his face and grimaced at the blood.

Orrin stepped back. 'You deserved that, you bastard.'

'Probably,' Dominic said after a moment. He pulled out a large piece of white cloth and held it to his nose.

'I've never known you to lie, Dominic.' Evelyn's disapproval was clear.

'I was trying to protect you from yourself,' Dominic said, dabbing at his nose.

Orrin growled and took a step forward.

Dominic sighed. 'And from him.' He looked at Evelyn. 'We've known each other for a long time, Evelyn. I don't understand—'

Evelyn gave him a steady look. 'You will, Dominic. When you too find the one you love.'

Dominic looked away. 'Please reconsider your decision. Maybe not as to this man, but as to the Church. Eidam is dying, and a conclave must be called to choose a new archbishop. It will take time to summon the high-ranking clerics of both the Lord and the Lady. You could ask to be reinstated, Evelyn. Regain what you have lost and—'

'Stop,' Evelyn said, her tone firm and resolute. 'I lost nothing. I chose this path for myself, Dominic.'

She looked every inch the regal lady as she sat there. 'How can I serve a church which supported a woman who used Odium? How can I serve a church where status and rank are more important than the needs of the people?'

Evelyn looked down at her hands. 'I was so busy plotting to put the Chosen on the throne that I didn't see what was happening around me.' She lifted her head and gave Dominic a sad smile. 'I cannot deny that I will miss the spiritual aspects. But not the secular ones, Dominic.'

Dominic sighed. 'And I am stuck with the secular problems. Eidam cannot be replaced until he is dead and that may take some time. There is manoeuvring to see who will act in his stead in the meantime and—'

'We wish you luck with that,' Orrin said as he opened the door.

Dominic stiffened, then spun on his heel and headed for the door, the cloth still held to his nose. 'You might do me one courtesy. One of the Lady's high priests was last seen in the Black Hills. If you could get word to him—'

'Dorne?' Evelyn said sharply.

'Yes, that's his name.' Dominic dabbed at his nose. 'The man hates the formal organisational requirements of the Church. But if you could get word to him, convince him to attend . . .'

Orrin gestured out the door, then closed it firmly behind Dominic and bolted it closed. He turned back to look at Evelyn. 'He deserved it,' he said, determined to defend himself.

Evelyn tilted her head. 'Orrin, I love you as you are. I really didn't expect you were going to turn into a nice man because you love me.'

Orrin frowned. 'So, you don't think I'm nice? I can be nice. If I want to be.'

'Really?' Evelyn climbed onto the bed. 'Come show me.'

Orrin growled deep in his throat and managed two steps before there was another knock at the door.

Evelyn fell back on the bed with a groan.

He cursed again, stomping back. 'Who the hells is it?'

'Bethral,' came the reply.

Orrin unbolted the door again and threw it open. Bethral was standing there with Orrin's weapons in her hands. 'I thought you might feel more comfortable with these by your side.'

'Thank you.' Orrin took them gratefully.

Bethral gave Evelyn an amused glance. 'Is there anything you need before you retire?' When they both shook their heads, she gave them a nod. 'Your men will be here in the morning, Blackhart. And High Mage Marlon will be here at midmorning to open a portal for both of us.' Bethral stepped into the hall. 'Sleep well,' she said, arching an eyebrow. 'If you sleep at all.'

Orrin closed the door firmly on her faint chuckle.

'Finally,' he said.

Evelyn watched him as he set his weapons close to the bed and started to disrobe. 'I'm not surprised that Dorne is of such a high rank,' she said. 'His brooch marks him, if his manner does not.'

Orrin frowned as he set aside his chain shirt. 'Are you sure? I never saw him wield any magics.'

'Each of us – of *them* – has different gifts. In some, the power of the Gods flows strongly. In others, not so much, or not at all.' Evelyn crawled off the bed and pulled back the bedding. 'Just as warriors have different skills.'

Orrin stripped down, setting his clothes neatly aside and crawled into bed. Evelyn slipped out of her white clothing and joined him. They met in the centre, to lie in each other's arms, skin to skin.

'I didn't think I'd ever feel this again.' Orrin breathed in her scent as he stroked her soft skin. 'I thought we'd have just that one night.'

'A thousand nights will not be enough,' Evelyn murmured as she kissed him. 'But this night we can take our time. Go slow.'

'Slow might just kill me, love.' Orrin kissed her chin and she lifted her head so that he could plant kisses down the length of her neck and over her chest. 'There's just one thing, before we start.'

Evelyn looked into his eyes.

'Who is the real Red Gloves?'

Evelyn blinked in shock. 'How did you—?'

'Little things.' Orrin rolled onto his back, pulling Evelyn over so that her head rested on his chest. 'But most of all, I can't see Gloriana cutting Elanore's throat. I saw that wound. So tell me, who *is* Red Gloves?'

When they woke, breakfast was brought to their room, along with clothing for Evelyn: a dark blue tunic and trous, with cloak and leather boots. Orrin watched with appreciation as she donned the garments. They made her blue eyes even brighter.

They went to Vembar's chambers and found him finishing his breakfast by the fire. Evelyn accepted the position of Guardian for the Barony of the Black Hills.

Eyes twinkling, Vembar held up a packet of documents, already drawn up and signed, appointing her to the position.

Evelyn shook her head and took the documents from him.

Vembar chuckled. 'Blackhart, your men are in the rear court-yard. Lady Bethral said something about not letting them wander the halls of the castle.'

'Smart woman,' Orrin said under his breath.

'Marlon should be along soon to open the portal. I'll be along with Gloriana to see you off.'

Evelyn led the way to the courtyard. Orrin recognised it once they stepped outside. This was the same courtyard where he'd stood naked in the rain.

His men and their horses were at the far side. They all had idiotic grins on their faces as they spotted Evelyn at his side. He was fairly sure that they'd got word of what had happened. As he started over, he noticed that there were far more horses than they'd brought with them.

Orrin looked at Archer with suspicion. 'Where did the extra horses come from?'

'That's a fine way to greet us,' Archer said. 'Ya well, Lady?'

'I am.' Evelyn smiled at them all. 'And glad to see you all.' She glanced at Sidian. 'It looks like your eyebrows are coming back.'

Sidian laughed.

'The horses?' Orrin growled.

'Remounts,' Archer said, a little too quickly. 'We figured we'd need them for the return trip, what with her coming back with us and all. So we picked up a few.'

'A few?' Orrin looked them over. 'It's a damned herd – with saddles and bridles. Did you buy them?'

Archer's eyes went wide as he looked at something over Orrin's shoulder. 'Lord of Light, look at that horse armour.'

Orrin knew full well he was being diverted, but he looked over his shoulder anyway. Another group of men was gathered on the other side of the courtyard – Lady Bethral's men, no doubt – loading their horses with supplies. One of the horses being led from the stable was a fine, tall mare with the most amazing barding Orrin had ever seen. It matched Lady Bethral's plate, come to think of it. 'It's called "barding", not "horse armour",' he said absently, admiring the sight. But then he had to smile.

Perched on the saddlebags was a barn cat, one of the ugliest he'd ever seen. The creature sat there as if it owned the castle and all the lands around.

'Ain't that something. Never seen anything like that,' Archer breathed.

'Wait until you see her owner.' Orrin nodded in the direction of the castle.

Lady Bethral stood there in the sun, her plate gleaming. Gloriana had come to bid her warriors farewell, and she was under the watchful eye of her guards as she came across the courtyard towards them.

Gloriana gave Evelyn a warm hug. 'All we need now is High Mage Marlon.'

'My father is not known for his promptness.' Evelyn returned the hug.

Bethral had a strange look on her face as she stared at Sidian's scarring. She tilted her head, then asked a question in a language that Orrin didn't understand.

Sidian's eyes widened.

Ezren Silvertongue came out through the doors, looking about. 'Blackhart' – his cracked voice rang over the courtyard – 'About your men and their activities.'

'Uh-oh,' said Reader.

'Told you not to put it on account,' Archer said.

'What did you—?' Orrin turned to them, but cut off his words at the sight of Sidian's face. The black man had gone grey, his eyes wide as he stared at Ezren.

'About these charges.' Ezren came right up to them, a piece of parchment in his hand. 'It seems—' Before he could finish, he stopped with a gasp, as if in pain, clutching at his chest. 'What—?'

Bethral turned to look at him.

Evelyn reached for him. 'Ezren, what's wrong?'

Ezren yanked back on his sleeve, revealing a bracelet . . . no . . . the manacle of a spell chain. Orrin recognised it now, but it looked odd, like dry old bread crumbling off his wrist. But that meant it had absorbed—

A pop, and High Mage Marlon appeared out of nowhere. 'Ready?' he said. 'I can't be all day—'

White-hot flames surged around Ezren, exploding with power.

THIRTY-NINE

Orrin reacted first, pulling Evelyn away from Ezren.

Ezren pressed his hands over his heart, the piece of paper falling from his hands. He stumbled back as the manacles crumbled away. With a cry he collapsed in the centre of the courtyard, barely able to keep his head up. 'No, no, no . . .' he rasped.

With a roar, more light surged up from his chest, a huge column of light and fire that started to spin. A wave of heat and force washed over the courtyard, knocking everyone off their feet and sending the horses into fits.

Orrin scrambled over the cobblestones, reached for Evelyn and covered her body with his own. He blinked hard, trying to see, but there was a roaring wind buffeting his head.

The power had begun to turn, spiralling in on itself with a sound like a thousand running horses. The stones beneath them vibrated with its fury.

Orrin looked behind him. The horses had fled to the farthest corner of the yard, milling in the corner, neighing in terror. His men were all pressed to the cobblestones, with Mage the closest.

'Rogue,' Marlon bellowed. He was on the ground. Bethral had Gloriana stuffed between herself and Marlon. Arent and Vembar were beyond, curled around each other. Marlon was looking at Evelyn.

Evelyn had turned her head and Orrin could feel her nod of agreement to her father.

Ezren had rolled to his side and Orrin saw a flash of his green eyes. White-hot power flared about his body and the sound grew louder. The power lashed out, hitting the area around him. His eyes closed and he started convulsing.

Orrin leaned into Evelyn and spoke into her ear. 'What can we do?' he shouted over the noise.

'Nothing,' she shouted back, 'it's the wild magic. We can't control it, can't channel it—'

The flares were brighter now, painful to the eyes. Mage crawled up beside them, his eyes wide with fear. 'I could try to drain . . .'

'No.' Evelyn shook her head. 'Father is going to have to—'

Orrin lifted his head and realised that Marlon was going to kill Ezren. He was staring at Ezren, reaching out as if to—

Bethral raised up on her knees, reached over and jerked Marlon's arm to the side. 'No!'

Marlon didn't struggle. He just turned to look up at her. 'He'll kill us all.'

Bethral caught Evelyn's gaze, her eyes wide and desperate. 'Open a portal,' she screamed, 'as far distant as you can.'

The wind whipped at their hair and clothes, and the fury of the power grew.

Evelyn's head came up, and Orrin eased back so that she could move. 'You'll be killed,' Evelyn cried out.

Orrin sucked in a breath as Bethral's face grew calm and determined. 'As far, as remote as you can,' Bethral yelled again. She released Marlon's hand and looked at the white-hot flares where Ezren lay sprawled on the ground, her face etched with pain. 'Where he'll not kill anyone else.'

Marlon nodded to Evelyn.

Gloriana lifted her head. 'Bethral, no, no. Don't leave me!'

Bethral ignored her and rose to her feet, fighting the winds. Marlon reached out and wrapped his arms around Gloriana, keeping her down. He was talking, but she was protesting, struggling against him.

Evelyn reached her hand out to Mage and they both turned to face the fury rising around Ezren.

Orrin knew that Evelyn was still drained from their battle with Elanore; Mage was going to lend her his strength. He looked around at his men as he crawled forward to try to protect Evelyn and Mage. 'Everyone stay down.'

Just in time. The power lashed out, striking cobblestones with white shards of lightning, as if the magic sensed a threat.

A portal appeared behind the fury, its soft curtains a contrast to the chaos around them. It wavered, then solidified. Mage and Evelyn's hands were locked tight together, knuckles white.

Bethral fought her way forward through the waves of raging power around Ezren. The flares danced around her, striking her again and again. She took the blows, staggering as she lifted the unconscious man into her arms, heaving him over her shoulder.

The winds grew wilder still, their roaring almost a scream in Orrin's ears. His eyes watered as he watched Bethral try to walk into the portal. She had her head down, her feet braced, but when she tried to step forward, she staggered, almost falling.

Orrin looked away to clear his eyes, then looked back.

Her horse was there.

The roan mare was by her mistress, standing firm. Her mane and tail were caught with the wind, whipping around. The cat was on all fours, claws hooked in the saddlebags, every inch of fur standing on end, mouth open in what had to be a hiss of defiance.

Orrin could have sworn that Bethral leaped into the saddle with Ezren, so fast did she mount. One minute she was on the ground, the next in the saddle with Ezren before her.

The light, the wild magic surged around them and Ezren's entire body convulsed in Bethral's arms. She struggled to keep her hold. Orrin saw her lean forward, crying out something and digging her heels into the horse, urging her forward.

The horse gathered her hind legs and started to obey.

The raging fury lashed out, striking both at the portal and at Evelyn and Mage. A thick strand of impossibly bright white whipped out. Orrin saw it coming and pulled himself up and over their heads, trying to—

Sidian stepped in front of them.

The big black man was naked from the waist up. He stood, arms wide, shouting something that Orrin didn't understand.

The white strand struck his chest at the same moment it hit the portal.

The force threw Sidian off his feet. Like a cloth doll, he was hurled over them and slammed to the ground.

The portal exploded as Bethral, Ezren and the horse disappeared. Blinded, Orrin froze as a hot, biting wind blew over his face, bearing the impression of open skies and the scent of endless grasslands.

Then silence.

The blindness passed. They were all left blinking, staring at the courtyard.

Empty.

'What was that?' Mage asked in a hushed voice. 'What just happened here?'

'Where did they go?' Gloriana asked, her face streaked with tears. Marlon helped her to her feet.

'I don't know,' Evelyn said. She sounded exhausted. Orrin helped her stand. 'I focused on the shrine I was exiled to, the one in Farentell, but it shifted. I don't know where they ended up, if anywhere at all.' She looked at her father. 'They might be dead.'

'Wild magic and a portal.' Marlon shook his head. 'They are surely dead. Wild magic is lethal when built to those levels.'

Archer and Reader were pulling Sidian to his feet. He came up with a grunt, his chest unharmed and unmarked. 'I do not think they are dead,' he said.

'And how would you know?' Marlon looked at him with scorn. 'Are you a mage?'

'No.' Sidian shook his head. 'I am a warrior-priest of the Plains.'

FORTY

'The Plains,' Evelyn repeated, tired and drained and feeling stupid. The words didn't seem to make any sense. Thankfully, everyone around her had the same stunned expression on their faces.

'Yes,' Sidian replied, 'one of many sent to wander the world, searching for that which was lost.'

'What was lost?' Mage asked.

'That which is now found,' Sidian said, his face etched with worry. 'Or so I believe. I must now return to the Plains, to bring word of this. But the way is a long one, and who knows what will have happened before I can reach the Heart?'

Evelyn frowned, confused. She was full of questions, but a wave of exhaustion swept over her. She swayed, and Orrin's arm wrapped around her waist. She leaned her head on his shoulder, grateful for the support.

'I thought people on the Plains had weird names,' Reader said.

They all looked at him. 'And yours is so normal?' Archer asked.

'Obsidian Blade,' Sidian said, 'that is my full name.'

Orrin frowned. 'There is no route to the Plains through the mountains. At least, not from the Black Hills.'

'Yes, there is.' Sidian's confidence was clear. 'Not much more than a gurtle path, but a path nonetheless. I will show you, if you will come.'

'I will,' Mage piped up.

Orrin glanced at Evelyn. 'We shall see.'

'They're gone?' Gloriana asked as she stood. Her cheek was smudged with dirt and her eyes looked lost. 'Can't we try to find them?'

'No,' Evelyn said. 'The wild magic ripped the portal away. I have no idea where they are.'

'What will I do without them?' The confident Queen was

gone. Evelyn again saw the uncertain child standing before her. 'Aunt Evie, do you have to go?' Gloriana asked. 'I've lost Bethral and Ezren and I—'

Evelyn found the strength to reach out and hug her. 'We can't stay, Gloriana. It would cause you more problems than it would be worth. I can come back for quick visits, but not much more.'

'We are still here, child.' Two of the guardsmen were helping Vembar and Arent to their feet. 'Arent and I won't leave you.'

Gloriana ran over to them and wrapped Vembar in a hug. He staggered a bit, but held on just as tight.

'Do you still want to send this force after the bandits?' Marlon nodded at the warriors milling about.

'Bandits?' Archer asked, raising an eyebrow.

'About twenty men, raiding along the road?' Reader enquired.

'Yes.' Gloriana raised her head. 'They are causing problems on the main road between here and Radaback's Rill.'

'No worries there, Your Ladyship,' Reader said.

'Your Majesty,' Marlon corrected.

'Your Majesty.' Reader gave a quick nod of his head. 'We had a bit of time on our hands, you see.'

'And they took homage to us, being from the Black Hills and all,' Archer said.

'Umbrage,' Evelyn murmured.

'Well, Mage here had to open his mouth and—'

'Your Majesty' – one of the guards approached – 'Lady Bethral . . . Is she—?'

Gloriana drew a breath, stepped back from Vembar and straightened her shoulders. 'Tell the men to stand down, Hakes. We need to deal with her absence before we do anything else. It might be awhile before she can return.' She gave Evelyn a nod, then turned to go.

'If ever,' Marlon said as Gloriana crossed the courtyard with Vembar, Arent and her guards.

'I wish I could help her,' Evelyn said. 'She's so alone.'

Marlon snorted. 'You can't, daughter.' He turned and glared at Mage. 'You, what is your name?'

Mage froze. 'Lord High Mage, I'm . . .'

'Come, lad,' Marlon huffed impatiently, 'you've a pardon. What is your name?'

'Rhys, sir.' Mage straightened his shoulders. 'Rhys of the Black Hills.'

'Rhys, eh?' Marlon said. 'You'd be welcome to the Guild for extra training, if you wish. Although I suspect you could teach us a thing or two as well. Think on it.' Marlon turned back to Evelyn. 'Let's open a portal and get you and these men out of here before the entire place comes down, shall we? The question is – where? I can send you to the keep, but—'

Evelyn shuddered. 'Please, no, Father.' She leaned her head on Orrin's shoulder.

'Understandable,' Marlon said. 'What about . . . There is a town I remember, with an inn. Have you ever heard of the Great Bed of Wareington?'

Archer was the first one through the portal, leading a string of horses. It opened up in Wareington's town square, just as the old mage had said it would. Men were coming at a run, weapons in hand, but they relaxed when they recognised him.

'Hey, take these horses, and there's more coming,' Archer said. He handed off the leading rein and grabbed a horn from one of the watch. He sounded it once, a long, clear call.

Mage came through, with more horses.

People were coming at a run now, and windows were being opened in every house. Archer looked up in pleasure at the sight. 'Gather around, call everyone together. Blackhart's got our pardons—'

More people came running, and Archer couldn't help but grin at their stunned faces. 'He's got our pardons—'

Dorne and Bella popped out of the inn's doors. 'What's that?' Dorne demanded.

Sidian came through the portal, leading another group of horses. Archer had to yell to be heard. 'Blackhart's got our pardons, and he's got his lady—'

Cheers rose as others gathered. These horses were led off as well, as soon as they emerged. People were leaning out the windows, hanging on every word.

'He's got his lady, and the Queen has named her our Baroness!' Archer yelled, and though it wasn't quite true, damned if he was gonna explain the whole Guardian thing. That was

Blackhart's problem. Never let truth get in the way of a really good gossip.

Another round of cheers filled the air as Reader came through, his string of horses rearing at the noise. It took some effort to get them all headed in the right direction, but everyone reached out to calm them and get them out of the square.

'And . . .' Archer bellowed, raising his hands for silence.

The crowd quieted, holding its breath, expectant.

'They went and got married,' Archer announced just as Blackhart and Evelyn walked through the portal and it disappeared behind them.

The crowd roared then, startling Blackhart. He looked around, focused on Archer and glared.

Archer just grinned.

Dorne and Bella walked forward to greet the happy couple. 'Congratulations!' Dorne was all smiles. 'This calls for a celebration. A dance tonight, here in the square. Let everyone gather at sunset!'

That set them to cheering. Archer grinned happily as those closest pounded him on the back.

There were those who wanted to speak to them, but Orrin held them off, working their way through the crowd. 'My lady wife is still recovering and needs to rest before tonight's celebration. Tomorrow we can speak of all that needs to be done.'

No one demurred, and he swept Evelyn up into his arms and carried her into the inn and up the stairs. Bella was at the door to the room, smiling at both of them. 'There's a fire laid and ready. Give me a moment and I'll bring some fresh bread and butter and hot kav.'

Evelyn yawned, then blinked at her. 'I'm more tired than hungry, Bella.'

'Then I won't be bothering you. Crawl in and get some sleep. I'll wake you just before supper.' Bella started to pull the door closed behind her, then hesitated. 'Maybe you could look in on the little ones before the dance. One's fussing and we've run out of our own remedies.'

Evelyn opened her mouth, but Bella was gone before she could speak.

She gave Orrin a stricken look. 'They don't know.'

'We'll explain later,' Orrin said as he set her on her feet.

Evelyn sighed and released the clasp of her cloak. 'Just that little bit of magic and I feel like I could sleep for a week.'

'That little bit of magic was damned impressive.' Orrin took her cloak and set it aside. She sat on the edge of the bed and he pulled off her slippers. 'We'd have been killed, but for you.'

'Mage helped,' Evelyn insisted. She stood long enough to skim out of her trous. Watching her took Orrin's breath away.

Evelyn left her trous in a heap on the floor and started to pull back the bedding. Orrin reached for them and started to fold them on the chair.

Evelyn took off her tunic and crawled into the bed with a sigh of pure contentment. She shifted to the centre of the huge mattress, then pulled the bedding up over her shoulders, relaxing into the softness. She smiled drowsily at Orrin and patted the bed next to her. 'Join me?'

Orrin wasted no time stripping down, but he left his trous on before climbing into bed. He settled next to Evelyn and she curled against him, head on his chest. 'You feel so good,' she whispered as her hand slid lower under the blankets.

'Rest, Evelyn,' Orrin said firmly, catching her hand before it could move lower.

'Awww,' Evelyn said, but it was ruined by a yawn. 'When we wake?'

'We'll see.' Orrin paused. 'Evelyn . . . have you thought . . . about . . .'

'About what?' she asked.

'About children,' he said, his voice cracking. He cleared his throat. 'We haven't taken any precautions.'

She lifted her head to look at him, worrying her lip with her teeth. 'I didn't think. I used to be able to regulate my courses with the healing magics, but now . . .' She settled her head back down. 'I'm fine until the end of this month, love. After that . . .'

'We should think about it,' Orrin said.

Evelyn's head came up again, her gaze sharper. 'What's wrong? You sound worried.'

'We can talk later, love.' Orrin stroked her cheek with his knuckles. 'Sleep now.'

Evelyn nodded and with a soft snort she drifted off to sleep.

It took him a while longer.

Evelyn woke first. The room was warm, the bed warmer still, and she felt so comfortable. Orrin had shifted to face her at some point, lying on his side. He looked younger when sleeping, relaxed and free of care. She smiled, a silent thrill running through her. She'd spend her days with this man, seeing him in all lights, in all moods, learning, loving. She closed her eyes and gave a quiet prayer of thanks to the Lord of Light and the Lady of Laughter. Especially the Lady, for the gift of this man.

But then her stomach grumbled. She caught a faint whiff of baking bread from the kitchen below.

She slipped out of the bedding and pulled on the tunic and trous. She opened the door quietly and walked down the back stairs that went directly to the kitchens.

Dorne was there, kneading dough, and the brick ovens behind him glowed with heat. He gestured to one of the stools and with a quick gesture served up a slice of warm bread, a crock of butter and hot kav.

Evelyn smiled her thanks and spread the butter thick, taking a sip of kav while waiting for it to melt. Then she took a big bite and closed her eyes at the wonderful yeasty taste.

Dorne didn't speak but let her eat as he kneaded and shaped the loaves into round mounds, then covered them with cloths to let them rise. He refilled her mug and cut another slice of bread to put on her platter.

The faint sound of music came through the walls. Evelyn gave Dorne a questioning look, and he grimaced. 'Everyone's excited about the news, and all and sundry who think they can toot a pipe or bang a drum can and will, tonight. There's those who are good at it and those who aren't, and we'll have to endure them all, more than like.'

'After so much sorrow, it's good to see joy.'

'And relief,' Dorne added. 'They're just as pleased that you are Baroness.'

Evelyn shook her head. 'No, I'm just the temporary Guardian for the Black Hills, until Gloriana can find someone she can trust to be the new Baron.'

Dorne rolled his eyes. 'That's not what Archer announced. And good luck explaining that to an excited crowd.'

'He didn't tell them that I am no longer a priestess,' Evelyn said. 'I'm going to have to tell them that as well.'

Dorne gave her a sharp look. 'Oh?'

Evelyn sighed, pushing a strand of her hair behind her ear. 'I renounced the priesthood before Queen Gloriana and the entire Court. The Archbishop excommunicated me just before he collapsed.'

'Fat bastard keeled over in his own spew.' Orrin walked into the room, a grim look on his face. 'Served him right.' He pulled a stool over and sat close to Evelyn. She smiled at him; his hair was slightly ruffled from their nap.

'I warned Eidam that he was headed for trouble.' Dorne covered the last of the bread. 'The man was fixated on the glory of the Lord and reducing the influence of the Lady and her priesthood. I warned him about the spiced wine too, but he wouldn't listen.' Dorne started to slice more bread.

'Priest Dominic asked us to tell you that he would summon a conclave as soon as Eidam dies,' Evelyn said.

'Oh, joy,' Dorne snorted as he took poured kav for Orrin. 'Long, tedious hours of discussion as various idiots manoeuvre for position.' Dorne stopped to consider. 'I think I'll walk to Edenrich.'

Evelyn fought a grin. 'It would take months to walk to Edenrich.'

'Wouldn't it?' Dorne had a very smug look on his face. 'More's the pity. But there's not a horse to spare for an old country priest.'

'Never mind the twenty or so my men looted.' Orrin said.

'You keep silent – they're needed for ploughing—'

'We could spare—' Orrin started.

'Ploughing, or such other tasks as need doing.' Dorne repeated firmly.

Evelyn laughed. 'Besides, who will care for the spiritual needs of your charges while you're gone, High Priest Dorne?'

Dorne locked eyes with her. 'Why, you, Lady High Priestess.' He reached under his floury apron, then pushed something across the table to her.

It was a silver brooch, a half-moon set around with several silver stars.

FORTY-ONE

Orrin frowned as Evelyn's mouth dropped open. 'But . . . I renounced my vows.'

'No,' Dorne said, 'you renounced a corrupt Church, Evelyn, not the Lord or the Lady. Think back on what you said.'

Orrin scowled at him. 'How would you know what she said?'

Dorne rolled his eyes. 'Don't be stupid.'

'I left the priesthood. I . . .' Evelyn's voice wavered as she stared at the brooch.

'You are a priestess,' Dorne said, 'if you want to be.' He straightened, starting to gather up the bowls. 'Those who serve the Light see to the order of our lives. They maintain the churches and shrines, administer the sacraments, teach the young, keep the hours and see to the business of the faith.'

'Yes, but—'

'Those who follow the Laughter wander the Kingdom, seeking out the work that needs to be done, bringing the sacraments to those who need them, caring more for the people than the structures. We are the ears and the eyes of the Lord and the Lady. There is less order, less restriction on us.'

'You wear black,' Orrin said, his mouth dry.

'Damn sight easier to keep clean than white.' Dorne snorted. 'But you can wear stripes for all that anyone cares.' He looked at Evelyn. 'The Lord and the Lady aren't done with you, Evelyn of Edenrich. Nor you, Orrin of the Black Hills. Serve the Lady, both of you. Go among the people and do Her work. No glory. No riches. Wandering and labour is our way and our calling.' Dorne smiled. 'There's plenty that needs doing.'

Orrin watched as Evelyn looked up, her eyes bright with tears. 'I'm still—'

'Ask your heart, if you doubt me,' Dorne said gently. 'Better yet, ask the Gods.'

Evelyn turned to look at Orrin.

'What does your heart tell you, Evie?' he asked.

She reached out and closed her trembling fingers over the brooch, bringing it to her breast. Then she closed her eyes, and her lips moved silently as she prayed.

Orrin held his breath, waiting.

She opened her eyes, her face aglow. 'Oh, Orrin, I—' She reached out her hand. 'Come with me!'

'Save me a dance tonight,' Dorne called as they left the kitchen.

Evelyn pulled Orrin up the back stairs, almost running all the way to the nursery in the attic. She pushed open the door.

Bella looked up, her face brightening with a smile. In her arms was a fussing babe, arms and legs waving in the air.

Evelyn walked over to her, leaving Orrin in the shadows by the door. She took the child and went to the stool in the corner, by the fireplace. She sat, cooing at the babe, whose wails made it clear he wanted nothing to do with any comfort she might offer.

Orrin watched as she closed her eyes and started to pray.

The glow was soft, and hard to see in the firelight, but it was there. Surrounding the babe, reflecting in Evelyn's face, the power of the Gods flowed through her hands. The babe kicked again, its little legs beating on Evie's stomach as it started to coo and laugh.

Orrin felt something ease in his chest as his lady looked up and smiled at him through her tears.

Archer thought it was a damn fine party, all things considered. Of course, a couple of bottles of mead put a glow on anything. He burped, and tried to remember how many bottles he'd actually had.

He was sprawled on one of the hay bales that had been set around the Wareington town square. The music was in full swing, with a small group banging out a tune and some others singing at the tops of their lungs. Sounded just fine to him.

He suspected the mead helped with that, too.

Nice to see everyone getting along, relaxing. Been too long since he'd relaxed. He lolled back against the hay and took another swig.

Of course, Orrin wasn't relaxing. Wasn't drinking, either. One minute he was checking the watch; the next doting on his lady.

Made Archer smile to see it. He looked around, to see if he could spot them.

Most of the night, Evelyn had been surrounded, talking to the people of the town, getting to know them better. A few had asked for healing, and she'd obliged, going off to see to them. But she and Blackhart had managed a few dances.

Mage was not far off, surrounded by a group of young girls, all laughing and admiring him as he sat gesturing and talking. From the looks of a few of his admirers, the boy was going to get himself some tonight. Archer grinned and gave him a salute with his bottle.

Sidian was trying to figure out how to dance with a partner. The big man had earlier stripped down to show them some dancing from the Plains and had just about everyone's eyes popping out of their heads. But he claimed he'd never danced a simple reel with a woman in his arms before. Archer suspected that he'd learned faster than he'd let on, but all the women were having great fun trying to teach him, so the big black man wasn't about to tell them.

Obsidian Blade. Odd kinda name. Of course, that was the pot talking to the kettle, wasn't it? Who was he to point a finger?

Archer burped and scratched his stomach. Of course, there was the pardon. They could go back to their own names, couldn't they? Except he'd been Archer so long, there was no sense changing. He'd have to think on that awhile. Once he was sober.

Reader was dancing a reel with a chubby woman in his arms, with kinda the same expression on his face as when the Baroness tortured him. Poor guy, probably too polite to run away. Archer wished Reader luck with that. The lady looked determined.

He looked around for Thomas and Timothy, before he remembered. That hurt. Those boys had been good friends. Archer lifted his bottle to the starry sky, then drained it dry.

He caught a glimpse of Dorne and Bella whirling around the dance floor, smiling and laughing. Other townsfolk were there as well, scattered around the square. People were coming and going and there was a lot of talk and laughter in the air. He could feel the relief and the absence of fear, in everyone. Made him smile to think he was part of the reason for it. And that Thomas and Timothy had not given their lives in vain.

Archer yawned and scratched his extended stomach. He'd

eaten too damn much, which felt good. He'd drunk too much too, but that was fine. He looked at his empty bottle with regret, but it was time for him to head to bed.

It had been a good night. He'd danced with some of the young bucks in town and flirted with them, but for some reason, no one had really appealed. Archer slumped down on the hay bale. Maybe it was seeing Blackhart and Evelyn together that made him envious. Not that he had any interest in Blackhart as a mate. Gods above, the man had a foul temper.

But those two shone with more than just their physical attractions. Archer envied them that. Kinda put a man off a casual fling in the dark. Maybe it was supposed to mean more than that.

Maybe he was drunk.

Archer set his bottle down and thought about standing up, then thought better of it. He was warm, the straw was comfortable, the stars were wheeling overhead. Maybe he'd just lie here for a while and—

Blackhart's face loomed into sight, blocking the stars. He looked grim and frowning. 'Have you seen Evie?'

Archer went from drunk to stone cold sober in an instant as a thin thread of chill went down his spine. He sat up. 'You ain't seen her?'

Blackhart was scanning the crowd. He shook his head. 'I went to release some of the watch and came back. We were going to dance again, then go back to the inn and—' Blackhart stopped.

Archer got to his feet. 'She might have missed the dance, but I doubt she'd have skipped the "and" without telling you why. I'll get the others and we'll find her.'

They searched for an hour before they found the note on the Great Bed.

'Should've looked here first,' Archer said. He glanced at the silent man next to him. Blackhart's face was a mask as he stared at the note. 'What're you gonna do?'

'Exactly what they tell me to.'

Outside the slaughterhouse, Orrin removed his boots, feeling the cool stones of the street beneath his feet. He tossed them on the pile with the rest of his gear.

'Don't like this,' Archer growled from behind him.

Orrin turned to look at his men, clustered in the street. 'Once she's clear, you get her out of here. Understood?'

Four grim faces met his eye; none looked away. 'Any reason we don't just rush in and take her back?' Reader asked, testing the edge of his dagger with his thumb.

'I won't risk her. We do it their way.' Orrin stripped off his tunic. 'It's a fair trade. A life for a life.'

'Yours for hers,' Sidian observed. 'I'm not sure she will agree.'

'Do I have your word? All of you?' Orrin demanded. 'Or shall I just fall on my sword here and let you trade my body?'

Four grim looks, then four nods.

'Well, then.' Orrin turned and put his hands behind his back.

Archer bound them with a length of rope.

Sidian pulled open the door, and Orrin slid into the darkness. The building felt big, echoing. Orrin took a few cautious steps, then stopped. 'I'm here.'

There was a click, and a lantern flared. Orrin blinked at the light, then his heart stopped in his breast.

Evelyn was tied to a chair in the centre of the room, gagged and blindfolded. He could see spell chains binding her wrists and cursed himself for not having all of those things destroyed. 'Evie?'

She cried out through the gag, but her words were indistinct. Orrin scanned the darkness beyond, sensing the presence of someone else. He moved forward into the light. 'I'm here, no weapons, no armour. Let her go.'

A man stepped forward then, directly behind Evelyn, a dagger in his hand. It took a minute, but Orrin recognised him. 'Torren, isn't it? You served in the kitchen at the inn.'

'Torren of Farentell,' the man said. 'I toted your water and chopped your wood and waited for my chance.' His hand tightened on the handle of the dagger.

'Did you hurt her?' Orrin asked, staring at Evie.

Evelyn shook her head and struggled against the ropes.

'No,' Torren said. 'Got no complaint against her. It's you I'll see dead.'

'I'm yours,' Orrin said. 'Release her.'

'You bring any men? Any weapons?'

'My men are outside,' Orrin said. 'But only to see her safe. I give you my word.'

'Like that's any good,' Torren scoffed. 'Kneel.'

Orrin got down on his knees.

Torren watched him for a moment, then pulled the blindfold off Evelyn. Her hair was in her eyes and she had to toss her head back to see. Orrin watched as the anger in her eyes faded to fear at the sight of him, helpless, on his knees.

Torren loosened the gag and pulled it gently away from her mouth. 'I'm going to cut you loose, Priestess. You need to leave.'

'No, no.' Evelyn staggered forward as the ropes fell away, throwing herself at Orrin, on her knees beside him. 'Orrin, you can't let him—'

Orrin leaned into her arms, breathing in the scent of her hair for the last time. 'Archer's just outside,' he whispered. 'He'll know what to do.'

Evelyn cast a terrified glance at Torren, then ran for the door, her wrists still bound in the spell chains. She banged through the door, calling Archer's name. The door swung shut behind her.

'So much for your word.' Torren stepped forward, his hand clenching on the hilt of the dagger.

From outside, Evelyn screamed in anger and disbelief. 'Let me go, let me go!'

'I kept my word,' Orrin said. 'They won't interfere. They won't let her interfere, either.'

Torren just looked at him.

'Kill me,' Orrin said.

Torren hesitated. 'I don't—'

'Do it,' Orrin said. 'I may not be so lucky next time.' He sat back on his heels and shook his head. 'I love that woman, but all it takes is the mention of a fevered child or, Gods help me, a plague and off she goes with no care for her own skin. The next man to take revenge on me might just kill her outright.'

Evelyn was crying now, calling out, begging Torren not to kill him. Orrin's heart clutched in his chest. 'Thank you for not harming her.'

'I couldn't. She's done nothing to—' Torren took a step towards Orrin. 'You, on the other hand – you I can kill.'

'Not easy, to kill a man in cold blood.'

'I've slaughtered many a pig,' Torren said. 'That's all you are. A pig that needs putting down.'

Orrin closed his eyes and exposed his neck. He felt the man move closer and then there was a long moment of silence.

'Lord of Light,' Torren breathed, 'how you must love her.'

Orrin grimaced, then nodded, still keeping his eyes closed tight. 'I do. I believe the Lady of Laughter now has her revenge, for now I know the loss that all suffered at my hands. That woman is my hostage to fortune, my love and my life. I'd rather die here and now than risk her further.' Orrin's voice cracked. 'And what terrifies me even more is the idea that we might have children. That they would suffer for my past sins leaves me cold and terrified.'

'You have the forgiveness of the Queen and of the Gods, and that's not right.' Torren's voice was the barest of whispers as he stepped next to Orrin. He could feel the heat of the man's body against his bare arm. Fingers wound through his hair and pulled his head back, exposing his throat yet again. Cold steel pressed to his neck.

'I may have their pardon' – Orrin opened his eyes and he looked up at Torren – 'but I don't know that I will ever forgive myself for what I have done.'

Evelyn was weeping now. They could hear her though the walls.

Orrin closed his eyes and waited.

FORTY-TWO

There was a long pause. Orrin swallowed hard.

'She's in pain,' Torren whispered as Evelyn cried out again.

She was struggling as well. Orrin could hear the thud of flesh on flesh. She was fighting to get back to his side as she cried out his name.

Torren sighed. The cold metal of his knife fell away from Orrin's neck. 'I won't do to her what you did to me.' He moved away. 'I thought that killing you would . . . may the Gods forgive me.'

'I'm sorry.' Orrin stayed on his knees.

Torren glared at him. 'Don't think I've forgiven you. I can't do that, either.'

'Don't.' Orrin stood. 'Hold me accountable. Don't let me forget. I'm not asking for forgiveness. But . . .' Orrin looked over his shoulder. 'Don't let anyone else harm her. Because there will be others.'

Torren shook his head. 'I can't stay here. Can't watch the two of you—' His face filled with pain. 'Get up.'

Orrin got to his feet, the rope cutting into his wrists as he rose. 'Where will you go?'

Torren sliced through the ropes and stepped back into the shadows. 'I don't know. I was so intent on hating you, I hadn't given any thought to . . .' His voice trailed off. 'Go. See to your lady.'

For someone so small, she sure fought dirty. Archer had to admire when Evelyn's foot caught Mage under the chin and sent him sprawling.

Archer was hanging onto one arm. Reader had the other. If they could just get her off her feet, they'd be able to carry—

Evelyn stomped down on his foot as she cried out. 'Help him, damn it. Orrin! ORRIN!'

'You could help,' Archer growled at Sidian, who stood there, his arms crossed over his chest.

'No,' Sidian said, 'I promised not to attempt a rescue, but this is absurd.'

'You get her feet,' Reader said.

'Four of you and you can't subdue one priestess?' Orrin's voice came from behind. 'You're losing your touch.'

Evelyn jerked her head around. 'Orrin!'

Archer released her with a sigh of relief and watched as she ran to Blackhart. 'Are you all right?' Evelyn asked.

'Where's the bastard?' Archer demanded.

'Gone,' Orrin said. He stood for a moment as Evelyn ran frantic hands over his bare chest. He reached out and hugged her close. 'He didn't harm me.'

'Well, that's nice an all,' Reader said, 'but—'

'Let him go,' Blackhart commanded. 'I can't blame him for lashing out at me.' He hugged Evelyn closer, tucking her head under his chin. 'Besides, we should pardon him, as we were pardoned.'

Archer wrinkled his nose and exchanged glances with the others. 'Well, there's pardoned and then there's pardoned. If you get my drift.'

Blackhart gave him a glare. 'I don't. But I'm serious. Let him go.' He drew in a deep breath. 'I just want to get back to the inn and go to bed.'

Evelyn stepped back from his arms and for the first time Archer realised that her face was stony with rage. 'Reader, get me out of these chains.'

'You're not going to hurt us, are you?' Reader cast a frantic look at Archer, who took a prudent step back. 'We was just trying to protect—'

'Evelyn' – Orrin rubbed the chafe marks on his wrists – 'I understand that you're angry.'

'How could you be such an idiot?' she snapped.

Dorne looked up as Evelyn stomped across the town square, her expression as black as thunder. He watched as she went into the inn, slamming the door behind her.

He turned to see Blackhart following, his expression as dark as

Evelyn's. He too went into the inn and slammed the door behind him.

Blackhart's men slowly entered the square, then came over to stand in front of Dorne, their expressions rather woebegone. 'What's wrong, lads? Aren't you enjoying the party?'

'We were,' Archer grumbled.

'The Lady High Priestess is kinda upset with us,' Reader said.

'Ah,' Dorne nodded, then waited, looking at each man in turn.

'We need to ask ya something,' Archer said.

'It's important,' Reader emphasised. 'Kinda private.'

'She wouldn't really do that, would she?' Mage asked.

Dorne gave them a puzzled look. 'She wouldn't do what?'

Sidian leaned over and whispered in his ear.

'Ah.' Dorne struggled to keep his face straight. 'I can see how that would be important.' He coughed slightly. 'But I'm sure, once she's calmed down a bit, you won't have anything to fear. A true priestess would not curse you with crotch rot.'

There were sighs of relief all around.

Evelyn marched through the main room of the inn and up the stairs to their bedroom. She was so angry she almost couldn't see. The door to the room slammed with a satisfying sound and she threw her cloak into the corner, turning to pace before the fire.

She'd finished only one circle when Orrin slid into the room. He looked grim and started to say something, but she cut him off before he could utter a sound. 'You stupid man, what were you thinking?'

'Evie.'

'You walked into that building weaponless, half naked, your hands tied.' Evelyn rounded on him. 'Are you insane? He could have killed you.'

'Let me guess.' Orrin crossed his arms over his chest. 'You were sitting in the square and he came up and said, "Oh, please, Priestess, my friend Ulfgar was drinking and now he's fallen and broken his leg. Help us, help us." And off you went.'

'It was an arm,' Evelyn said, trying to keep her voice even and calm. 'And that's not the point.'

'Thrice damned it isn't,' Orrin growled. 'You went off with someone without so much as a by-your-leave, much less a note or a message or—'

250

'He didn't hurt me.' Evelyn lost control of her voice. 'HE WAS GOING TO KILL YOU, AND YOU WERE GOING TO LET HIM!'

'Yes,' Orrin said. 'Better me than you, my love.'

Evelyn stood there, struck silent by those words. She stared at his face, seeing the terrible pain there. 'Orrin—'

'If you die, Evie, I die with you.' Orrin lowered his arms, his shoulders slumping. 'I'm terrified that another with a grudge will target you to get to me. Better to give myself over than risk—'

'Orrin.' Evelyn moved over then, to wrap her arms around his waist.

He returned the hug with a sigh, and they stood there for a moment, wrapped in each other's arms. 'I am so scared. Better, perhaps that I leave you . . .'

Evelyn tilted her head back and looked at him. 'Do you regret loving me? Marrying me?'

Orrin studied her face for a moment, then reached to stroke her hair. 'Oh, no, Evelyn. My life started when I met you. But the idea that you might suffer for my sins, or that our child might . . . how do I live with that possibility?'

Evelyn took his hands and tugged him over to the bed to sit beside her. 'Orrin, I love you. I promise to take more care in the future.'

'But—'

She reached out and touched his lips. 'I can control my courses, love. A baby is something we can deal with later. But it will be our decision whether or not to have children and we will make that decision together.'

Orrin nodded. 'But Evie, you are still vulnerable . . . still at risk.'

'Orrin, don't you see?' She took his strong hand in hers. 'If I am at risk because of loving you, then so be it. There are no promises in this life. We can only make choices and live our lives and hope for the best. I chose to love you and be loved in return, come what may.' Evelyn smiled. 'Everyone who loves, they take that risk. You're just not used to it.'

Orrin frowned. 'I cared for my men.'

She nodded. 'You did, and you still do. But love is different, Orrin. It leaves us vulnerable, weak. Naked in so many ways, not just naked physically. It exposes us to pain, heartache and loss.' She leaned her head on his shoulder. 'But it makes us stronger, too. A gift between two hearts.'

She lifted her head and kissed him gently. 'There are no promises in this life, Orrin. We can only make choices. I choose to love you, come what may.'

Orrin sighed and lowered them both backwards until they were lying on the bed. 'I can't let you go, Evelyn, as much as I'd like to believe it would make you safer.' He sighed and lifted her hand to kiss her palm. 'I'd rather love you and risk my heart, than refuse to be loved.'

'I should hope so,' Evelyn said, her smile bright. 'Since we are married, my lord husband.'

'That's true.' Orrin turned his head, hazel eyes sparkling. 'And we are on the Great Bed of Wareington.'

Evelyn kissed him. 'And the door is bolted.'

'That it is, lady wife.' Orrin rolled over, covering her with his body. His eyes danced, the hazel flaring bright. 'Now, then, didn't you just say something about being naked?'